It was Evan.

What in the world was he *doing* here? Was this a mirage?

The last time I'd seen Evan, we'd stood outside on the docks, shrouded in fog, hugging, and I was crying because summer was over and he was leaving the island.

"Hey, you." He slid off the freezer and wrapped his arms around my waist.

And there it was. What it had taken me so many months to forget. That feeling.

"So. Are you working here?" I asked. "Nobody said you were working here." I can be a bit blunt when I'm feeling cornered.

"What, am I required to file papers with the government?" Evan joked. "The island's cracking down on outsiders?"

No, I thought, *but maybe they should be.*

MAINE SQUEEZE

Catherine Clark

AVON BOOKS
An Imprint of HarperCollins*Publishers*

Maine Squeeze
Copyright © 2004 by Catherine Clark
All rights reserved. No part of this book may
be used or reproduced in any manner
whatsoever without written permission except
in the case of brief quotations embodied
in critical articles and reviews.
Printed in the United States of America.
For information address HarperCollins Children's Books,
a division of HarperCollins Publishers,
1350 Avenue of the Americas, New York, NY 10019.

Library of Congress Cataloging-in-Publication Data
Clark, Catherine, date.
  Maine squeeze / Catherine Clark.— 1st Avon ed.
    p.   cm.
  Summary: Colleen Templeton spends a romantic
summer before starting college working at Bobb's Lobster,
sorting out her feelings for two possible boyfriends, and
sharing a house with friends on the tiny Maine island she
calls home.
  ISBN 0-06-056725-2
  [1. Dating (Social customs)—Fiction. 2. Islands—
Fiction. 3. Maine—Fiction.] I. Title.
PZ7.C5412Mai 2004   2003022232
[Fic]—dc22   CIP
                                                  AC

First Avon edition, 2004
AVON TRADEMARK REG. U.S. PAT. OFF. AND IN OTHER COUNTRIES,
MARCA REGISTRADA, HECHO EN U.S.A.

❖

Visit us on the World Wide Web!
www.harperteen.com

Many thanks to Amanda Maciel
for her thoughtful editing and for her
ability to appreciate endless
food references.
And thanks to Sherren Clark,
John and Barbara Clark, Herb and Grace
Mitchell, Ted Davis, Sally Suhr,
and Ruth Koeppel.

Chapter 1

"You're not just going to leave me behind, are you? You're not going to strand me on this island. Are you?"

"Don't make fun of me. Just don't." I looked at my boyfriend, Ben, and raised one eyebrow. "But are you seriously that upset about my being gone for a day?"

"Well, no. But it is kind of lousy," Ben said.

Ben and I had just gone for an early-morning walk so we could have a little time together before I drove my parents to the airport. When they first told me they were leaving the island for the summer, I'd had that exact same reaction, which was why Ben was teasing me about it.

I'd kind of panicked at first. I don't know why. It wasn't like it was a deserted island or that I would be stranded—I lived there year-round. By the way, it's just referred to as "the island," like a lot of islands off the coast of Maine, and I'll keep it that way because (a) I'm too lazy to change everyone's names, and (b) I don't want to incriminate anyone. If you've been there, you might recognize it, but I'm going to keep some things mysterious in that Jessica Fletcher/Cabot Cove/*Murder She Wrote*–reruns kind of way.

Not that there will be any murder in this story. Unless crimes of passion, crimes of the heart, count.

Anyway, my parents would be landing in Frankfurt, Germany, tomorrow, while I'd be showing up for my first day of work at Bobb's Lobster. Something about it didn't seem quite fair.

"When do you think you'll be back tonight?" Ben lingered in the doorway of my house, his hands on my waist.

"Maybe seven? Not too late," I said. I'd drop my parents at the airport in Portland—from there they'd fly to Boston, then overseas—then I'd pick up my friend Erica and drive back.

"I wish I could go with you."

"Would you really want to listen to my parents chanting along to German-language tapes in the car because they haven't quite mastered the language yet?" I asked. Not that they'd gotten the hang of French, Spanish, or Italian, for that matter, but that wouldn't keep them from spending ten weeks in Europe. Nothing would. Not even the prospect of leaving me and Ben alone all summer. (Well, only if *his* parents would leave, too . . . .) I wasn't actually going to be "alone" alone, anyway, because three of my best friends were moving in.

I thought back to the night two months before when my parents told me they were going to Europe for ten weeks. At first I thought we were all going together. I was really excited, but then I realized I was not included, that they'd be sipping wine in the Alps while I schlepped melted butter at sea level.

But I couldn't begrudge them this second honeymoon concept—they deserved it. And did I really want to trek all over the world with my parents? I pictured my dad wearing a pair of lederhosen and doing a jig around a beer hall in Austria, while I cowered in the corner, hoping no one would guess we were related.

Then I pictured me, here, alone in this house. Me and Ben. Alone. It sounded too good to be true. I was afraid that they'd make me stay with my Uncle Frank and Aunt Sue.

It's not that I don't like my aunt and uncle. I just didn't want to live with them. My aunt has this blueberry addiction—she spends the whole summer trying to invent new recipes using blueberries. She eats so many that I could swear her skin sometimes has a blue tint. And if my uncle told me one more time that I should *paint* instead of doing collage art . . . I would go nuts.

Fortunately, my parents suggested my friends move in here, rather than me move in with my aunt and uncle. I'd be eternally grateful for that.

Ben smiled. "You're right. I can probably skip the German lesson in the car."

"Yeah," I said.

"But it's our first day off from school—and our last day off before we start working full-time. It'd be great if we could just go hang out on the beach or something."

"Tell me about it," I said. "We'll just have to make up for it—we'll find an extra day somewhere," I said. "We'll both call in sick or something. Middle of July."

"Okay, it's a plan." Ben nodded. "Maybe we'll be sick for two or three days. No, wait. I don't want to lose my job."

Ben was so psyched about his first summer on the island. He'd gotten a job working on the ferry, which we called "Moby" for obvious reasons—it was large, white, swam, and carried lots of people inside it. He'd be one of the guys taking tickets, tying up at the dock, loading bags of mail and unloading carts of groceries and other supplies, handing out life jackets in the event of an emergency—whatever was needed, except for the actual navigation and driving of the ferry. That was left to a few guys on the mainland and a couple on the island: John Hyland, a grumpy, retired fisherman who hated "summer people" and never smiled (his wife, Molly, ran the island post office and wasn't much friendlier), and "Cap" Green, who talked your ear off and told you more about the tide, the neighbors, and his health than you ever wanted to know.

Ben and I actually met on the ferry to school one morning. Everyone from seventh grade and up goes to the mainland for school, which means I'd been catching the ferry at seven o'clock every morning for the past six years for the forty-five-minute trip. But enough about my tragic life.

Meeting someone on the ferry probably sounds really romantic, but you haven't known nausea until you've ridden a ferry that smelled like diesel and you've had to sit inside because it was cold and raining very hard. Even someone like me, who'd been taking the boat for years, had trouble on days like that.

Ben was new to the island, and he was looking *completely* green. My friend Haley and I felt so sorry for him that we went over to him and asked how he was doing. Haley told him to look at the horizon, which is a trick for not getting seasick. Then I gave him some of my still-half-frozen cinnamon-raisin bagel and told him to come stand in the doorway with me, because it's better when you have something in your stomach and when you get a little fresh air, even if it's cold and wet outside.

"What's your name?" I asked him.

"B—Ben," he stammered, looking around nervously.

"Colleen Templeton," I said, shaking his hand, trying to distract him by making small talk and introducing myself.

"Colleen?" He nodded, biting his lip. "I really don't want to puke on my first day."

"You won't," I assured him. "Just have another bite of the bagel and you won't. But at least if you do? We're all wearing raincoats."

He laughed and then clutched his stomach.

6

I don't know how I could have found someone so green, so cute. But he was.

And I don't know if he asked me out a couple of months later out of gratitude for that day, or what. By that time I was starting to realize Evan—who I thought was the love of my life *last* summer—had moved on, so I decided I might as well, too. It was good timing, which was a first for me. My family's notorious for bad timing.

So now it was kind of funny that Ben would be spending eight to ten hours a day on the ferry. There's an expression, "getting your sea legs." Ben had those now, and very nice sea legs at that.

I was really looking forward to spending the summer with him. This year would be so different from last year. I wouldn't have any big ups and downs, like with Evan, who my friend Samantha had dubbed "the drama king." I wouldn't have to worry about how Evan felt about me, or whether Evan and I were going to get together, or whether, after we *did* get together, anyone would catch us making out in the walk-in fridge at work, which in retrospect seems a little tacky. Fun at the time, though, I have to admit. But my life was a lot less racy, now. I was a lot calmer—and happier.

As Ben and I were standing on the porch, saying good-bye, an old, faded blue-and-white pickup truck came rattling up the road. "Here comes trouble," Ben said as Haley Boudreau pulled into the driveway.

Haley slammed the driver's door shut. "What are you doing here?" she asked Ben.

"He came over for breakfast—to say good-bye to my parents," I told her, looking at all the boxes and bags in the back of the truck. Haley was moving into my brother Richard's old room, and Samantha would be coming up from Boston tomorrow and taking the guest room. I was going to pick up Erica when I drove my parents to the Portland airport that afternoon.

"You knew I was here, right? That's why you came over, so I could help you carry all that stuff in," Ben said as Haley unlatched the truck's tailgate.

"Yeah. Do you think you can lift this?" Haley picked up a small duffel bag and tossed it to Ben. "We'll do the heavy stuff. What do you think, we're not strong enough?"

Haley could be so stubbornly independent. You'd never know from the way she was talking to Ben that they were such good friends. The three of us did practically everything together.

She pulled a large cardboard box out of the back of her family's beat-up pickup truck. "How much did you *bring*?" I asked as I went over to help.

"I'm glad this is the last box," I said as we climbed the stairs. "Remind me again why we told Ben to leave and let us do this on our own?"

"Come on, it's good for you," Haley said. "You'll be ready to carry those big heavy trays."

"Strength training? Okay. Consider me strong." I dropped the box of CDs onto the floor in Richard's old room. It was funny to think of Haley moving in here when she only lived about five minutes away. It was like when we were ten and had sleepovers at each other's houses every Saturday night. We used to annoy Richard to no end; I wondered how he'd feel about "Horrible Haley" living in his room.

Haley and I have been friends ever since my family moved to the island, when I was eight. My mom grew up here, but went away to college and lived in Chicago for a while, which is where she met my dad and where Richard and I were born. Then her parents needed help, and Mom and Dad were sick of big-city life, so they turned their summer vacations on the island into year-round living. First one job at the elementary school on the island opened, and my dad took it, and then another, and my mom took that. (They're like the tag team of silliness when it comes to working with little kids. Maybe it's because they spend so much time with little kids that they're slightly, well, goofy. I mean, they've definitely spent too much time inhaling glue, paste, and Magic Markers.)

Haley is the shortest person I know—not that it matters, but it's a fact. Her father and her uncle are lobstermen, just like her grandfather, and his father before him, etc. etc. They've been on the island for decades—probably a century or two, for all I know. They call everyone who arrived since 1900 "from away." But they're not stand-offish about it, the way some people can be.

I once asked her why she'd decided to work at the Landing, instead of with her family, this summer. "My family's crazy," she'd said. "You know that. They wouldn't even *pay* me. Or they'd say they were going to, but then they'd tell me they needed the money for something else, and would I mind waiting a few weeks . . . you know how it was last summer. I made about ten dollars."

Haley had a strong Maine accent, so when she said words like *summer* and *dollar*, they sounded like "summah" and "dollah."

"So you'd rather sell postcards and ice cream cones?" I'd asked. "Really?"

"Yes, really," she'd said. "You have no idea how stubborn my mother can be."

Actually, I did, because I knew how stubborn *Haley* could be. Like this latest standoff with her mother—it could last for months. Haley and I had had a few standoffs ourselves over the years. We always got over them and apologized to each other, but sometimes it had taken weeks.

"Good. Finc," Mrs. Boudreau had said when Haley told her about our summer plan to share the house. She was already mad about Haley's going to work for someone else, and it showed. "Have a wonderful time," she said coldly. "See you in September." Which, of course, sounded like "Septembah."

I'll quit talking about their accent now—I just really like the way it sounds. I always wanted to have an accent, but I could never pull

11

it off since I wasn't born here.

Unlike me, Haley didn't have a serious boyfriend. She was determined not to get too serious or tied down with anybody while she was still young. Her older sister had gotten married by the time she was twenty, and then had two kids right away. Haley wanted to get off the island and go to college and see the world before she did that. She'd earned a scholarship to Dartmouth—she was brilliant in science and calculus—and was looking forward to getting off the island and meeting people who'd never even heard of it. Or so she said. I wondered how she was going to handle being so far away from the ocean when she'd never lived anywhere else. (I'd be attending Bates College, which isn't on the coast, either, but it's not far from it.)

"So, how do you think Richard's going to take the news?" Haley asked as she sat on the bed. "Do you think he'll even come out here this summer?"

I fixed the bulletin board, which was hanging crooked. The board was covered with photos of Richard and his freshman-year girlfriend, Richard and his sophomore-year girlfriend. . . . He always went out with beautiful girls, but he had a time limit on his relationships, it seemed. Two or three months and he was moving on. *Tick, tick, tick.*

It was hard to think that my big brother, who I'd worshiped for years (because he was five years older, he was just old enough to be really nice toward me most of the time, at least once he got past the new-baby-hatred phase—and I really looked up to him), was maybe not all that different from other guys, or that he did typical guy things that made him sort of a jerk.

"He's supposed to be coming for July Fourth. He doesn't get much vacation time because he's so new at his job," I told Haley. "So he's only coming for the long weekends—Labor Day, too."

"But we'll be gone then," Haley said. "Isn't that weird to think about?" She opened the box on the bed beside her and pulled out a few books. "Did I say weird? I meant incredibly great."

"And we'll be unpacking then, too," I said. "Is that why you brought so much stuff? Are you practicing?"

"I brought my favorite things," Haley said. "Because who knows when my mother's going to get mad at me again and decide to throw out all of my stuff."

"She wouldn't do that," I said.

"She would. When my sister announced she was getting married, my mother put all of her belongings at the end of the driveway. Remember that?"

"She doesn't like being left . . . I guess," I said.

"What does she think? That we're going to stay home and live with her forever?" Haley started putting books into Richard's empty bookcase. "I wish *she* would go to Europe for the summer, instead of your parents."

In a way, I almost wished that, too. Now that my parents were actually leaving that afternoon, I was thinking about how much I would miss them.

There was a knock on the door. "Colleen? Could you come downstairs?" my mother asked.

"Is it time to go?"

"Not yet. But there's something important we have to discuss before we leave."

"What to do when Starsky and Hutch get upset when they realize that you're gone?" I asked, referring to our cats. My dad named them after his favorite old television show.

"No. The house rules," my mother said.

Haley and I exchanged a look. *What* house rules?

Chapter 2

Haley drove off in the truck, the shocks bouncing along as she backed down the bumpy gravel driveway.

I saw that my parents had loaded their luggage into the back of the old Volvo wagon. (You almost don't need a car on the island, really— you could practically walk everywhere you need to. Mostly you just need cars and trucks to haul things. But if you want one when you get to the mainland, you have to keep it somewhere.)

Dad was sitting on the top porch step, petting Starsky and saying good-bye. Starsky always seemed to know when someone was going away, and then he tried not to let you out of his sight.

"Hutch is obviously crushed you're leaving." I pointed at Hutch, who was sprawled on top of one of the Adirondack chair cushions, his legs hanging off, about to fall but completely oblivious to the world.

My family had this ongoing debate about

how cats ever got onto the island in the first place. My mother theorized that the original feline residents of the island must have sneaked off a pirate ship in search of a better life. My father always said, "Actually, there was that one cat that took the ferry. No, wait. There had to be two." He was working on a children's picture book about a ferry cat and an ex-pirate cat that fell madly in love. As I said, he can be pretty goofy. Naturally, the two cats in his book looked exactly like Starsky and Hutch. Starsky is a gray tortoiseshell tabby with a white tail, and Hutch is a blond marmalade-colored tabby cat. They're brothers.

I wondered which one was more like a pirate. Starsky did have a habit of knocking my earrings from the top of my dresser to the floor, so maybe he had more of a yearning for stealing—and wearing—gold. Hutch had a habit of sleeping through everything, major and minor.

"You know what? Hutch is great. Hutch is cool. I yearn to be as relaxed as he is sometime in my life," Dad said, and I laughed.

Mom came outside, carrying a large sheet of hot pink poster board.

"What's that?" I asked.

"This is your contract," she said, looking it over. "Just want to make sure I didn't leave anything out. Honey, do you have a pen?"

My dad pulled a felt-tip marker out of his pants pocket. I don't think he's written with an actual pen in years. He even writes and signs checks with Magic Markers.

"You know how we talked about setting some ground rules, so we wrote them down to make them official and binding. This is a very big deal, you know. Us leaving you here by yourself. In fact, I'm almost having second thoughts about it." Mom tapped the marker against the porch railing.

Second thoughts? She couldn't. She wouldn't. Haley had already moved in. And I had the perfect picture of my perfect summer in my head. It definitely did not include Mom and Dad hanging around, crowding in at the corners of the photograph, waving hello.

"Mom, we've been over this. I'll be responsible," I said.

"Yes, I think you will be," she said, "but I'm not so sure about the other girls. I just . . . I'd hate it if anything happened."

"To the house?" I asked.

"Not just the house. To *them*," she said. "And to *you*."

"Oh." She did have a point there. "But, Mom, we'll all look after each other—we always do."

"But I won't be here to make sure of it," she said, her voice quavering.

"Mom, don't worry." I put my arm around her shoulder and gave her a little squeeze. It was a warm and fuzzy moment.

Then she stepped out of the hug and slapped the poster board on the slatted table. "Read, initial, and sign."

RULES—SUMMER RESIDENCE

1. No drugs or alcohol allowed.
2. No sleepovers. Especially of the boyfriend variety.
3. The house will be kept clean. To that end, the house will be cleaned once weekly. Uncle Frank and Aunt Sue will be dropping by for random inspections. In fact, the house is subject to inspections by your aunt and uncle at any time.
4. No loud parties. Small gatherings

are fine, but do not annoy the neighbors.

5. Each girl will be responsible for her own long-distance phone calls made on the house phone, as well as for excessive Internet connection charges.

6. Any damage done to the house—not that there will be any—will be repaired by the time we get home.

7. The Volvo is only to be driven by you and Colleen—nobody else.

8. No changes will be made around the house.

9. Anyone breaking any of the above rules will be asked to leave the house.

10. I don't have anything else; it just seemed like there should be 10. Have fun!

I smiled as I scrawled my signature in purple ink on the first line marked "Signed and Agreed By."

Mom carefully inspected my signature, as if I could have forged it. "It's up to you to post the rules in the kitchen—and get each girl to sign this." Then, out of nowhere, she started crying. "I don't want to go," she said, hugging me, her tears dropping onto my shoulders.

"Mom, please," I said. "You *do* want to go. You're not setting Dad loose on the Continent by himself, are you? I mean, he could really give Americans a bad name."

My father cleared his throat. "Ahem."

"Okay, a worse name," I amended.

"That's not what I was thinking about!" he said with a laugh. "Anyway, it's not as if I'm an embarrassment to anyone." He stood there, saying this, wearing a long-sleeved T-shirt Mom had given him last Christmas that said "I'm a Mainiac" over the outline of a moose.

"Are you wearing that on the *plane*?" I asked.

"Good point." He ran upstairs to get changed into his traveling clothes, and Mom and I just laughed as we taped the poster board onto the kitchen door.

I headed to Erica's house in Portland that afternoon around four o'clock, after a dreadfully sobby drop-off at the airport.

Dad kept cracking bad jokes about what souvenirs

he would bring home for the cats, and Mom kept telling me how to look after the garden, even though she knew I was hopeless when it came to having a green thumb. And she kept crying, too. I guess we never had been separated for as long as we would be that summer. Maybe it was good practice for my leaving home in the fall, like she said, but neither one of us liked it. And okay, so I cried, too. Miserably. Embarrassingly.

Now, while I was at a stoplight, I glanced in the rearview mirror and saw that my eyes were only starting to unpuff. I reached over to the passenger seat for my sunglasses and slipped them back on, then stuffed a crumpled Kleenex into the pocket on the driver's-side door.

I wasn't going to cry—I didn't think I would. But after we unloaded their suitcases and bags, as Mom and Dad were hugging me good-bye, this police officer started yelling at us because we were staying in the pickup and drop-off area too long and we were getting in the way of other people. Also, I hadn't parked quite as close to the curb as a person should, and this hotel shuttle bus was sort of stuck until the driver went up onto the *other* curb. It was chaotic, to say the least. I was about to be blamed for something.

Naturally, I burst into tears.

I think in some weird way that made my parents happy, though, because then they shifted into their "take care of Colleen" mode and suddenly stopped being upset themselves. Mom gave me a tissue (with a teddy bear print, of course) from her purse, and Dad gave me a Lifesaver, and off they went through the doors for their first flight. They just whisked away and left me there with the scowling police officer and a wet face. They'd land in Frankfurt in the morning. I'd wake up at home, without them. It was a bit hard to fathom.

Good thing my three best friends in the world would be there with me.

I pulled up in front of Erica's house and parked. She lived on top of a hill, in a large brick colonial house with a great view of the water. The last time I'd seen Erica was in May, when she came out to the island for her grandfather's birthday. We usually saw each other every other month or so—either she came up or I went to Portland with my mom and dad to shop, or eat out, or visit their friends.

Erica was going to the University of New Hampshire in the fall, so she could be close to home. Erica's parents were a tad overprotective.

Erica was the sweetest, nicest person in the world. She worked as a hostess at Bobb's, which was a perfect fit for her. Even when people got angry about waiting too long for a table or were rude to her, she'd just "kill them with kindness," as the saying goes. She earned a lot of overtime money because she couldn't say no when others asked her to cover their shifts—great for the money part, but bad because she'd work too many hours and get completely exhausted. (Being too nice occasionally has its downsides. That's why I try not to go overboard. That, and the fact it doesn't come naturally to me.)

"Look who's here!" Erica's mother cried when she opened the front door. "It's Colleen Templeton!" She always says this, as if she's announcing my arrival at a fancy dress ball. Instead, I was standing on their doorstep wearing cut-off khaki shorts, a bright pink tank top, and unlaced sneakers.

Erica came running to the door and we gave each other a quick hug. After talking to her for a few minutes, we quickly tossed two large duffel bags and a box of Erica's stuff into the back of the car, grabbed some juice and sodas from the fridge, and were about to be on our way when

Mrs. Kuhar caught up to us.

Erica's parents were coming up to the island the next weekend, but her mom acted as though Erica was leaving the country when she said good-bye (and I knew what that looked like, having just been through it myself). She gave Erica several instructions on when to call home, how to dress for the changing weather, how to arrange her schedule at Bobb's so she didn't get overworked like last summer. . . . Then Erica and her mother hugged, then her mother hugged *me*, and eventually we were on the road.

"We're on the way!" Erica said, putting down her window and resting her arm on the door as we hit Interstate 295. "Wow, what a nice day, huh?"

"Can you believe we're really doing this? I mean, we've been talking about it since April, and now it's finally happening." I took a sip of orange soda. "Isn't this great? This summer is going to be *so* amazing." I reached down to turn up the radio.

Seconds later, Erica leaned over and turned down the radio. "The thing is, Colleen," she said, sounding a little nervous. "I can't actually live with you."

Chapter 3

"You can't?"

Already there were some glitches in the perfect plan, some "flies in the ointment," as my father would say, only he always made a point of mentioning they were black flies, because that's the fly variety here in Maine that will bite you until it hurts.

Anyway. The fact that Erica wasn't going to live in the house with us came as a complete and utter shock to me. She was more reliable, nice, and—maybe it's shallow to say, but she's really skilled at cooking, and I'd been relying on her to feed me all summer—than the rest of us put together. What would we do without her? What would I eat? Toast only got you so far. Now I was looking at toast and leftovers from Bobb's. Leftover reheated lobster stew on toast. Yuck.

I told myself to stop thinking about my stomach and get this figured out. "But wait. If your parents won't let you live with us, then how come they're letting you ride up with me today?" I asked. It didn't sound exactly logical.

"I needed to get there?" she said meekly. "And you were coming down anyway to drop off your parents?"

I laughed. "Well, true. But why are they against the idea of you living at my house? I mean, when have you ever given them a reason not to trust you?" I asked.

Erica fiddled with the knob on the glove compartment. "Well, uh . . ."

I couldn't believe it—Erica was almost acting guilty. "What? Did you do something?"

"No! I was going to say . . . well, it's not me they're worried about," Erica said slowly.

I nearly slammed on the brakes, which was not a good thing because we were on the highway. "What? It's *me*?" I felt terrible. Did Mr. and Mrs. Kuhar really think so poorly of me? They'd always acted so friendly toward me, so *nice*. Just like Erica—they were almost *too* nice sometimes. And since when could I not be trusted? I was extremely . . . trusty. Trustworthy. Whatever.

"No, no! I mean, it's not you," Erica assured me. "It's the entire situation. Four girls on their own. My parents think I'm still too young for something like that. You know how they treat me as if I'm ten sometimes. Plus, they said that they want me to look after my grandparents this summer."

"Your grandparents are sixty-five, going on thirty!" I said. "I held the door for your grandmother last week at the store? And she stared at me and said, 'Are you working here now? Well, what are you waiting for? Are you doing arm-strengthening exercises? No? Then go *in* already.'"

Erica laughed as she leaned down to adjust the back straps of her brown sandals. "Yeah, that sounds like her, all right. I know, they're completely self-reliant. And, Coll, I'm *really* sorry. I should have told you sooner. I just kept hoping I'd convince my parents to change their minds."

"Don't apologize!" I said. "I mean, I'm disappointed. I wish you *could* live with us. But it's perfectly fine. You'll be over all the time anyway. Right?"

"Of course! I just won't be able to sleep there, that's all. And hey, that means you'll have a guest room now."

I swear, she could put a positive spin on anything. She was amazing that way.

*   *   *

When we pulled up in front of the house it was getting close to seven thirty and dusk was falling, but I immediately spotted Samantha sitting on the porch with Haley.

"Sam!" I closed the car door and ran over to the porch steps. We could unpack the groceries later.

"Colleen!" Samantha jumped up and gave me a big hug. "How's it going?"

"Wow, you look fantastic," I said, stepping back to admire her. She wore faded stretch boot-cut jeans, boots, and a light-orange T-shirt with cap sleeves that looked great against her dark brown skin. She wore her hair pulled back in a gold barrette at the base of her neck. "Did you get taller over the winter or what?"

"No, you got shorter," she replied. "It's the heels, of course. Hey, Erica!" Sam quickly hugged Erica, and then Erica hugged Haley.

I ran inside and brought out four glasses and a pitcher of iced tea while Erica put all the cold groceries in the fridge and freezer. Then we all sat on the porch, talking and laughing. It felt exactly like the end of last summer, sort of like no time had elapsed at all. I love that about summer.

Sam and her family had rented a place on

the island last summer, after coming the year before that for a shorter vacation and falling in love with the place. They lived in Richmond, Virginia, for the rest of the year, and her parents were both university professors, which gave them the summers off. I've never been to Virginia, but from what Sam has told me, it sounds pretty different from here. I know it's a lot *warmer*, which is why Sam had decided to stay down there for college and attend the University of Virginia. I was kind of envious of that, and planned on visiting her during key months of the year—like February. And March. And April. (It usually doesn't get really warm and springlike here until May.)

Sam and I e-mailed each other once a week, at least, so we knew everything that had been going on over the past year in each other's lives. I knew how she'd done on her college entrance exams, who she'd gone to her prom with, how her parents had taken her cell phone away during finals week, which senior awards she'd won, that she was still addicted to Heath candy bars, and that her parents were spending a week in late August on the island and the rest of the summer researching new books.

So catching up when she got to the island didn't take long. But of course we went over it all again anyway. Sometimes it was hard for us to shut up and let someone else do the talking.

One thing I really like about Sam is that she always speaks her mind. You don't have to worry about where you stand or what she thinks of a person or a situation. She'll tell you. But not in a mean way—she's just very honest and forthright. You can trust her not to lie to you. If you ask her, "Does this shirt look all right?" she might say, "It's perfect," or she might say, "Not with those pants, no." And she'd immediately go to your—or her—closet and find something that looked better.

She could even make her Bobb's outfit look okay. And she was such a good server, too. She could remember twenty orders and get all the details right. Her tips always outnumbered mine, but she didn't brag about it.

She was the kind of person who'd pitch in when someone else got slammed with too many tables wanting too many things. And she always tipped out the bussers and dishwashers really well. She was generous to a fault, sort of like

Erica, but it was a great fault when you were her friend.

At the end of last summer, Samantha had treated me, Erica, Haley, and some other friends to an all-day sailboat cruise on the ocean. It was something tourists always did, but we never thought of doing it ourselves. For one thing, it was expensive. For another, it was . . . touristy. It was the equivalent of us tying on plastic lobster-eating bibs and saddling up at picnic tables outside Bobb's for the Friday night early-bird special lobster boil: "Reserve Now—the Early Bird Catches the Lobster!" As if birds caught lobsters. But whatever.

After we got over feeling slightly embarrassed, we had an amazing time, cruising from the island over to and around other islands, making our way along the rocky coast, sitting in the sun drinking spritzers and eating a gourmet lunch while getting what was essentially a tour of our own backyard.

"Genius. Pure genius. You're coming back next year—you *have* to," Haley had told her—Haley, who'd initially thought the sailboat cruise idea was ludicrous and a waste of time.

I suddenly remembered that Evan had been there on the sailboat, too. I remembered leaning back against him and the wind whipping my hair and him giving me his baseball cap and the sun sparkling on the water and the sound of the hull slicing through the water.

There were so many memories with Evan that I'd been trying to forget over the last year. Fortunately, he wouldn't be around this summer to remind me. Nobody had heard he was coming—not my boss, Trudy; and not his cousin Jake, who he lived with last summer. And especially not *me*. I hadn't heard he was coming—or what he was doing this summer.

Of course, he'd quit writing me back in November. Not that I was feeling angry and bitter about it—at least, not anymore. I was taking the whole fun-while-it-lasted approach. Apparently, Evan was the type of guy who was completely and utterly devoted to you—until suddenly one day he wasn't, and you never heard from him again.

You know that type. A terrible, horrible person.

* * *

"So. Now what?" I asked after we'd drained the pitcher of iced tea, the ice in our glasses had melted, and we'd gone through the short versions of all of our lives.

"Now we unpack the rest of the groceries," Erica said. She had helped me stock up on things at the supermarket before we caught the ferry to the island. We have only a small market here, and it's more expensive, so we'd tried to buy in bulk. "Then we decide what we're grilling for dinner. But first I'd better call my grandparents and tell them I'm here, so they don't worry—and so they don't call my parents and make *them* worry."

We all filed into the house, and while Erica was on the telephone with her grandparents, Haley, Sam, and I went upstairs. "So, which room did you choose?" I asked Sam as we stood at the top of the stairs.

"The guest room," she said. "Since I slept in it a few times last summer, it sort of felt like home already."

"Okay. So that leaves my parents' room open, since Erica won't be here. Maybe one of you guys wants to move in there?"

Wait a second. It was the biggest room in the house, with the best view. Maybe *I* wanted to move in there.

But no, that would be weird. It would have my parents' vibes. Not that there was anything wrong with them, but it would just feel strange, and giving up my room would be strange, too.

"No. Let's just keep this room vacant," Sam suggested. "That way, when people come to visit they'll have a really nice place to stay."

"Who's coming to visit?" I asked.

"I don't know. Your brother. My parents. Orlando Bloom." Samantha smiled.

Haley and I laughed. We'd all thought we saw Orlando Bloom getting off the ferry last year, and had been convinced he was summering somewhere on the island. We rode our bikes all over the place, hung out at the general store, stalked a few B&Bs, did everything we could to find out where he might be staying. But we never spotted Orlando—or his very-good-looking look-alike—again, until someone reported they'd seen him getting back *on* the ferry and leaving the island.

I brushed my hair and headed downstairs to help get dinner ready. I was good at setting the table. I could do that, and dishes, quite well. The rest of the meal should be left to other people with actual skill.

Almost as soon as Erica hung up the phone, promising her grandparents she'd be over when we finished dinner, it rang again. I grabbed it.

"Hey, you're there!" Ben said. "I thought you were going to call when you got home from Portland."

"I was, I was! But I kind of got caught up in . . . catching up. You know." I laughed.

"So how was the drive? Did it go okay? How's Erica?" Ben asked.

"You know, it was fine, but my parents got pretty upset at the airport." Best to lay it all on my parents. After all, they were in Europe now and couldn't defend themselves. "And then it turns out Erica can't live with us, but that's okay—she's here now, making dinner. I'll take her over to her grandparents' later."

"So what are you doing tonight?" Ben asked.

"We're just going to eat and hang out," I said. "I think it's kind of a girls' night thing. But I'll see you tomorrow—after work?"

"Sounds good. Hey, tell Sam I'm looking forward to meeting her, okay?"

"I will. I missed you today. Bye, sweetie!" I clicked off the phone. "That was Ben. He said to tell you he's looking forward to meeting you tomorrow."

"So what's this Ben guy *really* like?" Sam asked as she chopped vegetables for a salad.

"He's great. We hang out all the time," Haley said as she got four glasses out of the cabinet. "And he treats Colleen really well. In comparison to certain other boyfriends she's had."

I groaned. "Did you have to mention him? I've been trying so hard not to think about him."

"So don't. He's not worth it," Haley declared. "Ben's taller. And nicer. Sweeter. I like him a lot more than I ever liked Evan," she said. "And you can actually trust him, too."

"What? All that and a cute face, too? Sounds too good to be true," Sam commented. "How did you get so lucky, Coll?"

"I know!" Haley said. "Not that I think Evan was great, but this is a place with a limited population. We get one new, nice, cute guy, and she gets to go out with him. *Again*."

"Come on!" I laughed. "There are a lot more guys around here. Or at least there will be this summer."

"And who cares, really? Because it's not all about the guys. In fact, it's not even *half* about them," Sam declared.

"Yeah. It's about earning tons of money for next year—"

"And hanging out together—"

"And the book club."

"Of course. We can't forget the book club."

"When's our first meeting?" Haley asked.

"Friday at three. Of course, just like always," Sam said with a smile.

Chapter 4

The next morning at ten o'clock, Sam, Erica, and I walked to work together. Erica had come over at nine to make sure Sam and I were awake and getting ready—she had a tendency to look after other people like that.

Sam and I had stayed up so late talking and watching TV the night before that the walk to Bobb's felt a lot longer than a mile to me. I had no energy, which wasn't exactly a good way to start off a forty-plus-hour workweek.

"We should have driven," I said as we trudged down the road for our first lunch shift of the summer. Bobb's was only open on weekends during the off-season, and wasn't busy enough to hire me for that. It would be hard, getting back into the swing of work again. I felt more like lying in bed until noon, then taking a long, hot shower, then sitting in the sun. Eventually getting around to making something to eat. Meeting Ben when he got through with work. You know.

"We're going to walk to Bobb's all summer. It's our exercise plan, remember?" Sam said. "One of them, anyway."

"Whose dumb idea was that," I grumbled.

"Mine," Sam said. "Thanks."

"Sorry." I reached up to push a lock of hair off my cheek. I have these short parts in my hair that are layered, and they insist on escaping barrettes. My hair was shaping up to be a real frizzone that day. Frizzone, by the way, isn't an Italian pastry; it's the name we came up with last summer for out-of-control hair after we kept calling the island the Frizz Zone. In fact, you can pretty much forecast the weather here by what your hair does. It would be humid today, with a chance of rain tonight. Those of us with long-ish, wavy-ish hair were natural-born forecasters.

I'd been working at Bobb's since I was fourteen years old. I started out behind the takeout window, taking and ringing up customer orders. "To go or to eat here?" was the line of that summer. (At the takeout window, "here" meant sitting at a couple of picnic tables right beside the parking lot, so not very glam.) When it was slow, we'd watch people walk up toward the restaurant and we'd bet on whether they were coming in to eat or would get their food to go and sit at the little picnic area.

Yes, we were bored.

Personally, my favorite Bobb's item was the fried haddock sandwich. Whenever a customer asked, "What's good here?" I'd tell them to get the sandwich. Then they'd say, "I'll have the fried clam basket." Somehow I wasn't convincing in my pitch, but oh well, that left more haddock for me.

At Bobb's we didn't use computers. Everything was shorthand, abbreviations, or had a nickname. We used white notepads to take orders. "You're actually writing this down? How quaint," tourists would say when they saw me jotting on the notepad.

Quaint was a top-ten tourist word. Some of the others were: *clam chowdah*, which they loved pronouncing in a bad fake accent; and *gift shop*. Trudy had even started selling Bobb's T-shirts and ball caps because customers kept asking for them. She sold two tees with goofy slogans, but luckily our uniform tees just had a logo on the front and a red lobster on the back.

We had an old cash register, too—not a computer, just a big, fat calculator with a cash drawer attached. "It works. Why replace it?" Trudy would say.

That was the philosophy of a lot of people on the island. For instance, my parents and this twenty-five-year-old Volvo with 200,000 miles on the odometer that I now drove. There was no point replacing something that still worked because you'd probably have to leave the island to find whatever it was you wanted. And then you'd have to haul whatever you didn't want *off* of the island, or else find someone else on the island who wanted your old stuff. Which was weird, when you saw someone walking down the road pushing the very stroller that you, Colleen Templeton, once graced, wearing your old baby clothes. I'm all in favor of recycling everything we can, but it's still strange to see your past walking around with a new identity.

Anyway, Trudy put a lot of money into having good food at the restaurant, the best and freshest seafood catches, along with some cool, old standard family recipes.

There were old wooden booths near the windows, and long tables in the middle of the restaurant for large groups. There was also a "banquet room," where people had private parties for weddings, birthdays, promotions . . . basically, any excuse would do. There were little lamps fashioned after lighthouses on each table. For a while the salt and pepper shakers were shaped like lobster claws, but they were so cute that people kept stealing them, so Trudy went back to using plain glass ones. One of my jobs when I was fifteen used to be Salt and Pepper Girl, which was nothing at all like the groundbreaking rap hip-hop group Salt-N-Pepa. It involved refilling and pouring and wiping off greasy fingerprints.

There used to be a lobster tank near the salad bar, but it caused too much confusion because some people didn't understand why the lobsters were dark blue-green instead of red. They only turn red when they're cooked, which I think is a very good metaphor—I know *I* turn red when I'm cooked, figuratively.

So anyway, back to the Bobb's language. Here were some of the order nicknames: fried clams were rubberneckers; a tuna sandwich was shark on toast; sea scallops were bottomfeeders; a fried seafood basket was a frantic Atlantic; lobster stew was floating fish; a lobster roll was a rock 'n' roll.

This didn't make sense to me at first because

the nicknames were just as long as the actual order names, but Trudy explained that it was part of the restaurant culture, that having nicknames made us close as a team, because we had our own language. So, okay. But you definitely didn't want the out-of-town customers to hear you calling out some of your orders in the kitchen. For one thing, some of them didn't sound all that appetizing. For another, they'd probably say, "How quaint!"

"They should say 'How *Maint*,' not 'How quaint,'" Sam had said last summer.

"We're not quaint. We're Maine-ahs," one of the cooks said.

"Did you hear that accent? How *quaint*!" Sam had teased him.

Despite the goofy names, the food at Bobb's *was* incredibly good. We always had people waiting for tables, crowding the dock outside, mingling, and sipping drinks in plastic cups while they waited, and once or twice falling into the water.

You didn't want to fall in, not out there. The water near Bobb's and the marina was not only as cold as the rest of the ocean could be, and full of seaweed, but it was also tainted with boat engine fuel run-off, scraps of fish, etc. It was rather disgusting, if you really stopped to look at it.

Cats roamed around the docks; kittens lounged on the docks in the sun. They lived for, and on, the fish that escaped from nets being hauled in, bait that was dropped out of buckets, and of course, dropped fried shrimp and clams. They had to compete with some very fast seagulls, the pigeons of the ocean.

I stepped around a couple of cats now, as we walked into Bobb's.

"You know, some places you can be away from for months, and then as soon as you see them again, it's like you never left. Know what I mean?" Sam commented. "I swear, this same loop of rope was lying here when I left last August."

"That's because we don't actually do anything in the off-season," I said. "We wait for the tourists like you to come back before we actually—"

"Tourists like me? Excuse me, but I worked side by side with you last summer," Sam replied. "I'm no tourist."

"So define what you are exactly," I teased.

"She's a part-time resident," Erica said.

We were arguing about how to define a

Maine native—which, technically, I wasn't, since I hadn't been born here, which meant I too was "from away"—when we walked into the kitchen and I lost my breath completely. It wasn't the smell of bleach, from everything being disinfected to the umpteenth level of cleanliness for opening day. It wasn't the onions on the chopping board, or the tomato bisque simmering on the stove.

It was Evan.

What in the world was he *doing* here? Was this a mirage? I exchanged panicked looks with Sam and Erica. No, it couldn't be Evan.

But it was.

He was sitting on top of the stainless steel ice cream freezer. He had a semi-scruffy look, like he hadn't shaved in a day or two. He could make stubble look good. I hated that about him.

He was wearing a faded yellow long-sleeved T-shirt with a hole in it, and long khaki shorts. His long legs nearly stretched down to the floor.

I found myself staring at his legs, at his feet. So he had nice ankles. So what? How could I be so shallow as to fall for someone because of his *ankles*? Ankles didn't mean anything. They just held you up. Shinbone connected to the anklebone connected to the footbone, etc.

He was wearing the same Birkenstock sandals he wore last summer.

Last summer. The last time I'd seen Evan, we'd stood outside on the docks at five A.M., shrouded in fog, hugging each other, and I was crying because summer was over and he was catching the ferry and leaving the island to go back to Philadelphia.

It was like something out of my grandmother Templeton's favorite movie, *Casablanca*, which I must have watched with her at least ten times. Instead of the ferry, there should have been an airplane whirring its propeller blades behind us. We should have been in black-and-white, not color. And Evan should have been wearing a fedora hat and a trench coat, instead of a T-shirt and shorts and Birkenstocks, and talking about our problems not amounting to a hill of beans.

What is a hill of beans, anyway?

A hill of blueberries I could understand.

Anyway, whenever I thought about that awful morning, I remembered Evan's faded blue T-shirt, and pressing my face against his chest, how soft the cotton shirt was and how it smelled.

I used to think Evan wore this really cool

cologne, because he always smelled so good, no matter what. But it turned out to be his Ultimate Endurance antiperspirant.

I could have used some Ultimate Endurance right about then.

"What—what are you . . . doing here?" I stammered.

"Hey, you." He slid off the freezer and wrapped his arms around my waist.

And there it was. What it had taken me so many months to forget. That feeling. That scent. Us. Lying on the beach together. Swimming together. Walking together. Being together.

"Are you . . . working here?" I finally managed to get out. "Or something?" My voice came out as a pathetic whisper, as if the words *or something* could ever be sultry.

Without answering me, he stepped back and spotted Samantha standing behind me. "Hey you, too." He gave her a quick hug, and she playfully kicked up her leg behind her as if this was her prom, or an end-of-World-War-II V-Day photo. Evan dipped her, lowering her toward the freezer, and they both laughed.

Why was their hug more romantic than ours? No fair.

Erica acknowledged him with a shy nod. "Hi."

"Hey, Erica. How's it going? What's up?" Evan replied.

He had the nerve to ask what was *up*. How about my *pulse*, buddy?

"So. Are you working here?" I asked. "Nobody said you were working here." I can be a bit blunt when I'm feeling cornered.

"What, am I required to file papers with the government?" Evan joked. "The island's cracking down on outsiders?"

No, I thought, *but maybe they should be*.

"Funny, we were just talking about that," Sam started to tell him.

"But . . . *are* you working here?" I asked again.

Evan raised his eyebrows.

"Because, I mean, Trudy said you weren't working here." In fact, I think I asked her to swear to it in blood, like something out of *The Adventures of Huckleberry Finn*. We had a pact, or at least I did. Since when did Trudy lie to me? I'd been working here for four years, and I couldn't ever remember her lying to me. Well, except for that one time when she told me Saturday nights would not be "all that busy."

Evan shrugged. "I changed my mind. My other plans fell through—"

"What other plans?" I asked.

I couldn't help feeling angry to see him again. He'd blown me off. He'd dropped me. Completely. Sure, we were hundreds of miles apart, and maybe it *was* pointless to have a long-distance relationship. But he could have kept in touch. He could have warned me he'd be here again. Not to mention the fact that Trudy and Robert could have warned me when I asked them, repeatedly, whether they'd heard from him and whether he'd be back. I was furious with Trudy and Robert, I decided. I'd quit if I didn't like working here so much.

Not, I guess, that I would have planned my summer any differently if I'd known Evan was returning. I wanted to be here with my friends—and with Ben. This could be the last time it'd be so easy for us all to be here together. If I'd known Evan was coming, I wouldn't have run off to, say, Europe or something. At least not without seriously thinking it over first and deciding it was the best possible move.

"So. When did you get here?" I asked Evan.

"Well, I got in last night—but it was dicey," he said.

About as dicey as this is, right now? I just stared at the freezer, wishing it wasn't as newly cleaned as it was, that it was the end of the season, not the beginning, and that I couldn't see my distorted reflection on its side. Was my hair seriously going to look that bad on the day I saw him, after nine months of perfect hair and not seeing him? (Maybe the two things were related. He really was evil.)

"Dicey?" I finally said. "How?"

"I was supposed to catch a ride with a friend heading up north to work at a summer camp," he said. "But his car broke down outside Boston." Evan laughed. "It was such a rust heap that we took out our bags, and he just sold it to a junkyard for twenty-five bucks. They towed it away and we just stood there on the side of the highway. Then it started raining. Not just raining, actually—pouring. With lightning flashing and these huge cracks of thunder. So it was impossible to hitch a ride when we were crouched down, holding our backpacks over our heads."

What an amusing little story, I thought. But I

was dying inside, dying. I'd never had heartburn in my life, so I wasn't sure if that nauseous churning in the pit of my stomach was heartburn or just disgust.

Soon Evan had Sam, Erica, and the rest of the summer crew laughing at his tale of hitching a ride from a police officer to the train station, getting as far as they could with what little money they had, then camping at a New Hampshire rest area, and finally finding a ride the next day with two nuns and mistakenly swearing as they got into the car because Evan's friend hit his head on the door.

"So, anyway, I made it, safe and sound. Someone was looking out for me, I guess," Evan said.

Darn that someone.

"Technically, I was supposed to be here three days ago," he said.

And what a loss for all of us that you weren't, I thought. I was so (a) angry at the nuns, which is horrible, I know; (b) angry at his attitude; (c) angry at the way he was telling this long, drawn-out story that really only illustrated his stupidity and poor planning. When a random nun has to save your butt—I'm sorry, but you're really counting on luck or divine intervention.

Nuns. Come on! Like they'd let Evan ride with them for more than ten minutes. Didn't they automatically recognize Satan? Weren't they specifically trained for that sort of thing?

Then again, maybe the nun bit wasn't even true—Evan had a habit of embellishing things, of saying things that were obviously exaggerated. Such as: "I love you, Colleen."

"Why didn't you just call someone to come pick you up?" I asked.

"What would the fun in that be?" He stepped closer to me. "Unless, of course, you were the one who came. Still got that Volvo?"

No. I drove it into the ocean when you broke my heart. Sadly, however, I survived.

"Of course," I said.

And there we were, the last place I expected to be, just standing in Bobb's kitchen, looking into each other's eyes.

And I was thinking:

I will kill Trudy with my own bare hands for hiring him back.

"Well, I'm not starting until tomorrow, so I guess I'll see you then," Evan said. "Bye for now."

"Okay. Whatever," I mumbled under my breath.

As he walked away, I looked over at Sam, who was studying the schedule, which was on a clipboard hanging from the back of the store-room door. Trudy did the schedule in pencil. Sometimes it was tempting to erase an entire week . . . like now, for instance.

When Sam met my gaze, I mouthed the words, "What the . . ."

And she whispered back, "I know!"

It was a good thing the lunch shift at the restaurant was beginning. I kept my mind off Evan by visiting with the kitchen staff, the cooks and busboys and dishwashers—most of them had worked at Bobb's the summers before, like I had, so it was more of a reunion.

Even though it was a Tuesday, the restaurant was very busy. Lots of islanders came in to celebrate the beginning of summer, to mark the fact that Bobb's was even open for lunch. And there was a ferry full of retirees from Florida who were traveling together across New England on a bus tour. They kept making jokes about the ferry being worse even than the bus, which was saying a lot, apparently.

One table took so long to order that my mind completely started to wander. I couldn't get over the fact that Evan was here, that I'd just talked to him. I had a hundred questions I wanted to ask him. I was so angry and so excited at the same time. It was a really bad combination; I wanted to talk to him, but if I did, I'd only yell and scream at him.

There it was, that intense pull I felt toward Evan. I could say I'd keep my distance from him. But this was Bobb's, where we both worked. And we were on the island. There weren't that many places to hide.

For some reason I suddenly remembered how we'd sneaked into the old, abandoned lighthouse last summer, after an open-house party at our neighbors' place. We'd sprinted up to the top, climbing up the circular stairs, laughing and pushing each other, until we were standing on the little ledge, looking out at the water. Then we started kissing and soon we were moving on to other things. "Nobody can see in, don't worry," Evan had whispered in my ear.

We'd gotten into enough trouble when my parents were around to keep an eye on me. What would it be like *now*?

But wait! Colleen! I scolded myself. Evan and I weren't together, and I didn't want to be. He'd been fun last summer—but that was all it ever was with him. Fun. Ben and I had something deeper, more serious. Everyone thought we'd get married one day, and we probably would.

I smiled and looked at the first retiree to finally decide on her order. "Would you like soup or coleslaw with that?"

Behind her, I saw Evan outside through the plate glass window. He was standing on the dock, talking and laughing with Stan Mathews, one of the lobstermen who supplied the restaurant. As they talked, Evan was skipping rocks on the water.

The older woman cleared her throat. "Excuse me, doll. But what's the soup again?"

"Oh! Ah." I had to glance at my order pad to remember, which was rather pathetic. We had the same soups every Tuesday last summer. "Clam chowder or tomato bisque," I said.

"Did you say *chowdah*?" a man at the table asked. "Come on, say it. Chowdah!"

I smiled politely, said "Chowdah" as best as I could, and finished taking everyone's orders.

Then I went into the kitchen, clipped the slip to the carousel, and came back to the table with rolls in a plastic basket shaped like a lobster trap.

"Look at that! Oh, Bill, look at that. How quaint!" one of the women said.

Before I could go over to the bar for their drinks, I caught Evan looking at me through the window. When he saw me looking at him, he smiled and waved.

How quaint, indeed. How ridiculously, nauseatingly, shockingly quaint.

Chapter 5

"So. *That* was awkward," Sam said as we walked to the house that night after the dinner shift, at about ten o'clock. She smoothed back her dark brown hair and refastened one of her small gold barrettes.

My feet were so tired from being on them all day that I was starting to rethink this walk-to-work-and-back exercise plan. I was going to need new sneakers. I was going to need a new bike, and not the one-speed hand-me-down from my grandmother that I usually rode all over the island. (Though I couldn't imagine getting rid of the cute wicker basket on the handlebars. My grandmother made it herself. She was so multi-talented—she could sew, knit, and draw like nobody's business.)

"What was awkward?" I asked. "Running out of the special at five thirty and then having to tell everyone we were out of clams at six? I mean, what seafood restaurant runs out of clams? Trudy must have lost her predicting skills over the winter."

"No, it wasn't about the *menu* selections." Sam laughed. "You know what I'm talking about, Coll!"

"Oh, right. When that guy at table nine asked you if you would be working tomorrow, too? What was he . . . like, forty, forty-five?" I'd seen a guy wearing a goofy khaki hat with earflaps smiling and flirting with Sam.

"If I were working tomorrow, which of course I *am*, do you think I'd tell him?" Sam shuddered.

"Too bad there aren't more restaurants on the island," I said—and as soon as I did, I realized how very, very, very true that was. More places to eat would mean more places to *work*. And that would mean I wouldn't have to work with Evan again.

"Yeah, we know that," Sam said, sounding exasperated. "So anyway. What about *Evan*?"

Sam and I had had a brief chance to talk in the kitchen about how freaked out I was, but it wasn't easy to really dish while Cole, the dishwasher, was trying to eavesdrop (and not dishdrop). We were short two people that night, and things had gotten so busy that I hadn't spent that much time thinking about Evan. Which was a blessing not even in disguise, but a flat-out obvious blessing for which I would be eternally grateful.

"I mean, how shocked were you when you saw him?" Sam asked.

"Let's just say that my blood pressure hasn't quite gone back to normal yet." In fact, it felt as though maybe there was a *new* normal that was going to be a lot higher than it used to be. Evan and Ben and me. In the same town. Surrounded by water. Oh, joy.

"He looks, I hate to say it, good," Sam commented. "Really good. He's definitely still working out a lot, or doing triathlons or whatever—you can tell."

"Maybe you should go out with him this summer, then," I suggested.

"Are you serious? No way!"

"Come on, I saw the way you guys were hugging each other."

"Yeah. Very moving, wasn't it?" Sam scoffed. "He was just being a drama king, as always. You said he wanted to major in drama, right?"

"Last I knew, yeah." I let out a sigh. "He looks . . . older or something." I thought about Evan's face. I thought about the way Evan had put his hands on my waist when he saw me. I thought about our tragic good-bye scene in the fog, on the docks, last summer, when I felt like I would fall apart when I saw him get onto the ferry. And how did I not go *with* him, so I could draw the pain out another forty-five minutes?

Then again, it was okay to make a fool of myself on the island—people knew me here. It wouldn't be okay to be crying the entire way there and back on the ferry.

"You're right, he did look older. Except I think he was wearing the same exact things he wore last year. But then, maybe I am, too," Sam said.

"Just the Bobb's uniform. That doesn't count."

"At least they got us a few new T-shirts. My old ones were so worn out, it was ridiculous. But okay, why did he just show up like that? Why do you think he didn't tell anyone, like *you*?"

"He probably feels too guilty for blowing me off last fall. You know?" I asked.

"Evan? Guilty?" Sam shook her head. "He doesn't strike me as the kind of person to feel guilt. Or remorse. Or have regrets."

"Or feelings," I added.

Sam laughed. "Come on, don't get upset. All I meant was that he's more of a live-for-the-moment type."

"Yeah, live for *his* moments, anyway," I said. "He could care less about my . . . moments. Whatever that means. God, listen to me, I'm ranting about *moments* now."

"So the summer's not starting off exactly as we expected," Sam said. "But you know, Evan can go his way this year, and you can go yours. You don't have to worry about him—you're with Ben now."

I smiled, thinking what perfect revenge it was that I had an even better boyfriend now. Ben never ignored me; he was never rude to me; he respected me; he loved me; he'd never cheated on me; we'd never even fought about anything more serious than what pizza toppings to get. Ben wasn't like Evan, and I loved that about him. He was dependable, reliable, and even unflappable when I got into my anxious college-application-due mode and yelled at him for photocopying my collage art in the wrong reduction size.

(Temperamental artist. Yuck, I know. I try not to live up—or is it down—to that stereotype, but sometimes I can't help myself. Honestly.)

Anyway, it all boiled down to one thing: Evan was more flash, less substance.

Flash was overrated.

Flash was like a tall hot fudge brownie sundae with extra whipped cream that tasted great at the time but gave you a stomachache later.

Flash left you sobbing as you stared at your empty e-mail inbox.

I was through with flash.

When we walked up the driveway, Haley and Ben were sitting on the front porch of the house, talking and laughing.

"Hey!" I said, walking up to them. "No fair having fun without us, while we're still wiping down tables."

"And no fair sleeping in, while *we're* already at work for two and a half hours," Haley replied. "Right?" she asked, turning to Ben.

"Yeah, we have a much worse deal. Do you know how cold it is at six A.M.?" He smiled at Samantha and got to his feet. He was wearing a hooded sweatshirt, shorts, and untied basketball sneakers. "You must be Sam. Hi."

"Hey, Ben, nice to meet you." Sam shook his hand.

"I've heard a lot about you," Ben said, smiling. "I'm sure about half of it is true, right?"

"Well, all of the *good* stories are true, anyway," Sam said. "Disregard any of the others."

"Come on, there aren't any bad stories about you," I said. "Unless you count the time you made the tartest lemonade in history for a rude customer."

Sam grinned. "Well, that wasn't necessarily bad. She left, didn't she?"

"Hey, what's that?" I asked, pointing to a familiar-looking orange backpack that was sitting beside the porch swing.

"I heard you have an extra spot in the house, so . . ." Ben shrugged.

"Uh-huh. *Right*," I replied.

"No, actually, I brought back some books I borrowed from your dad," Ben said.

"*The Very Hungry Caterpillar*?" Haley joked. "Or *The Cat in the Hat Comes Back*?"

"Ha ha," Ben said.

"It's nice to meet you, Ben, but I'm beat," Sam said. "I've got to go take a shower and hit the sack—I'll see you guys tomorrow, okay?" She walked over to the door.

Haley covered her mouth as she yawned. "Yeah, I was thinking of turning in, myself. Good night, Ben. Night, Coll."

"Good night," we both said. I felt bad that Haley and Sam felt they had to bolt as soon as Ben and I were together. I mean, I wanted time alone with him, but hanging out as a group was okay with me, too. This was their house for the summer, and they should be able to hang out wherever and whenever they wanted.

"So, how was work?" Ben asked once we were by ourselves.

"Work was—" Suddenly I remembered. *Evan*. Sitting on the freezer, giving me a hug, waving at me through the window. Reminding me of his stupid nice ankles. "Um. It wasn't exactly what I expected."

"Why not?" Ben asked. "Come on, how much could that place change?"

"You'd be surprised," I said with a faint smile. I really needed to tell Ben about Evan. I'd have to tell Ben who he was, that we'd dated, that he was back in town. Sooner or later, I'd have to tell Ben the whole story, or at least part of it.

But as he wrapped his arms around my waist, I decided the story could wait. I snuggled close to him, enjoying the feeling of being in his arms. I felt safe and warm.

"You know what? You smell like . . . lobster

and melted butter," he said.

I stepped out of his embrace and slapped him on the shoulder. "You'll never be asked to live here if you go around saying things like that."

"Sorry," he said, laughing. "I was only joking."

"No, you're not. You know what? Let me go change and I'll be right down," I said.

"Okay, but hurry—I can only stay for another half hour at the most," Ben said. He gave me a quick kiss, then went back over to the porch swing and sat down.

Upstairs, I ran into Sam in the hallway outside the bathroom. "Coll, I know we have the extra room, but . . . he's not really moving in," she said. "Is he?"

"No!" I laughed. "It's just this running joke we have."

"Okay. But is he staying over? I mean . . . is that cool with your parents?"

"No, definitely not. It's on the list, remember? 'No sleepovers, especially of the boyfriend variety,'" I quoted.

"Then again, they *are* a few thousand miles away," Sam said. "How would they—"

"Don't even think it," I said. "Well, okay, think it, but don't do anything else. Anyway,

Ben and I aren't exactly . . . we don't. You know. Sleep together."

"No?" Sam asked.

"Not yet, anyway," I said. For some reason Ben and I were both still waiting to take that last step. Maybe I was waiting because I felt like I'd jumped into that too quickly with Evan and it had made the breakup that much worse. I was a little tentative now, I guess.

I quickly changed into a pair of striped pink Adidas workout pants and a long-sleeved navy fleece, and went back downstairs. On the way, I grabbed an apple from the bowl on the kitchen table.

"So did you really bring a change of clothes?" I asked, pointing to the backpack, now propped against the porch chair. I sat next to him on the porch swing and took a bite of the apple.

"Sure. I mean, why not? I can always sleep out here on the porch." Ben laughed. "No, *your* parents might be gone, but mine are still very much here. And they're expecting me home in a half hour."

"Right. Parents." I snuggled a little closer to him. "I remember those."

Ben put his arm around my shoulders and

squeezed me tightly. Then he turned and started to nuzzle my neck, giving me little kisses. I turned to him and kissed his chin, his cheeks, his mouth. I just needed to be reminded of how wonderful Ben was, how he was nothing like Evan, how he worshiped me completely . . . ?

Suddenly the telephone rang, jarring me out of the fantasy that I was worshiped by—well, anybody. Who was calling so late at night? Maybe Haley's mom, I thought. To tell her to go to bed or she'd be tired tomorrow.

"Ignore it," Ben whispered in my ear as the phone rang again.

"Done," I said, trying to lose myself in his kisses.

The phone stopped ringing. Seconds later, there was a loud knock on the screen door. "Um, sorry," Haley said. I pulled away from Ben and looked up to see Haley standing there holding the telephone out to me. "Coll? It's your parents."

"What? My parents?" Somehow they knew that if they called right now, they'd ruin the one half hour I had to spend with Ben. It was amazing.

"Hello?" I said into the receiver.

"Colleen!" my father's voice cried. "How are you?"

"I'm fine—but are you? I mean, is there an emergency or something?" I asked.

"Goodness, no."

"Then why are you calling *now*? It's like four in the morning there—isn't it?"

"It costs less to call now," my father said. "Plus, we have jet lag, and knew you'd just be getting home from work. How was it?"

"Fine, the same as always," I said, my brain flashing back to the freezer moment, when I first saw Evan. In some ways, yes, work was the same as always, but in some ways it was completely different. I decided to spare my father that particular detail—and it wasn't just that Ben was still sitting beside me. It was that my dad wouldn't enjoy hearing about Evan any more than Ben would.

"And how are all the girls? Did everyone arrive okay?" he asked.

I got up off the swing and went into the house to grab a glass of water. "Yes. One thing, though—Erica is going to live at her grandparents' house instead of here. So we have a free bedroom—yours, in case you decide to come home early."

Why did I say that? I missed them, but I didn't want them to come home early.

"Oh, no chance of that. I mean, we aren't planning to cut the trip short—but if there's an emergency, or if you need us—"

"No, don't worry, everything's fine. It's going to *stay* fine, too," I told him.

My mother got onto the phone next, and I talked to her for a couple of minutes. Before I hung up, I had to promise her that I'd stick to every single one of the posted rules and that everyone in the house would stick to them, too—and everyone on the island would, too. I'm actually not sure what I promised. I was really tired, and I wanted to get back to Ben, who was patiently waiting outside for me, even though it was getting chilly. "Yes, Mom. Love you, too. Good-bye!"

She rattled off a few German phrases and then she was gone. Despite the fact they had kind of annoyed me, I was really glad they'd called. It was great to hear their voices. It was just . . . couldn't I have heard their voices the next morning?

"Your parents have incredibly bad timing," Ben said when I rejoined him on the porch. I sat on the swing and cuddled up next to him. "Do you think they have a web cam set up or something?

You know, 'Let's see what Colleen's up to'?"

"No, you know what it is. My family, my entire extended gene pool, has really poor timing," I said. I patted my mouth to cover a wide yawn. "You know that."

"And yet, I still hang out with you." Ben lightly rubbed my shoulders. "Why do you think that is?"

"I have no idea," I said. "Maybe because you know you owe me."

Ben laughed. "I *owe* you?"

"Yes. You'd never have your summer job now if you'd puked on the ferry that first day of school," I reminded him.

"You're so romantic." Ben tilted my face toward his and we kissed.

Telling Ben about Evan now would be a case of bad Templeton timing. Wouldn't it? I mean, here we were, enjoying ourselves, feeling really close. If I told him now, it would be a horrible end to a pleasant evening. We only had about ten minutes left before Ben had to go home.

So, it was settled. I'd tell Ben about Evan tomorrow.

Chapter 6

When Erica, Samantha, and I walked into Bobb's for our staff meeting the next day, I expected to see everyone sitting in the dining room, where we usually got together for these occasional meetings.

Instead, the meeting was in the kitchen. Evan was sitting on top of the stainless freezer once again. Standing beside him was a girl I'd never seen before. I felt my heart start pounding nervously, and my palms got sweaty. *Don't tell me that's his new girlfriend, I thought. Please don't tell me it's bring-your-latest-conquest-to-work day.*

She had long, straight blond hair, and wore khaki capris, white sneakers, and a Bobb's T-shirt with the sleeves rolled up, showing off tan, sculpted arms. She looked like a tennis player. Maybe it was the K-Swiss court shoes that made me think that.

Trudy started off by saying something about

how being in the kitchen brought us closer to the heart of the restaurant, and how that would bring us all closer together. She talked a lot about needing to be *close*. She was somewhat of a hippie, but she'd also apparently read a lot of business books over the winter and she was just dying to try out their theories.

"So, crew, there are a few new people I want you all to meet. Well, one is new, and one is a returning favorite." Trudy winked at Evan.

I nearly tossed my cookies into the sink I was standing beside. "Returning favorite"? As if this were a game show and Evan was a former champion or something. Or a feature on the menu. Tonight's returning favorite: Evan the cold-hearted. Served with a side of slaw, also cold.

Maybe I felt so grumpy because I was sleepy from staying up so late with Ben the night before. I couldn't imagine how *he* felt—he'd already been at work for four hours. Poor Ben. He had to be at work at six. Our summer schedules weren't going to work very well together. He kept trying to get the later shift, but since he was the new guy he got last choice.

The new person at Bobb's was the blond-haired girl standing beside Evan. Her name was

Blair, and she was taking the place of Kelley, who'd decided at the last minute to work at the Spindrift B&B instead of at Bobb's. (Why anyone would want to make beds and muffins is beyond me, but to each her own, I guess.)

"Blair came to visit for a weekend but decided to stay on," Trudy said.

That still didn't answer my question: Did she *know* Evan before now? What did she know and when did she know it? Etc.

"Where are you from?" I asked her, smiling and trying to be polite about the fact I was prying.

"The most boring town in the United States," she said with a sigh. "I am *so* glad to be here."

Everyone laughed, and I thought, Could she be a little *less* forthcoming? That description didn't sound like Philadelphia, Evan's hometown. But you never knew. Anyhow, my invitation to visit that particular city had been rescinded, so what did *I* know?

"Is this the first time you've ever been here?" I asked.

She nodded. "Yeah."

"What made you want to stay for the whole summer?" I went on.

"Isn't it obvious?" she asked.

I just smiled at her. *Um, no? That's why I'm asking?. Because if it has anything to do with Freezer Boy there, I need to know. Now.*

"This place is heaven!" she said. "I love the ocean, and I love the feel of it here."

"Yeah, well—see how you feel in July, when you're waiting on a table of spoiled ten-year-olds who just flew in from New York and they expect you to shell their lobsters *for* them," Evan told her.

"Now, Evan, that's enough of that," Trudy scolded. "We don't need any negatives here in this kitchen, just positives." She smiled at everyone, and Evan looked at me and the corner of his mouth curled up in a half smile.

I just looked at him, remembering the day last summer when that happened, and how hard we'd laughed when Evan had intentionally cracked a claw so that it shot pulpy liquid into one of the kids' faces.

Then Trudy was off on one of her let's-all-pretend-we're-crustaceans-and-bond lectures.

"Remember, we all have to work together as a team if we're going to make it through another crazy summer. A lobster has eight legs and two claws, and needs every one of them to walk." Trudy was constantly trying to integrate things about lobsters into her management technique. It was funny—when it wasn't extremely annoying. Because right now there were some legs on this team that I wouldn't mind losing. Legs with Birks attached to them. Why did he have to be in such good shape? I hated that about him. Running around the island, Little Mr. Triathlon.

It was appropriate that he was sitting on the freezer all the time. He could be so cold. All those times I called him, E-mailed him, told him that I wanted to visit. And he totally encouraged me, until push came to shove and it was time to set a date, and then he dropped me.

"Colleen?" Trudy asked.

"Oh. Yes?"

"Are you still with us?" Trudy waved her hand in front of my face.

For the moment, I thought. If I could find another job on the island, then . . . no.

"Are you getting enough sleep?"

"Not last night," Samantha commented.

"Oh, really." Trudy frowned at me.

Evan was staring at me, and I felt this heat rising from my toes all the way up to my face, and I knew I was turning bright red. Almost cooked-lobster-like.

"Well, I was wondering: If you could be a sea creature, Colleen, what would you be?"

"Anything with a hard shell," Evan said before I could think of anything, and everyone laughed. Me, with a hard shell? He was the one who'd retreated, not me. I was the one who'd gotten hurt.

"Soft-shell crab," I said, staring right back at Evan, who had this idiotic grin on his face. "With a baked potato on the side."

"Yeah, well, I think I'm more of a squid," Evan said. "Squids are the smart ones, right?"

No, squids are the slippery, elusive ones. So yes, that fits you perfectly, I thought.

"Now, one last announcement before we throw open the doors and meet our public," Trudy said when she wrapped up the meeting about five minutes later. "Blair is still looking for a place to live this summer. For now she's camped out on our living room floor, but I'm sure she'd like something a little more permanent and private. If anyone knows of anything . . . please don't hesitate to speak up. All right, you guys. Let's have a great summer!"

Erica, Samantha, and I immediately headed off to a corner of the kitchen where we could talk privately.

"So what do you think?" Sam asked me. "Should we tell her we have space in the house? Would you be okay with that?"

"We don't really know her. I mean, we don't know her, period," I pointed out. "We have no idea what she's like."

"No, but she seems nice," Erica said. "Doesn't she? And you have that empty bedroom that used to be for me, right?"

"Unless Ben sneaked in there when we weren't looking," Sam joked.

"I don't know, Erica. My parents . . . they wanted to approve of everyone living there," I said.

"So what's not to approve?" Sam asked. "She's employed. She must be okay or Trudy wouldn't have hired her. How about we invite her over and show her the rules? Ask if she wants to agree to the terms? If she does, great. If not, then no big deal—she can keep looking. But . . . you know how hard it is to find a place to stay here, Coll."

"And she seems really nice," Erica said again. "She even volunteered for the Monday and Tuesday lunches because no one else did, because everyone knows you don't make good money."

"I wonder if her parents would let her live with three total strangers," I said.

"We're not strangers, we're co-workers," Sam said. "All you can do is ask." As I said earlier, she has a way of cutting to the chase and making things seem simple—things that I could obsess and worry about.

I nodded. "Okay." The three of us approached Blair, who was studying the back-of-the-house menu of abbreviations, no doubt trying to memorize some of Trudy's bizarre nicknames.

"Blair? How about living with us?" I asked. "We're all splitting a house, and we have an extra bedroom."

"You're kidding. Really?" Blair asked.

"I was going to live there, but then my parents changed their minds and said I had to stay with my grandparents instead," Erica said. "So yes, really. It's available."

"There's no rent," I said, "but you'd have to kick in some money for basic house expenses, split the groceries, all that. It's about a mile from here—" I felt a tap on my shoulder, and turned to see Evan standing at my elbow.

"What are you talking about—you're all living at your house?" Evan asked. "Where are your parents, Coll?"

"In Europe," I said, trying to ignore the fact that (a) he had just called me "Coll," (b) he still had his hand on my shoulder, and (c) it was making me feel very uncomfortable.

"You're kidding!" Evan said. "They left for the whole summer?"

"Practically, yeah," I said. "They'll be back at the end of August."

"Oh. That's too bad. I was looking forward to seeing them again," Evan said.

Don't take that tone with me, I thought. That I-know-your-family tone. So aggravating. "Yeah, well. Too bad."

Actually, if my parents had known Evan was coming back, they probably wouldn't have left me here by myself. They thought he was "semi-dangerous." At least that was how my dad put it when he was trying to console me during the days when I was trying to get over Evan and spent every spare moment moping around the house.

Maybe I should spare them the bad news and not tell them Evan was back for the summer, so they didn't spend time worrying on the Continent and ruin their trip. He wasn't that important.

Evan shrugged. "I guess there's a lot that's

been going on that we don't know about each other."

Um . . . yeah. For instance, I didn't know if he had a heart or whether he was running on battery power. How many Duracells would it take to make someone appear human?

Suddenly I realized that Sam, Blair, and Erica had drifted away, leaving me and Evan alone. "Um, yeah," I said. "There probably is a lot we don't know. For instance, where are you going to college?"

"Actually, I'm going to B—"

"Not Bates," I interrupted him. "You're not going to Bates. You can't."

"I can't?" he asked.

"No—"

"Can I finish what I was going to say?" he asked.

"But Bates—that's not fair, because *I'm* going to Bates—"

"Oh, and you have to approve who can be there at the same time with you? You're on the admissions board?" Evan asked.

"No. I just thought . . . maybe we shouldn't be at the same college because maybe that would be weird. Right?"

"Maybe it would be. Yeah, it probably would be," Evan said. "But you don't have to worry about that, because what I was trying to say was that I'm going to Boston University," he said. "That's where I'm going. BU."

"Oh." I felt like a complete idiot. Why couldn't I just shut up now and then and wait for people to speak? Did I have to rush in and embarrass myself like that? "So, BU." I smiled weakly. "That sounds great."

"Yeah. What is that—a three-hour road trip from Bates?" he mused.

As if it mattered, I thought. As if I were going there, or he would come see me. "More like two and a half," I said, and then I could have kicked myself. Why did I want it to sound shorter?

We exchanged awkward glances. The last time we discussed a road trip, it was me to Philadelphia. And as we both knew, that never happened, which was part of the reason I was standing there feeling like I wanted to shove him into the walk-in freezer and lock the door behind him.

Not that I would. But picturing icicles on his stupid stubbled face *really* made me smile.

Evan, not knowing what I was thinking, smiled back at me.

"It really is good to see you."

Don't! Don't be nice like that, I thought. "Yeah. You too," I said.

And then the lunch shift began. It was completely busy, and I didn't get a chance to take a break until two thirty. Sam was finishing up with a large party, so I signaled to her that I was heading outside, and grabbed a bottle of chocolate milk from the fridge. Then I went outside to get some fresh air. The air doesn't circulate all that well at Bobb's—or at least not in the kitchen, with the giant steaming pots of hot water and soup simmering all day long.

I got a shock when I opened the back door. The wind had shifted direction so that it was now blowing off the water towards, well, *me*—and it was getting really cold. It felt good, though, and I knew I would cool down in about two minutes. Then I could go back inside, wipe down my section's tables, and wrap some silverware in napkins (Trudy called it "bundling") before the end of my first shift of the day.

I cracked open the twist top on the chocolate milk and leaned back in the doorway, taking a few gulps. I was in mid swallow when Evan came up to me, carrying a bag of garbage for the Dumpster.

I was going to offer to move when he squeezed past me in the narrow doorway. And then he stopped and stood there for a second.

"So. Still got milk, huh?" he asked.

I just glared at him. He thought he was so funny. Him and his Ultimate Endurance, which somehow got activated to smell even better when he was standing that close to me. He wore it, he lived it . . . and I had to suffer because of it. I didn't have high endurance for this. I had low tolerance. And now he was cracking jokes about my beverage preference.

"What? Why are you looking at me like that?" Evan smiled.

"You know why," I said.

"Not really, no," he said.

And there was this electric feeling in the air all of a sudden, as if a storm were about to hit. Suddenly it didn't feel chilly.

"That trash bag is touching my leg," I said. "What else?" I wriggled out from the doorway and went back into the kitchen to safety. I wasn't ready to be alone with Evan like that. I didn't think I'd ever be ready for that again.

Chapter 7

"This is it? No way!" Blair said as we walked up to the house. The four of us were sneaking in a visit between shifts at the restaurant so we could show Blair the place. "How long have you lived here? You're so lucky!"

"Well, we moved here about ten years ago," I said. "When my grandparents died, we moved into their old house. Well, first we moved back to help take care of my grandfather, and then we stayed here."

"Your grandparents died?" Blair gave me a sympathetic look. "I'm sorry. They must have been pretty young."

"Yeah, they were. In their sixties." I still missed them, and I wished we could have all lived here together—if not in this house, then at least on the island. I had lots of great memories of the weeks we'd spent here together when I was little.

I'd inherited not only my grandmother's bike,

but also a little of her artistic skill. She had done illustrations for a book about the island, and it had become so popular that she'd been asked to work on a few other books—one was all botanical illustrations, and another was about the ocean. She'd had a fatal stroke about ten years ago, and I'd always regretted that I hadn't gotten to know her better. After she passed away, my grandfather didn't do very well. He ended up with heart trouble, and he died about two years later.

"Wow. That's terrible," Blair said when I told her the story. "Sorry if I brought up a painful subject."

"It's okay," I said. "I don't mind talking about it."

"Still, you live here all year? That is so cool. I'd love to do that. This makes my town look pathetic—well, more pathetic than it *usually* does." She laughed.

It was fun to watch someone new to the island see the place for the first time. You know how you get so used to something that you don't realize how great it is until someone else points it out?

"Wait until you see your room," I told Blair as we walked through the kitchen. On the way in, I grabbed the sheet of poster board off the bulletin board. Blair was so busy looking around the house that she didn't notice.

After a quick tour of the first floor, she and I headed up the stairs together. "It's usually my parents' bedroom, so you'll have to be really careful and make sure you don't, um, wreck anything."

"No problem," Blair replied.

During a break at work, I'd called my parents and asked them whether it was okay for me to offer the extra room to Blair, since Erica couldn't take it. They'd said it was fine, that they trusted my judgment.

Sometimes I wished they didn't trust me or my judgment so much. It felt as if I could only go *down* in their estimation of me—and that it might happen fairly soon. But Blair seemed cool, and I just couldn't see that we'd have any problems. She was really making an effort to get to know all of us, and so far she was a great co-worker. Okay, so we'd only worked together one shift so far, but you could learn a lot about a person in that short time.

"It's huge!" Blair cried when she walked into the bedroom. She wandered around the room and looked out the windows. "Ocean view. King-size bed. The color's a little drab, but I can deal with that. So why has no one else taken this gorgeous room?"

"Well, it was set aside for Erica, remember?" I explained again how her family had decided she should stay with her grandparents this summer instead of here. "And then we decided to leave this room vacant for guests."

"Wow. And you'd really let me just live here? Free of charge?" Blair looked at me.

"Well, yeah—I mean, you'd need to pitch in on house stuff with the rest of us, like groceries and the phone bill," I said.

"You're the best!" Blair said, throwing her arms around me.

"Okay, but before we go any further, there's something you have to see."

"The bathroom? Oooh, is it connected—a master bath?"

"No, not quite." I laughed. "Feel free to go check it out, though, third door on your right. But I was talking about this." I handed her the poster board. "It's a list of house rules, which my parents wrote up and made me agree to. It's important to them, so if you could look at it and make sure you're okay with the ground rules, that'd be great."

"Ground rules?" she said, beginning to scan the list.

"Yeah. If you don't mind. Just review them. I know it sounds dumb, but—"

"No, it's fine. I know how parents can be."

"I'm going downstairs. Come on down when you're ready," I said.

As I started down the stairs, I heard Haley's voice. She didn't sound happy.

"You guys asked her to *live* here? Without asking me about it first? Without even letting me meet her?"

I gulped. Oh, no. Why hadn't I thought of that? Of course Haley would have to approve of the plan, too. And there was nothing Haley hated more than being out of the loop.

"But she's really nice," Erica said.

"So what? You know, you don't even live here!" Haley cried. "How can you make decisions that affect the rest of us?"

"I'm so sorry," I said as I walked into the kitchen. "We shouldn't have asked her without asking you."

Haley just glared at me.

"Come on, Haley—I'm sorry. We got carried away—we just felt so bad because she didn't have a place to live. She's been sleeping on Trudy and Robert's living room floor," I explained.

"But we all agreed that we'd decide who was in the group together. We're fine with just the three of us, aren't we? It's not like we *need* a fourth person so we can pay less rent. We *have* no rent! And then *you* always have a place to sleep when you stay over," she said to Erica.

Erica shrugged. "I can sleep on the sofa."

Haley rolled her eyes. "Come on."

"Nothing's final yet," I told Haley. "Meet Blair first, okay? If for some reason you don't like her," I said in a soft voice, "we'll just tell her that we changed our minds."

"We can't do that," Sam said. "That'll come off really rude. We already *offered* it to her. And she really needs a place."

"What's she doing up there, anyway? Moving in already?" Haley asked.

"I'll go get her," I said. I headed for the stairs, but before I could go up them, I saw Blair heading down. "Hey, Haley's home—you've got to meet her."

"Oh, sure. Great. Love to," she said with a smile.

"So what did you think of the rules?" I asked as she reached the bottom of the stairs. "Are you going to be okay with them?"

Blair handed the poster board back to me. "They're exactly the kind of rules my father would write up for me. In fact, I think he has, already. So it's no problem. I'm ready to sign on, if you guys are."

"Um . . . well, let's see. Blair, this is Haley. Haley, Blair."

"Cool name." Blair smiled at Haley.

"Thanks." Haley wouldn't quite look at her, at first.

I went to the fridge and got out a pitcher of lemonade. I sliced a few fresh wedges of lemon and tossed them into the pitcher. "So, let's go outside and talk. We still have some time before we have to get back to work."

"Where are you working?" Blair asked Haley as we filed out onto the porch.

On the way, Samantha grabbed four wineglasses from the cupboard. "Just to make it fun," she said to me.

"Or, are you working, I guess I should ask,"

Blair said to Haley as she settled into a chair. "Not everyone has to."

"Oh, I have to, all right," Haley said. "I work at the Landing—you know, the shack down by the water with coffee and ice cream—"

"Where are you from?" Blair interrupted.

"Here," Haley said.

"You have that accent. I love that accent," Blair said.

Haley shrugged. "I can't help it. I'm going to try to get rid of it in college."

"Oh, yeah? Where are you going—Paris or something?"

"Not quite. Dartmouth."

"Oh, God. Dartmouth. I got rejected by them before I even submitted my application. When I requested a catalog they sent it to me with this big DON'T EVEN BOTHER sticker on the front cover."

Haley laughed. "They didn't."

"Pretty much," Blair said. "Ivy League . . . I mean, I'd kill to be Ivy League. I'm actually taking a year off so I can reapply and try to get in somewhere good next time."

"I don't care that much about whether it's Ivy League," Haley said. "I just want to be somewhere where the other people are smart. It's a lot of pressure, you know?"

"Yeah, but it's your ticket to everything when you graduate," Blair said.

"My ticket's going to be to Europe. One way," Sam said. "Right, Colleen? We're going to Europe for three months after we finish college."

"Right," I said. "Just as soon as my parents do all the groundwork this summer and figure out where we should go."

"Yeah, but you wouldn't want to go or stay where your *parents* like. Would you?" Blair asked.

"She has a point," Sam agreed.

"Colleen's parents think classical music is fun," Haley said. "They read about ten books a week, and their last big road trip was to . . . Where was it? Historic Colonial Inns of Massachusetts?"

Everyone laughed.

"Hey, at least they have a great house, and we're all really lucky to be here." Sam raised her glass. "To the Templetons."

"To Starsky and Hutch!" Haley grinned at me.

"Starsky and Hutch?" Blair said.

"Our cats. Are you okay with cats?" I asked.

"Um. Sure," Blair said. "Are they nice?"

"Supersweet." Erica raised her glass in the air. "To a great summer!" She turned to Blair. "Your turn."

"To . . . oh, my gosh, I can't think of anything original," Blair said. "To . . . the ocean! And my new view of it. Thanks, guys."

To ex-boyfriends, I thought. *To new boyfriends.* "To friends!" I said.

We all reached forward to clink our glasses together.

I guess I must have clinked too hard, because my wineglass splintered into a hundred pieces and we all jumped back to avoid the shattered glass.

Maybe I should have taken that as an omen, but I didn't. It just seemed like something clumsy at the time.

Chapter 8

"Colleen?" Trudy stopped me on my way back into the kitchen on Friday. I was done, for the moment, with my lunch tables. "Could you help me out with something? There was just a woman here who insisted on looking at every single T-shirt we had for sale, and she and her kids must have tried on about twenty shirts. Could you do me a favor and go refold them all?"

"Sure," I said.

"And there's some additional stock in the drawer underneath the cabinet. If you wouldn't mind restocking, too, while you're at it?"

"No problem." I quickly washed my hands in the sink and then went out front. No one was working at the register, and Erica was nowhere in sight, which was odd. But, knowing Erica, she was probably carrying leftover boxes of food out to someone's car, or driving them home, or something. The phrase "above and beyond" was created for her.

I picked up the pile of T-shirts from the counter and moved them over, away from the register, so they wouldn't be in the way. I shook the first one out and laid it on the counter, then neatly folded it into a small square, with the Bobb's logo showing above the pocket.

When I finished folding the first stack, I crouched down to put them into the glass display case. I was doing some rearranging when someone else walked behind the counter and legs slammed into my shoulder. "Ow!" I cried.

"Sorry!" a voice above me said. Evan reached down and put his hand on my shoulder. "Colleen, you okay?"

I pushed his hand away and resisted the urge to spit on his sandals before standing up. "I'm fine."

"How was everything today?" Evan asked as he ran through a credit card for a customer.

Everything was fine, I thought, pulling myself to my feet, *until you showed up*.

"Great. Delicious," the man said. "We'll definitely be back." After he'd signed the receipt, and after he and his family left the restaurant, Evan leaned against the counter, watching me fold shirts for a second.

"I can ring up the next person," I said. "I mean, I'm here. I could have rung up the *last* person."

"I didn't see you," Evan said. "I didn't think anyone was over here."

"Yeah, right," I murmured.

"What—you think I'd intentionally crash into you? Why would I do that?"

I shrugged and didn't say anything. I tried to slide open the cabinet door closest to him so I could put the size small T-shirts away. But it wouldn't open from the side I was on, so I looked up at him. "Do you mind? Moving?"

He took a few steps to get around me, but he didn't walk all the way out from behind the counter. In fact, he was standing about a foot away from me, giving me no room at all to work. "I don't want to leave because someone might come up, and, you know, you are busy with those shirts. Busy busy busy." He smiled at me.

I let out a deep, annoyed sigh and just kept restocking the case, trying to get it done as quickly as I could, and also trying to ignore what it felt like to be in such close proximity to him again. He smelled the same as always. And I caught myself looking at his ankles again as I crouched down to pull out overstock from the bottom drawer. And then I started thinking about the time he came to my house for dinner last year and I played footsie with those ankles under the table. Or would that be "anklesie." Whatever. Wrong, wrong, wrong to be thinking about it now.

I couldn't get those shirts folded quickly enough. As soon as I was done, I marched straight past him to Trudy's back office and knocked on the door. "Trudy? Could I maybe change my schedule around?" I asked.

"Sorry. No changes for the first month," she said.

"The first *month*? Why?"

"People need routine. A restaurant needs routine," she said.

Yes, but I need a routine that doesn't involve seeing Evan every day, I thought. Couldn't she be more sensitive?

"Why? Is there a problem?" Trudy asked.

"Yes. No—it's fine," I said. I closed her office door and went back down the hallway into the kitchen. Evan smiled at me as he walked past, carrying a tray of desserts out to the dining room.

Drop them, I thought, staring at the tray. *Drop them*.

After the lunch shift, Sam, Erica, and I headed down to the Landing. I was glad to be getting out of Bobb's for a while, and away from Evan.

The three of us were going to our weekly book club meeting with Haley—at least that's what we said we were doing when anyone asked, and occasionally we did talk about what books we were reading. But in reality we were going down there to watch the ferry come in. Later on Friday afternoons was when it got crowded with tourists coming for the weekend. Haley and I had started out as kids, watching people get off the ferry in order to write stories about them. We played a game of making up details about their lives; she wrote stories about them and I did sketches.

Then when we got older it became part celebrity watch and part looking for hotties who might be coming to the island for the weekend. We could also see people cruising into the harbor on their sailboats.

Not that I was looking for a guy now—in fact, I hadn't been for the past year, or for last summer, either. But that didn't mean I couldn't look. I mean, help my *friends* look.

We called it our book club so that we had an excuse for being there every Friday. *Book* was an acronym for "boys on our kiss-list." Okay, so we came up with that in the fifth grade and it sounds dumb now, but at the time? It was brilliant.

"Where are you guys going?" Blair asked when we didn't turn off on the road to our house. "Or am I totally lost?"

"We're going to the Landing," Erica said. "Want to come along? It's time for book club." I cast a sideways glance at Erica. I wasn't sure if I wanted to invite Blair, but it was too late now to take back the invitation.

Blair looked confused. "But I probably haven't read the book. What is it?"

Erica quickly explained what our book club was all about.

"I like the sound of this. But how about if we stop by the house and change our clothes first?" Blair suggested.

"I don't know," Sam said. "See, I kind of like letting people know where we work. Just in case, you know, it's Orlando Bloom for real this time, and he starts wondering where he should go for dinner, and he looks at our T-shirts and voilà. He's at Bobb's."

"You have it all planned, huh?" Blair teased.

"Anyway, we'll get all bogged down in changing, and then we'll miss the three o'clock, and we'll have to come back and change before we go back to work at four thirty . . ."

"Hey, say no more." Blair held up her hands. "Let's go! My parents are going to be so impressed when I tell them I'm in a book club." She grinned.

I'm sure Ben wondered why Haley and I were always there hanging out on Fridays, but we never told him the real reason, because that would ruin everything. We said it was our Friday-afternoon book club. "Then why don't you have books with you?" Ben had asked more than once.

"We remember it all—we just read the book this week. What do we need the book for?" Haley said.

Not very convincing, but he didn't push the issue. He was nice, and trusting, like that.

Last summer Evan had been a little more suspicious. He'd always asked, "What book is it this week?" and I'd have to come up with something, and then if it was something he'd already read and I hadn't, I'd have to read it just to keep from blowing our cover. Yes, our cover *was* that important. It was a fun game for us that we didn't want to see end.

Evan had even pulled up a chair once last summer and tried to butt in on our "meeting." Samantha politely told him it was a *female* book club.

When we got down to the Landing, Blair and Erica went over to Haley's window, while Sam and I sat down on one of the wooden benches facing the dock.

"So that was pretty uncomfortable at work today," Sam commented, loosening the laces on her sneakers.

"Your feet?" I asked.

"Um, no," she said. "You and Evan. There's so much *tension* between you guys—it's like painful to watch sometimes. Are you going to try to switch shifts, so you don't work with him so often?"

"I tried, but Trudy said she doesn't want anything to change for a month. She's anti-change. Which is odd, because lobsters get to molt, so shouldn't we be able to?"

"Molting isn't your problem, Coll. I mean, did you even *tell* Ben yet?" Sam asked.

"Tell him?" I asked.

"About Evan being here this summer." She slid her sunglasses down her nose and looked at me over the top of the frames. "Oh, no. You guys haven't talked about it, have you?"

I shifted uneasily in my chair. "Well . . . no, not exactly."

I was overdue on a couple of talks.

Evan and I hadn't had The Talk, or any talk, yet. Maybe there wasn't all that much to say, I thought. We were together . . . and now we're not. We were totally crazy about each other . . . and now we're not. We were in love . . . or so I thought.

It was all sounding like bad poetry. That was what bad poems were about: lost love, love in general. Of course, there were good poems about that subject, too. I'd had plenty of time to find them in my *Norton Anthology of Poetry* when Evan was not calling me.

And yes, I was procrastinating about telling Ben about Evan, and about the fact he was back and working at Bobb's with me. It wasn't as if I'd never said *anything*. I mean, before we went out the first time, I'd told him I'd had a couple of boyfriends before him. Of course, I'd focused more on Walter, my second grade sweetheart, and Clifford, who took me to our freshman winter formal.

"Walter and Clifford?" Ben had laughed. "You're making this up, right? Freshman winter formal? So what does that mean—down jackets and black ski pants?"

"It was a *very* sexy evening. Actually. Very sexy," I insisted.

"Not exactly?" Sam was saying now. "Meaning what?"

"Well, I did tell Ben that there were lots of, um, familiar returning employees at Bobb's."

Samantha raised her eyebrow. "*Familiar?* Is that seriously what you said? *Familiar?* How about extremely—"

"I know, I know," I interrupted her. "Slightly more than familiar." I tried to kick a rock with my sandal, but I ended up hitting it with my toe instead. "There just hasn't been a good time to talk to him about it yet."

"Ahem. You've spent at least a couple of nights hanging out with Ben this week," Sam pointed out. "Like last night. You've had time."

"Oh, sure, *time*. But not . . . the right time."

Sam laughed. "Listen to you—'the right time.' There's never going to be a *good* time! Just get it over with, because if you don't, he's going to hear about it from someone else, and that'll be really bad."

"I know. I know I have to tell him. It's just . . . I don't want it to be awkward. I don't want him to feel threatened. That's why I have to pick the perfect time. I know—why don't you come with me when I talk to him?" I said.

"Yeah. Right," Sam said. "*That's* what I want to do."

"Why not?"

"I don't even know Ben yet. Do you know how awkward that would be? And why would I be there for such a personal conversation?"

"Because you're nosy?" I suggested.

"What are you being nosy about now?" Haley dropped into a chair beside me and handed us both fudge bars. "Make it quick, I only have a ten-minute break. As soon as everyone gets off Moby, I've got to run back."

"Oh, nothing," Sam said. "Just talking about some people at work." I knew she was covering for me so I wouldn't have to tell Blair and Haley what a coward I was being, which was awfully nice of her. Haley would be mad if she thought I was hiding *anything* from Ben.

"So I was wondering something. How come you don't work at Bobb's?" Blair asked Haley.

"It's kind of dumb. But my mother has this feud going with Trudy and Robert. I can't even remember how it started, but she'd disinherit me if I ever worked there. Not that there's anything to inherit," Haley said.

"So about this club. Have any of you ever actually met a celebrity getting off the ferry?" Blair asked as we watched the boat approaching.

"I met a senator once," Haley said. "That was pretty cool."

"Oh, yeah," Blair teased. "Bet he was a real hottie."

"She," Haley said. "And no."

We all laughed.

"Speaking of hotties, you know who's really cute?" Blair took a sip of water. "That Evan guy."

That Evan . . . guy. It was weird to hear someone else talk about him that way. Was Blair interested in him? Should I tell her that we'd gone out? Or should I just warn her about what a jerk he could be?

Blair and Evan . . . if they got involved, I wouldn't be able to handle it, I realized. Why hadn't I thought of that before I asked her to live with us? I mean, I knew none of my close friends would date him . . . but what if Blair did?

"Colleen went out with him last summer," Erica said before I could say anything myself. Because I was just sitting there having an anxiety attack and letting my Fudgsicle melt.

"Yeah, they had a *thing*. A pretty serious thing, actually," Sam added while I rubbed at the melted chocolate with a napkin.

"Oh, *really*." Blair gave me what seemed like a look of newfound respect. I smiled awkwardly. "A thing? Cool. So, what's he like? How long did you guys have this . . . thing?" She laughed.

"Um, well." I wondered how much I should tell her. We'd only met a couple of days ago, so I didn't feel comfortable going into complete detail. "He's . . . well, he *can* be . . . fun," I said. That was pretty vague. "We went out for a month or so."

"No, it was longer than that, wasn't it?" Erica said. "Two months."

"Yeah, I guess. But then summer ended and

he went home, and so . . . you know." I shrugged.

"No point keeping up a long-distance relationship," Blair said. "That's exactly how I feel about things."

I smiled. It wasn't exactly how *I'd* felt, but whatever. I really didn't feel comfortable talking about Evan with her. And even worse, now Blair knew about me and Evan, while Ben still didn't. That wasn't cool. What if it got back to Ben from her? Or what if Haley mentioned it? They were friends; they'd talk like that. But she knew I wanted to be the one to break the news, or at least I hoped she did.

The ferry pulled up and we all watched as first several cars drove off it, and then a varied collection of middle-aged-looking men and women strolled off the ramp and onto the dock. Small children screamed and raced each other to the end of the dock and were chased by their parents. A few teenaged boys were there, but they were boys we knew from the island—boys I knew nobody either would be, or should be, interested in.

In other words, no prospects.

"See you guys later!" Haley jumped up as she

saw someone approach the takeout window.

I smiled as I saw Ben helping an older woman walk carefully from one surface to another. He was carrying her luggage for her, too.

"You know what? Out of everyone?" Blair pointed toward Ben with her red straw. "*That's* the best-looking guy here."

I cleared my throat. Did we have the same taste in guys or what? "Blair? That's my boyfriend. Ben. You met him at the house the other night. Remember?"

"Oh, my gosh—I'm sorry. You're right—I didn't recognize him in his uniform. Sorry," Blair said. But she kept looking at him—staring, in fact.

He walked right up to where we were sitting. "Hey, guys. How's it going?"

"Good," I said, looking up at him and smiling. He leaned over and kissed me on the cheek. "How was work?"

"Crazy, as usual on Fridays," Ben said. "How's the book club?"

"We were just finishing up our discussion," Sam said. "Metaphors, similes. You know."

Ben stretched his arms over his head. "I'm so beat. I'm going home to take a shower and change—I'll see you when you get off work tonight, okay?" He gave me another quick kiss and went over to the bike rack to unlock his bike.

"Your schedules really suck this summer, huh?" Sam commented. "Not like when you were dating Evan and you could see each other at work all the time."

"Sh!" I said.

"Sh, what?" Blair asked.

"He doesn't know about Evan yet. I still have to tell him."

"Why would you do that?" Blair said.

"Uh, because I have to?" I said. "Because it's the only right and honest and decent thing to do?"

"Maybe, but it's stupid, too. I never tell guys about ex-boyfriends," Blair said. "It just makes them mad, or it makes them think they're better than him, or even worse, it makes them think they have to go out and *prove* that they're better than him."

Why did it sound as if she'd had a hundred boyfriends already? "So you just don't say anything?" I asked.

"I keep it vague. Extremely vague. I think secrecy is underrated these days," Blair said.

I nodded, smiling. Maybe she was onto something.

"I mean, has *he* told you about all of his ex-girlfriends?" Blair asked.

"I think so. I mean . . . well, how would I know? He only moved here last year."

"Exactly. And how would Ben know about Evan if you don't tell him?"

Sam cleared her throat. "He'd know."

"Why?" Blair asked.

"Because she and Evan act like freaks whenever they're around each other."

"Freaks?" I laughed. "We do not!"

"Okay, then. Whatever you say. But why don't you go walk Ben home?" Sam suggested.

I glanced over my shoulder and saw Ben talking to one of his neighbors. "Good idea. See you guys in an hour!"

I jogged over to catch Ben before he rode off on his bike. We walked down the road together, catching up on things.

Tell him! Tell him! my brain screamed as I babbled on about an E-mail from my parents and a description of Trudy's latest dessert concoction (a peanut butter fudge brownie sundae with fresh strawberries and whipped cream—what I'd had for lunch).

"I'm going to have to come by for that," Ben

110

said, sounding very interested. "I should do that, huh? Come see you at work sometime this weekend?"

"Um . . . maybe not this weekend, because it's going to be swamped," I said. "How about sometime during the week? Like, ah . . ." I hadn't seen the schedule yet for next week, but there must be a day that I worked and Evan didn't. And if there wasn't? I'd create one.

Tell him, tell him right now!

But we only had an hour to spend together. Why should I ruin it? I'd wait for my day off. Monday. I'd tell him then, for sure.

Chapter 9

Any day that starts off with you getting canned cat food on your sunglasses is not a good day.

Maybe I don't even have to point that out, because it's pretty obvious, but take my word for it: When your small, perfectly oval, slightly green and slightly pink framed sunglasses, that you found only after trying on fifty other pairs and annoying your mother to no end at a department store, because all the other shapes made your face look big, or small, or wrong, only she couldn't see that, only *you* could see that . . . well, when something happens to *those* glasses, you should take it as a sign.

I was feeding the cats before I went to work, and I had leaned over to set down the bowls, but my sunglasses were perched on my head and they tumbled right into the ocean fish catch (or, rather, can) of the day. The lenses went smush into the gloppy, fishy part. If that image isn't disgusting, I don't know what is. In fact, I could not stop thinking about it even after I washed them in hot soapy water for five minutes, so I wasn't wearing sunglasses, which could have been part of my problem. Any bright sunny day near the ocean without sunglasses? Not a good idea.

Also, someone had used up the coffee the day before without replacing it. I added Rule 11 to the pink poster board:

No using up coffee without buying more.

Then I made myself a cup of herbal spearmint tea—which is what I usually drink before going to sleep at night—and made a bowl of instant oatmeal, because we were also out of milk for cereal. Halfway through eating, I noticed the oatmeal had a strange-looking black seed floating in it. The rest of it went down the garbage disposal. Then I added Rule 12 to the list:

No using up the last of the milk without buying more to replace it.

It was my day off, but not Ben's, so I'd decided to do a round-trip on the ferry. That way, we could spend some time together. The way the day started off, maybe I should have given up on my plan to talk to Ben about Evan that afternoon, but I didn't. I even begged Sam for assistance, but she turned me down, saying she wanted to spend the day reading and hanging out on the beach. She promised to stop at the store for milk and coffee, so I was officially out of excuses.

I was riding my bike down to the Landing when I turned a corner in the road and saw Evan riding toward me. Could this island *get* any smaller? Could there not be more than three main roads?

Of course, as I got closer I noticed that Evan had a nice road bike, while I was cruising along on my trusty fifty-year-old one-speed.

"Hey!" He turned around and started riding beside me. "What's up?"

"Oh . . . not much." *Just going to tell my boyfriend about you.*

"You're not—" I stopped myself before I blurted it out, for once. If I told him where I was going, he'd probably follow me there, or ask me why I was going to the mainland.

"I'm not what?" he asked.

Not that nice. Not very considerate. Not as good-looking when your ankles are covered up with white socks. "You're not, ah, training for a triathlon, are you?"

Evan squinted at me, which was funny considering I couldn't stop squinting. Having light blue eyes makes you very sensitive to bright sunlight. "No, not right now. Why?"

"Just, you know . . ." I shrugged. "Wondering."

"And you? Where are you headed?"

"I'm, ah, going to visit Haley. At work."

"Oh, yeah? Well, tell her I said hi."

"Sure thing," I said. "I'll do that."

Haley was no fan of Evan's, though, so maybe I wouldn't do that. I heaved a sigh of relief as he turned back around and rode away.

"Could you get me two large root beers?" I asked Haley. "No, wait. Maybe I should make those banana splits."

"Having a bad day?" she teased.

"Not yet," I said. "Well, kind of." I explained about the cat food and the sunglasses while she filled the cups with root beer.

"Thanks for making me lose my appetite," she said as she handed me the large plastic cups.

"Thanks. I'm bringing one of these to Ben—I thought I'd catch Moby and ride a round-trip with him."

"That sounds like fun." Haley rested her

elbows on the takeout window and we both gazed out at the people getting off the ferry.

I saw Ben talking with a tall girl with long red hair who was carrying a classic off-white L. L. Bean "Boat and Tote" canvas bag. (I used to think they were stupid, until I realized how much stuff you could carry in them.) "Who is that girl?" I asked as I watched her give Ben a big smile and wave good-bye as she disembarked.

"I have no idea," Haley said.

"Isn't she on the ferry like every day?" I asked. I'd seen her every day that I came down here, anyway. Why was she boating and what was she toting? And did it have to be with Ben?

"Almost. Usually at three, though. She's early today."

As she walked past, I couldn't help noticing that she was flat-out gorgeous. She was tall, and she wore a black skirt, a pink-pattern wispy blouse, and black sandals. Her legs were model material. "Do we hate her, maybe?"

"Maybe a little bit." Haley nodded. "Yeah."

I stepped aside as a customer approached the window. "Wish me luck."

"Luck," she said. "For what? Drinking a root beer?"

"Yeah, something like that." I laughed. The way my day had begun, I wouldn't be surprised if I (a) dropped it off the boat, (b) got the hiccups after drinking it, or (c) laughed too hard while drinking it and had root beer come out my nose.

"Actually . . . I'm going to tell Ben about Evan," I confessed.

"Oh. Oh? Well, then. *Luck*," Haley said. "Lots of it."

When I stepped up to the ferry to get on, Ben just stared at me.

"Colleen? What are you doing here? What's this?"

I handed Ben a ticket. "For me." Then I handed him the root beer. "For you."

"Wow. Thanks."

"I'll go sit down. Come and find me when you get some free time, okay?" I said.

"More than okay." He smiled and kissed my cheek as I walked past him.

I sat up front, on the upper deck, enjoying the sun on my face with my eyes closed against the brightness of it. I was exhausted from last night's shift. We'd been fairly busy when a table of twelve came in without a reservation. It was a birthday party for a four-year-old, and by the time we could get them a table all of the kids were in pretty rotten moods. While I went to get their sodas, Evan had brought them a couple of trays of French fries to keep them happy, and then entertained them all by doing some simple magic tricks, like pulling out quarters from behind their ears. Then they'd laughed and yelled and made Evan be their waiter, instead of me. What can I say? They were easily entertained. I was a bit put out, until he shared his eighteen-percent tip with me.

"Hey."

I opened my eyes and saw Ben standing there. "Hi!"

He sat down beside me and we gave each other a hug. "This was so nice of you to come for a cruise. You didn't have to buy a ticket, though."

"Well, I didn't want to get you in trouble or anything," I said. I looked into his eyes, squinting against the bright sun. Why did I feel so guilty, like I had done something wrong? It was what I *hadn't* done that was the problem. I gave myself a mini pep talk while he finished off his root beer.

If I tell him about Evan, that will make it seem less weird. Once I tell him, it'll be out in the open and we can all go back to our normal, or semi-normal, lives.

"So, there's something I have to tell you," I began.

"This doesn't sound good. What's wrong?"

"Nothing! Nothing's *wrong*." I put my hand on his leg and gave his thigh a reassuring squeeze. "I just need to let you know about something that happened last summer, before you lived here." I paused for a second and then reminded him, "You didn't live here then. I didn't know you."

Ben just stared at me. "Yeah, I know I didn't live here last summer. I'm the one who moved."

"Right. Right!" I laughed nervously. "I really have to stop saying that so much. *Right*. I'm constantly saying that, aren't I? It must be annoying."

"Colleen? I only have a couple of minutes, so . . ."

"Okay. Last summer." A strong breeze blew the strap from my knapsack against the ferry railing. For a minute, I just sat there and listened to the sound of it snapping. "I probably mentioned I went out with this guy named Evan. Right?" Darn. I said it again.

"No, I don't remember anything about a guy named Evan," Ben said.

"Sure, I told you. Evan. From Philadelphia?"

I finally got the nerve to look at his face, and tried to gauge his reaction to this news. "Anyway, it wasn't like it was anything serious. We dated for a couple of months—you know, typical summer . . . fling. Thing."

"A couple of months isn't exactly a fling."

Darn Ben and his definitions.

He looked at me, then down at the deck, then back up at me. "One or two dates is a fling. Not two months."

"But see, sometimes the way you feel about a person is that they're like a fling, like that's how *un*important they are to you."

"And you spent two months with a guy you didn't care about. Wow. That really makes me feel good about us."

"No! I didn't mean . . . Sorry. Okay, so it wasn't just a fling. That was a poor choice of words. We . . . we went out last summer."

"So why are you telling me about this now?"

Because I have to? And because Sam won't be my friend if I don't? "Well, it's just . . . this guy, Evan? He came back this summer. I didn't *know* he was coming. I hadn't even heard from him in months. I mean, I'd barely heard from him since the day he left."

Annoyingly, the image of our painful good-bye scene actually had the nerve to flit through my brain the split second I said that. The early-morning fog, the long romantic hug, the never wanting to let go. . . .

"We didn't keep in touch," I said to Ben. Or at least I did, but he didn't. "So I had no idea he'd be here again. Which is maybe why I never mentioned him. Anyway, he's here."

"Really. Where did you see him?" Ben's voice was flat, almost like a monotone.

"Bobb's."

"He came in for dinner or something?" Ben asked.

"Well, uh, yeah. In a manner of speaking." This was going to be so, so awkward. "He works at Bobb's."

"When did he start? Last night?" Ben asked.

"Actually . . . maybe a few days ago."

"And you're just telling me this now," Ben said, not as a question.

Oh, no. I knew I shouldn't have waited so long. He was really angry. I'd never seen him like this. "We hardly have any of the same shifts, so I haven't seen him much, and I didn't think it was a big deal," I babbled. Now, on top of everything, I was lying.

"Just . . . don't. Look, I have stuff to do." Ben stood up and walked over to the steps that led down to the main deck.

That could have gone a lot better, I thought as I watched him glide down the steps. I mean, it could hardly have gone *worse*.

Right?

After a few minutes, I tried moving down to the lower deck to see if I could talk to him. First he walked past me without making eye contact. Then when he was standing beside Cap Green, I went to try to join the conversation. But Ben moved away, leaving me alone with Cap, the chatterbox of the ferry industry.

I was stuck on Moby with Ben, who hated me now. I looked longingly at the inflatable life rafts hanging on the wall and the preservers stacked beside the door. Making a run for it sounded tempting. Ben would probably help by giving me a push in the direction of the island.

I had a new rule. It didn't have anything to do with the house, but just for fun let's call it Rule 13, because it felt so unlucky.

Never have important discussions on a boat when you are halfway through a round-trip.

Chapter 10

"So, I'll see you later?" I asked.

Ben mumbled something as he leaned over to unlock his bicycle, but I didn't quite catch it. I decided not to push my luck right now. He was still angry with me. He probably didn't want to see me later, or even *think* about seeing me later. He hadn't spoken to me on the way back to the island. (Me, I had made small talk with tourists, and it was the longest forty-five minutes of my life.) I had to give him some time to let him deal with the news about Evan, and me and Evan.

"Okay, well, um, take care," I said awkwardly as he pulled his mountain bike out of the rack beside the Landing.

"Ben! Where are you going?" Haley shouted from the takeout window.

"Hi, Haley!" he called back.

Well, at least he was talking to *her*. He wasn't doing that hate-by-association thing.

"Where are you going?" Haley asked.

"I've got to get home," Ben said. He didn't explain what the big rush was. Obviously it involved getting away from me.

"Hey, you want a FrozFruit for the road?" Haley offered. "We got more coconut in today."

"No thanks. Tomorrow, though! See you later." Ben gave me a cursory glance, and immediately his grin faded. Then he climbed onto his bike and started pedaling away.

"Bye!" I called after him, trying to sound as sweet as I possibly could, hoping I'd erase this new, bad impression I'd apparently made on him. Then I walked over to Haley. No, more like crawled.

"So, how did it go?" Haley asked.

"Couldn't you tell? Ben hates me now."

"Hates you? Come on, be serious. What flavor do you want?"

"I'm not hungry. Anyway, you saw how he was," I said. "Not even talking to me." I stared at the tubs of ice cream. "Cookies and cream," I sighed.

Haley scooped ice cream into a sugar cone and molded the scoop so that it would stay in the cone. "So he's a little put out," she said. "I wouldn't worry about it."

"I don't know. I think I *would*," I said.

She dipped the ice cream into the bowl of chocolate sprinkles—we call them "jimmies," but I know not everyone does, because I ordered them that way once when we went back to Chicago to visit and everyone treated me like I was a freak. "How did he really react?"

"He kind of didn't say anything. I mean, he was mad at first. And he's still mad. That pretty much wraps it up, I think."

Haley handed me the cone, then rang up the sale and slipped a dollar into the register. "Don't worry. He'll be angry for a while, but he'll get over it. He loves you. He'll understand."

"Thanks for saying that." I started to lick the ice cream. "I hope you're right."

"Of course I'm right," Haley said. "I'm a Boudreau, and Boudreaus are always right. Or at least they always think they are."

I laughed. "Haley, what if he doesn't forgive me? What if he gets mad at—at Evan, and they fight or something?"

Haley looked at me and frowned. She seemed annoyed by the suggestion. "Ben's not like that. When he's mad at someone, he keeps his distance. Now be quiet and eat your ice cream and forget about those guys for a second. Put your feet up. Relax."

"Okay, Mom," I said.

"I'm not acting like—" Haley stopped as she noticed she was about to unfold a napkin for me. "Anyway, eat."

"So, speaking of. Have you seen your parents lately?" I asked.

"Oh, yeah. I went over there to see how they're doing. They're still mad I'm not working for them. They kept saying pitiful stuff like, 'Well, we're about to go under, not that you'd care about that.'"

I smiled. I could just picture Haley's mom saying that. "She thinks guilt is one of the food groups."

"Oh, yeah. She's horrible. And she's *good* at it, too, which is the worst part. So I'm going over there at two to help out." She rolled her eyes. "I cannot *wait* for September."

I was on my way back into the kitchen to put in two orders and grab some food when I saw Evan delivering a trayful of plates to one of my tables.

There. He was doing it again.

I hated how he kept bringing food to my

tables, as if I needed help, as if I couldn't handle it on my own.

Ten minutes later, I walked into the kitchen to pick up another order that was ready and caught him doing the same thing. "What are you doing?" I asked. "I can get those."

"I know, but I'm right here." Evan shrugged. "Besides, all my tables are parking right now. I don't have much to do."

"Yeah, but I can still handle it," I said. "I don't need your help."

Evan turned to look at me. "You know, last summer you loved it when I did this."

"Yeah, well, last summer I loved a lot of things you did," I said before I could stop myself. I bit my lip, wishing I could take it back. I couldn't believe I'd just said that. I had to follow up with a witty retort immediately. Danger, danger! Actual feelings emerging!

Evan was grinning at me in that annoyingly seductive way of his. It's amazing how far nice green-blue eyes can *get* a person in life. It's like a get-out-of-jail-free card.

"But, you know, as the saying goes . . . that was then. This is now." I gave him what I hoped was a withering, devastating look. Probably I just seemed really crabby. Not the soft-shell kind, either.

"Wow. Deep. *Insightful*." Evan nodded. "I bet Bates can't wait to get a hold of your mind."

I took the plates of food off his tray, briefly considered tossing them into his face, thought he might get burned, and instead started loading them onto my own. If only I were closer to the refrigerated pie case, I thought. I'd love to see his annoying, charming smile covered in blueberry or coconut cream.

"We *could* just swap trays," Evan said. "You know, an empty one for a full one? Or do you have a close personal attachment to that one— you guys go way back or something?"

I heard a laugh behind me, and glanced back at the coffee machine. Blair was standing there, laughing at Evan's ridiculous tray joke. Great. Now we were amusing other people. Even more than we usually did.

I hoisted the heavy tray and headed out to the dining room. When I walked through the swinging door, somehow the tray slipped from my fingers—sweaty, no doubt, from my Evan encounter—and tipped a little, and I jostled a side dish of coleslaw off the tray. Of all the luck.

It landed right on my foot, then I almost slipped on it and fell down.

I hate coleslaw. What or who is "cole" and what is "slaw" about cabbage and mayo, anyway? If I ever had a side dish named after me, I hoped it would not resembled a "slaw." Colleenslaw. That's about how good I felt about myself as I scraped it off the carpet five minutes later.

It was all Evan's fault. Everything was.

(a) The fact that I had coleslaw shoe.

(b) The fact that I'd just had to get up close and personal with the carpet.

(c) The fact that Ben wasn't speaking to me and probably wouldn't be for the rest of the day.

I pulled off my apron and tossed it into the laundry hamper beside the kitchen door. "What are you doing?" Evan asked. "You're not leaving, are you?"

"No. I'm taking a break." I walked through the kitchen to the back door and stepped outside. For some reason he was following me.

"You okay?" he asked.

"I'm fine." As I was walking onto the docks, it started to rain. As if my day could get any worse. I should have known it was about to rain because the kittens that hung around the docks were nowhere in sight. They have cat-dar. They can tell when storms are coming, sort of like my hair.

"This is all your fault, you know," I said.

"Me? What did I do?" Evan asked.

"You know, you have a way of ruining things just by standing there."

Evan started to laugh. "I think you're giving me a little too much credit. I can't actually make the weather change."

And then we just stood there for a minute, not saying anything. I couldn't think of anything *to* say. I was speechless. I'd spent hours rehearsing all the things I'd say if I ever saw him again, if we were ever alone again. Now I couldn't open my mouth. Which was so ridiculous, considering.

"So, what was your winter like?" Evan finally asked.

I knew he was trying to be nice, to make conversation, but it made me so angry that he had absolutely no clue what my winter had been like. *And my fall, and my spring?* I wanted to ask him. *And basically everything since last August 29th, or whatever day it was in November when you just vanished?*

"Colleen?"

"Oh—fine," I said. "Just fine."

"Fine. Really? Did you want to give me any details?"

"I just . . . I don't know why you're asking. Now. I mean, it's a little late. You could have asked me back when it was actually semi-relevant."

"Yeah, but what would be the fun in that?"

I was so sick of hearing him say that. The *fun*. Was that how it felt, completely ignoring someone by not keeping in touch? *Fun?*

I started thinking that I must have really bad taste when it came to boyfriends. Maybe that was it; maybe that was why I'd had two of them while my friends didn't, because I'd picked guys who were no doubt available because they were horrible, evil losers.

But that didn't make sense, because Ben was a totally nice person with zero flaws except (a) nearly vomiting when he met me, which technically had nothing to do with me, and (b) being too nice sometimes, to a fault.

Ben wasn't the problem. Evan was.

"I can't believe you're still wearing your Birks to work. I thought Trudy banned sandals as footwear. Didn't we go over that, like, a hundred times?"

Evan just looked at me with a small smile

turning up the corners of his mouth. "Funny."

"What?"

"You never struck me as the nagging girl-friend type."

"That's because (a), I'm not nagging, and (b), I'm not your girlfriend."

Before I knew what I was doing, I'd stepped closer to Evan, and I gave him a little shove, a bit more forceful a shove than I'd meant to. His sandals slipped on the slick docks, and he lost his balance. Then he plunged backward into the harbor, landing butt-first with a loud smack in the dirty, fishy, disgusting cold water.

"Oh, no—oh, Evan—I'm sorry!" I cried, running over to him when he surfaced.

I expected him to be coughing and sputtering and yelling at me, but he wasn't. He was actually smiling.

"Are you okay? Are you freezing?" I asked. "Come on, get out."

"You know what? It's refreshing, actually," he said.

"Refreshing? You're literally swimming with the fishes." I could see a fish skeleton bobbing in the water beside Evan.

Erica ran out of Bobb's toward us, holding a

couple of towels. "Evan, are you all right? Do you want help getting out?"

"Thanks, Erica. That would be nice." He swam toward the dock and held on to it with his fingers, which already looked slightly blue. I watched as he reached up for Erica's hand, while she dumped the towels in my arms.

Suddenly, Evan grabbed my ankles instead of Erica's hands—and pulled me facefirst into the water. I threw the towels over my head as I dove in.

The water hit me like a wall of ice cubes. I think my heart actually stopped beating for a second as my head submerged, and I closed my eyes and mouth against the freezing, murky water.

When I surfaced, I saw Evan smiling at me. He hadn't even started to get out of the water yet. "You . . . This is so dangerous!" I said.

"So . . . it's okay for *me*, but it might hurt you?" Evan's hair was slicked back, and he looked so good to me that for a few seconds I just tread water and stared at him. I started remembering a night last summer when we'd dared each other to go swimming. Not just swimming, actually. Skinny-dipping.

We were walking home from a party, and we took a detour down a dirt road, by this private cove, to check out the full moon.

And yeah, we both did the dare. And then—

Erica cleared her throat loudly. "So, don't you think you guys should get out now? We should all get back inside."

"Right!" I said quickly, swimming to the edge. I hauled myself up onto the dock, with Erica's help, and grabbed one of the towels from her, quickly covering the wet T-shirt and shorts that were now clinging to my body. I rubbed my hair with the towel, trying to dry it a little bit.

"I lost a sandal." Evan was crouching at the edge of the dock, peering into the water.

"So dive down and find it," I said.

"Like I could." He stood up and looked at me, giving a slight laugh as he reached down to slip off the one remaining Birkenstock. It was dripping wet. "It's your fault, and they're like ninety-dollar sandals."

"You only lost one. So that's forty-five."

"But I can't buy just one, I have to buy a new pair. So you owe me ninety bucks."

"Yeah, but they were at least two years old, so they weren't worth that much."

"So? Replacing them will still cost me ninety." Evan rubbed his head with a towel.

"You can start paying me tomorrow, out of your tips. Unless you have ninety on you right now."

I quickly reached into my pocket, hoping I hadn't lost my wad of bills to the harbor along with Evan's stupid sandal. Nope, it was still there. But I wasn't handing it over.

"No. I don't. And I can't give you all the money I make tomorrow. I need it."

"Well, you should have thought of that before you pushed me in." He turned and walked up the dock and then up the ramp to the restaurant's back door.

If I could have found that missing sandal, I would have thrown it at the back of his head.

We had a shower in the basement that he was probably going to use. I'd stay out of his way until he was finished. Me, maybe I'd just go home and shower, so I could change my clothes. And if I didn't work any more tonight, I wouldn't make any more tips, so then I wouldn't have to pay him back.

Right?

I started shivering and realized I needed to get inside. I called home and asked Haley if she could bring me a change of clothes.

"Why do you need new clothes?" she asked.

"Don't ask."

"I just asked."

I let out a sigh. "Because I fell into the water and my clothes are sopping wet and I smell like bait."

"Gross. Why didn't you just say so?"

As soon as she dropped off the clothes, and when Evan was done, I went into the bathroom and took a long, hot shower, trying to wash away the entire day: the cat food on my sunglasses, the bad talk on the ferry with Ben, the nasty harbor smell in my hair.

The way Evan had looked, treading water beside me. How it reminded me of last summer.

And how I shouldn't be thinking those kinds of things anymore.

Ben wasn't waiting for me when I got home that night, and I can't say I was surprised. In a way, I was a little relieved, because I was so exhausted that I didn't know if I could (a) deal with his being mad at me, (b) explain why my shoe smelled of coleslaw, and (c) explain why I'd acted so secretive about the whole thing with Evan.

I shouldn't have secrets from Ben. Should I?

But I did.

Chapter 11

It was still raining the next morning, so I decided to take advantage of the bad weather to work on a new collage piece.

I've been doing collage art since I was about nine. It started out as an art project for school— I'd always loved children's books by Eric Carle, Leo Lionni, and Lois Ehlert, to name a few. So I tried to imitate their techniques, but it didn't come out quite right. Dad helped me improve, though, and I started small, making Mother's Day and birthday cards, then worked up to bigger pieces. I made mini-yearbooks for my friends, and even taught art in my parents' classes a few times a year. We sometimes used discarded lobster, clam, and mussel shells and stones from the beach to make glued collages—a different type than I usually made, but it was still fun.

My dad, Magic Marker Man, couldn't have been more thrilled by my decision to pursue an

137

art major. After Richard gave up liberal arts to become a stockbroker, Dad had been convinced he'd failed somewhere along the line. Now, sadly, I would apparently uphold the Templeton tradition of doing lots of work for no pay.

But maybe it wouldn't come to that. I was working on some new pieces, and getting slides made of others so that I could start putting my portfolio together and maybe someday have a gallery show. Portland has a lot of galleries and a really active arts scene.

"Why don't you paint? You should paint," my Uncle Frank would say whenever he saw my work. "You know, Betty McGonagle sold over *fifty* paintings last summer."

Which might sound impressive, except that:

(a) Betty McGonagle paints only one thing.

(b) It's the ocean.

(c) She does the same thing over and over again and they're all 5"x7".

(d) They're sold at the Landing gift shop, and you could put old, expired, rancid *meat* at that gift shop and it would sell, as long as it had the word *Maine* imprinted on it. (People get desperate when they see the ferry about to leave, and they reach for something—anything—quaint.)

(e) Betty McGonagle is like seventy-five years old and has all day to paint.

Don't get me wrong. I love paintings of the ocean. Winslow Homer really knocks me out. But I just can't get excited about Betty McGonagle's paint-by-numbers . . . numbers.

Suddenly I realized there was a reason I was thinking so much about Betty McGonagle. And it wasn't jealousy over her sales figures or ability to capture moving water.

The smell of paint was wafting down the hallway and sneaking into my room. Was there another artist in residence that I didn't know about? I set down my glue and wandered out into the hall. Then I followed my nose to Blair's room. I knocked on the door. "What's that smell?"

"Paint!" she called out. "Come on in—check out how good it looks!"

I walked into my parents' bedroom and nearly tripped on a bucket of paint as Blair switched on the overhead light to give me a better view.

"Purple?" I cried. "You painted my parents' bedroom bright purple?"

"No. It's lupine, actually," she said. She

leaned down to look at the can of paint sitting on newspapers on the floor. "Late-afternoon lupine." She was wearing overalls and a white T-shirt, with a baseball cap over her hair.

"It's still . . . purple, though," I said.

In a way, it looked sort of cool. And my parents could be fun, and it fit into the category of playful elementary school colors. But she had a lot of nerve, painting a room that was only going to be hers for a couple of months. And who was going to get into trouble? Not her. *Me.* "How could you do this?"

"What?" She seemed surprised by the question.

"You just . . . paint someone's room? Without asking? You're only living here for two months!"

"But I needed a change," Blair said. "That light blue—it was bringing me down. So washed out. When I wake up in the morning, I need a blast of energy, not to look at myself in the mirror and just seem . . . faded and tired."

"But it was new. And it matches—excuse me, *matched*—everything," I said. "And it's my parents', and my mother picked out the color and she spent like a year choosing it." One of the most aggravating years of my *life*, I could add—the great Templeton redecorating project of the new millennium. Poring over home improvement books and comparing color palettes until the break of dawn, night after night. It was my mother's reaction to Richard leaving home for college. (Of course, she didn't finish all the work until well after he graduated.) I wondered what she was going to do when I left home.

First, probably repaint my room and turn it into something else.

Or maybe Mom would deal with my leaving home by going to Europe without me for the summer. Hold on. How did that make sense?

Anyway. Blair wasn't all that apologetic about it, and I wasn't the kind of person to fight and fight over it. I strongly believed in that old adage "What's done is done," maybe because my father said it all the time, usually whenever he botched a home improvement project. I told Blair that we'd have to repaint before the summer was over, then I went downstairs, took down the house rules list, and wrote:

13. Do not paint or redecorate any
    rooms without asking first.

It was too late, and it kind of repeated some other rules on the list, but whatever. Doing it made me feel better, as if I'd proved some sort of point, which of course I hadn't.

I went back up to my room and tried to work some more, but I couldn't stop racking my brain for the name of that light blue paint shade that my mother loved so much. I could ask her in an E-mail, but that might make her suspicious.

I knew—I'd ask at the hardware store. Eddie would remember the name of it, and I could see if he had some in stock. I grabbed the car keys from the counter and went outside.

I was about half a mile from the store when I saw him running on the side of the road.

My first thought was to pull over and ask if he wanted a ride. It was raining, after all.

My second thought was to swerve and hit him.

I decided to ignore both urges and just drive past with a friendly wave to Evan. I glanced in the rearview mirror to see if he recognized me. The mirror was tilted toward me, and I noticed that my hair was a complete frizzone. Naturally.

At the store, Eddie was busy helping another customer, so I picked up this big flip-book from the counter that showed hundreds of colors and tints of paint. I went through all of the blues, but none of them sounded familiar.

I kept flipping through colors, hoping I'd recognize it when I saw it. Then I gave up and wandered down the paint aisle. I was surprised I didn't see Betty McGonagle there, stocking up on a few gallons of Atlantic Ocean Blue and Sunset Sea Foam. She must buy her paint by the gallon.

"Colleen? What are you doing here?" Eddie asked when I drifted past the counter for the third or fourth time.

"I need paint. Do you remember the paint my mom bought? For the master bedroom?"

"Hm." Eddie scratched his head. "No, can't say as I do."

"You don't? Because I don't, either. And I've got to buy some more because I need to repaint."

"No sense painting in this weather," Eddie said.

The little bell above the entrance jingled, and I turned to see Evan walking into the store. He was sopping wet. Rain dripped from his hair to his shirt, from his shirt to the floor. His shoes made a squishy sound as he approached the counter.

"What did you need today, young man?" Eddie asked. "Besides a raincoat, an umbrella, and more sense than God gave a lobster."

Two points for Eddie, I thought with a smile.

Evan ran his hands through his hair. "Uh . . . ants." He pointed to the boxes stacked in the display rack beside the counter. "I mean, ant traps."

"Ant traps," I repeated. "You ran here in the rain for ant traps."

"The man's got a problem," Eddie said as he rang up the sale.

Man? No. Problem? Yes.

"All of a sudden, they're everywhere. My cousin's panicking," Evan said. "I told him I'd pick these up when I was out on my morning run."

"Right." I nodded as he pulled a ten-dollar bill from his shorts pocket.

"It might stop raining, you know," Eddie said. "I suspect we'll be done with this front in . . . oh, two, three days at most." He chuckled. His telephone rang, so he picked it up with a polite wave to both of us. So much for getting paint.

Evan and I walked to the doorway and stood

there for a second, watching the rain come down even harder now.

"Do you want a ride back to your house or anything?" I offered.

For a second he looked flustered, which was nice, because so far I felt like I was doing all the flustering. "Yeah. I'd better not get these traps wet," he said.

"You wouldn't want wet ant traps," I agreed. "Anything but that."

"Shut up," Evan said, and we both sprinted to the car, which was silly, considering he was already drenched and I was about to be. I slammed the door behind me and started the engine. A Volvo was a good thing to have in a flood.

"So. You still owe me for the sandals, you know," Evan said as we started down the road.

"What? I *gave* you money," I reminded him.

"No, you gave me half."

"Evan!" I slapped the steering wheel. "Come on. Do you really want to be like that?"

"Like what? Cheap? Like you're being?"

I ignored his "cheap" shot and drummed my thumbs against the steering wheel as I drove. "So, I have a question."

"Yes?" Evan asked.

"Why did you come back this year?"

"Where else would I want to be in the summer? This place is paradise," he replied.

"Paradise." I rolled down the window a little bit, and raindrops pelted my arm. Evan must have run pretty far. He didn't exactly smell . . . paradisiacal. Then, too, there was that Ultimate Endurance deodorant scent sort of hanging in the air. "Are you training for anything right now?" I asked. He'd run a few marathons already. I'd never even made it the whole way around the island, though some busy nights at work, I could have sworn I'd walked five miles— unfortunately, all of them back and forth from the dining room to the kitchen.

"No, not really. Well, I want to make the cross-country team at BU, so I guess I'm training for that. But if I don't make it . . . you know. I'll just transfer to Bates or something."

I laughed. "Yeah, right." I looked over at him. "You wouldn't."

"I wouldn't?" he said.

"Come on. Really. Would you?" I asked.

"I doubt it, Coll. Aren't Maine winters brutal?"

"They're cold, but they're not horrible," I said. "At least, I don't think so."

"Yeah, but you love sweaters. I don't do sweaters."

I smiled, because it was almost sweet of him to remember my stacks of sweaters in the hall closet.

Then I really remembered how he knew about them.

We'd been in my house; he had come over for dinner so he could finally meet Mom and Dad, and I'd brought him upstairs as part of the house tour.

"We keep this door open because Hutch likes to sleep on the sweaters," I had explained. And Evan had gently pushed me inside the closet and closed the accordion-style door behind us and started kissing me. I was thinking, Good idea, Mom, getting this walk-in closet added during the big home renovation! And we were still kissing in the dark when I stepped on Hutch and there was a loud cat "Yowl!"

We all jumped, and Evan flung open the door so quickly that it sprang back shut again—on Hutch's tail. "Yowl!" Hutch cried while we were laughing and kissing.

"Everything okay up there?" Mom called up the stairs.

"Fine! Everything's fine, Mom!" I yelled. "Hutch is just being funny."

Evan wiped a smudge of my lip gloss off his mouth while Hutch hissed at him as he finally bolted out of the closet to safety. That was one of the times we'd very nearly gotten caught. It wasn't the only one.

"Colleen?" Evan coughed. "The house is back there."

"What?" I suddenly snapped out of the memory. "Oh. Right. *Right.*"

"Were you thinking what I was thinking?" he asked as I did a U-turn.

"Um. What was that?" If he said anything about the closet incident, or asked how Hutch was doing, or said he wanted to visit the cats, I didn't know what I would do. I was still mad at him. But I also might jump him and head for the nearest closet.

I am such a bad person.

"With this weather? Work's going to be so dead tonight," Evan said. "Don't you think?"

"Oh, yeah. Really, incredibly dead."

The way I should be for thinking such disgusting things about an ex-boyfriend.

* * *

When I got home, Sam and Erica were huddled in front of the TV, watching a movie.

"Where've you been?" Sam asked when I walked in.

"Oh. Ah. The hardware store."

"What did you get?" Erica asked.

I looked around the living room for a minute, trying to remember. "Nothing. I guess."

Erica stared at me with a confused expression. "Oh."

"You seem kind of down," Sam commented. "Is everything okay?"

"Yeah, everything's fine," I said, but I was talking as if I were a prerecorded message.

"Coll. Really?" Erica pressed.

"Yeah." I didn't want to admit, not even to Sam and Erica, that I had no idea (a) what I was doing, (b) how I was feeling, (c) what I should do next, and (d) what it all meant.

I told myself I should call Ben. It was almost four and he'd be home from work, so we could talk before I went in at four thirty. But it was like I didn't even know what to talk to him about right now. I definitely wouldn't tell him how I spent my afternoon.

So I told Erica and Sam about the purple

lupine paint job Blair had done on my parents' bedroom, and we all ran upstairs to check it out.

"No wonder you were in such a bad mood," Sam commented.

"Don't worry—we'll fix it. My grandparents have tons of painting supplies," Erica said. "Masking tape, rollers, pans, all of it."

"What was she *thinking*?"

Blair walked out of the bathroom with a towel wrapped around her head. I'd had no idea she was home, and I don't think anyone else did, either.

"I was thinking I needed a change. I don't see what's so criminal in that. My parents always let me paint my room whatever color I choose."

"But . . . that's your house. Not her parents' actual bedroom," Sam pointed out.

"Look, it's okay—we'll just have to repaint before they get back. It's fine for now," I said.

As long as Aunt Sue and Uncle Frank didn't see it. I could just see Aunt Sue placing a pan-icked, late-night phone call to Spain—about paint.

Chapter 12

"Colleen, there's someone at the takeout window who wants to see you," Maggie said the next day as lunch was winding down.

Maggie was a fourteen-year-old girl with braces, here for the summer and getting her big break at the takeout window the same way that I had.

"Who is it?" I asked. For some reason I glanced over my shoulder to see where Evan was. As if he'd run outside to the takeout window or something to try to trick me. He was devious like that.

"A very cute guy," Maggie said. "So I'm really bummed that he wouldn't let me take his order. Now *go*. I'll do this."

She took over my salad prep work while I wiped my hands on my apron and crossed the kitchen, toward the windows. I looked through the screen and saw Ben standing there, arms folded in front of him.

"Hey," I said. "What are you doing here?"

"I came to see you?" Ben smiled.

It was so nice to see him smile like that. And at me, no less. He must not be angry anymore, but I wasn't going to push my luck. "Thanks," I said. "But what about work?"

"I'm done for the day," he said.

"Oh, my gosh, is it three already?"

"It's three thirty, actually," Ben said.

I couldn't believe it. We hadn't stopped being busy long enough for me to even take a short break, never mind look at the clock more than a few times.

"So could I get a lobster roll and fries?"

"To go or to eat here?" I asked.

"Coll, I was kind of hoping you could come outside for a break and eat with me," Ben said.

"You know what? That's a great idea," I said, smiling. "Hold on one second—grab a table and I'll be out with your food." I went back into the kitchen, placed an order for the two of us, and went to find Trudy so I could tell her I was taking my half-hour break. It was a good time, because the between-shifts lull was actually, finally, happening. An hour and a half later than usual.

By the time I found Trudy our food was

ready, so I carried it out the back door. I set the plates down on the picnic table where Ben was already sitting. "Oops—I forgot drinks. What do you want?"

"Lemonade or iced tea—whatever," Ben said.

"Be right back," I promised as I headed back inside. When I came back out, I realized I'd forgotten ketchup for Ben's fries, so I ran in to grab a couple of packets and some extra tartar sauce for my fried fish sandwich.

You might think I was doing all this because I was stalling. And probably I was, just a little bit. Ben and I hadn't talked much since the ferry incident two days ago, since I confessed to not telling him everything about my past. (Which sounds a lot more dramatic and soap opera–like than the actual situation. It wasn't as if I'd killed someone, or been married.)

"Why do they call it tartar sauce?" I asked as I spread a spoonful onto the bun. I knew that was harmful to my health, because tartar sauce must be higher in cholesterol than, say, fried fish pieces, which were also stacked high on my sandwich. "I mean, what is tartar about it? What is a tartar, anyway?"

"I don't know, but my toothpaste says it removes tartar." Ben grinned at me as he ripped open a straw and poked it into his lemonade.

"Gross!" I cracked open my little carton of milk. A child's portion. So unfair. I sipped my milk and looked across the picnic table at Ben. I tried to smile a little. I felt so vulnerable, sitting there. And it wasn't because seagulls were circling overhead, just hoping I was going to drop a crumb. It was the feeling that I had no idea what was going to happen next. Ben seemed to be okay with me now. If he was angry two days ago—and he was—then he'd somehow gotten past that. Or was he just being nice because he wanted to break up with me, and eating lunch together was the easiest and kindest way he could think of?

But no, Ben wouldn't be that heartless. He'd never tell me something difficult in public, least of all at my workplace. He'd come and find me, alone, or suggest we take a walk, or—

Wait a second. Why am I thinking of ways he could break up with me? I thought as I dabbed tartar sauce off the corner of my mouth. I had this tendency to think things through a little *too* much, envisioning things in the future while I completely missed the present.

Or, as my first grade report card said, "Prone to daydreaming."

"So, busy today?" Ben asked.

"Ridiculously busy, yeah. I think I had a snack at like eleven, and I haven't had a chance to sit down since," I said. "This is nice."

"Yeah, it is." Ben paused. "Sorry I've been kind of—"

"No, it's okay," I said quickly.

"Not really," he said. "I kind of acted like a jerk about it. It was just—it really came out of left field. I wasn't expecting it. I mean, I guess I remember you or Haley talking about someone from last summer . . ."

"You do?" I asked.

"Vaguely."

Phew. Vaguely *was* the best way to remember Evan, especially if you were Ben.

"But why didn't you tell me?" he asked.

"I really thought I'd never see him again. Maybe that was stupid, but that's what I thought. Trudy said he wasn't coming back this year. And I hadn't heard from him since last fall, so—"

"Yeah, but why didn't you tell me, like, the day he showed up? You waited a week," Ben said.

"I was nervous?" I said. In fact, I'm still nervous? And couldn't we have this conversation a *little* farther away from the building? And couldn't I get a few more shifts that weren't the same as Evan's? It was like a Trudy conspiracy.

"Yeah. Well, I can understand that, I guess. I was just really surprised. But I'm over it now. I realized that I probably haven't told you every single thing about my exes, either," Ben said.

"You haven't?" I asked. *Hold on a second,* I thought. What exes was he talking about? And why was it plural, as if there had been a lot of them?

"No. And I'm probably not going to, unless there's a point, unless there's some reason why I need to, because that's all in the past," Ben said. "Like you and that Evan guy. And I understand you had to tell me, since he showed up here unexpectedly."

Is Ben the greatest guy on the planet or what? Well, maybe not the planet, but definitely this one little self-enclosed subplanet.

"Thanks for understanding." I stood up and leaned across the table so I could kiss him on the cheek.

"You're welcome," he said.

I sat back down and started eating my sandwich again, this time with a little more appetite for it. So I had nothing to worry about. Ben knew now; case closed.

"So." Ben popped another French fry into his mouth. "Is he here?"

"Is who here?"

"Colleen."

"Oh, *him*. You mean . . . him him," I said.

Ben smiled. "I don't know. What does that mean?"

I had to laugh. I really was being slightly psycho about this, I knew that. "Well, he's inside still, I guess."

"Is he one of those guys?" Ben pointed with a French fry at the restaurant.

I looked over my shoulder as I heard the back door close. A group of co-workers had just come out of the restaurant, and they were walking over to take another picnic table. "Yeah. He's over there," I said.

"Well, which one *is* he?" Ben asked, laughing. "Or is this supposed to stay a secret? Well, hold on, I know Rick . . . and Chad—"

"He's the one with the . . . um . . ." Nice ankles? Somewhat handsome stubble? Triathlete body? How did you describe one boyfriend to another? "Birkenstocks."

"Colleen. I can't see *shoes* from here," Ben said. "They're all sitting down."

"Well, he's kind of . . ." I was about to mention the brown hair, green-blue eyes, and short sideburns when Evan noticed we were both staring at him. He popped a straw into his mouth and waved at us. "He's the one waving at us," I said as I quickly waved at him, then turned back around with a nervous feeling in my stomach.

Oh, God. This was the most uncomfortable situation I had ever been in, the most awkward minute of my entire life. Evan, waving at Ben. What next? Were they going to talk? Shake hands? Sit at the same table with me?

"Maybe I'd better head back inside to work," I said. "Since they're all taking breaks now, Trudy probably needs me."

"Okay, but what about tonight? Can we get together tonight?" Ben asked.

"Of—of course," I said. "I'd love that. I'll be home at ten—or do you want to pick me up here?"

"That sounds like a good idea. Maybe we can go down to the beach for a little while."

"See you then!"

I knew Ben wanted me to kiss him good-bye, but I just couldn't. I felt so awkward, like I didn't want Evan to see me with Ben, and I didn't want Ben to see me with Evan. But that was ridiculous, because I wasn't doing anything wrong, I wasn't cheating on anyone. It *felt* like it, though.

Even though everything was supposedly out in the open now, I still felt like I was keeping things from both of them. I was acting like someone in a cheesy love song, the kind my mom would play loudly while she was doing housework, the kind I usually said "ick" to.

Now I was living an ick life.

The rest of the day was just as crazy at work, which was okay with me. Keeping busy was a good thing—and I was making more money than I could count.

I bumped into Evan at around eight, when I was refilling my water and iced tea pitchers.

"Is this the busiest Saturday you can remember?" he asked. "My feet are killing me."

I glanced down at his sandals—a new pair, a different kind—and decided not to comment this time on the fact that he should wear running shoes, that he might be more comfortable, that sandals were banned. If he wanted to be in pain, fine, good, that was his business, not mine. Not this year.

"So, who was that guy you were eating lunch with?" Evan asked as he filled a couple of pitchers with ice.

Oh, no. Here it came. More ick. "That was Ben," I said.

"Ben," Evan repeated. "Ben . . . who?"

"Ben . . . my boyfriend Ben. My boyfriend," I stammered.

Evan stopped mid–ice shovel. "Oh. You have a boyfriend?"

"Well, yeah. I do." I dropped a couple of lemon slices into the pitcher of water, and realized I'd meant to drop them into the iced tea. So, the water would have a nice crisp taste now. I dropped lemon slices into the iced tea and was about to bring the pitchers out to my tables when Evan said, "Interesting. Very interesting."

I stopped and turned around. "Would you stop saying that about everything? What's interesting about it, anyway?"

"Aha! Are you saying he's not interesting? Or maybe you're not interested in him?"

"No." I shook my head. "Don't flatter yourself."

"I was flattering myself? I didn't realize. Usually I'm a lot more demonstrative when I do that. As in, Evan, you have the best—"

Ankles, I thought, but thankfully my mouth didn't open. *Stop that, brain. Stop that right now.*

The swinging doors flew open and Trudy stood there with a stack of menus in her arms. "Evan, Colleen, come on—you've got three new tables apiece."

"Aren't we supposed to get a break at some point?" Evan asked. "I mean, a lobster takes breaks, Trude. A lobster can't keep going and going and going. Not even with eight legs."

"Yeah, every now and then a lobster has to stop and smell the roe," I said, quoting a T-shirt joke Evan had come up with last summer, along with one that said "Dip Into Something More Comfortable," with a picture of a butter dish. He had even gotten a few fake T-shirts printed up with that slogan, to try to convince Trudy to use them, but the T-shirt shop had messed up and spelled Bobb's as "Boob's." So Trudy wasn't convinced, but he kept them and wore them for running.

We smiled at each other and then started laughing.

"You two." Trudy shook her head. "Same as always."

No, we're not, I wanted to say. We're not the same—things aren't the same! We weren't back here together because we were trying to sneak in a moment alone, so we could kiss by the fluorescent glow from the food-warming lamps.

Yeah, that *is* as tacky as it sounds, and we'd done it last year. How embarrassing.

"Come on, Trude. Cut us a break. Has anyone else been working since ten A.M. straight?" Evan asked.

"Well, I have," Trudy said. "Now run—your tables are waiting."

"I can't believe we're still seating people, and it's almost nine o'clock," Evan complained.

"We're not getting out of here at ten, are we?" I muttered.

I'd have to call Ben and cancel our plans. The way this summer was going so far, I was spending more time at work than I was with Ben. Which meant, in a way, that I was spending more time with Evan than with Ben, even if I was only constantly bumping into him in the kitchen.

This was a trend that had to change. Soon. But how?

That night, Haley borrowed her family's pickup truck and drove down to Bobb's to get us when we were finally released. She knew that if we weren't home yet, we'd all be too tired to walk when we finally did get out of work. Erica called her grandparents and told them she would be sleeping over at our house. Then she sat up front with Haley, while Sam, Blair, and I all piled into the back of the truck. When we got home, it turned out Haley had bought ice cream and cookies for all of us, and the five of us sat on the porch and ate and talked and laughed until long after midnight.

Chapter 13

Sunday afternoon I was exactly where I wanted to be: lying on a giant towel on the beach, right next to Ben. It was pretty warm, and very sunny, and we'd just eaten a late breakfast together over at his house. I hadn't seen Ben's family in a while because I'd been so busy. It was cool to catch up with everyone and remember how nice things used to be before the summer started and we both got overworked and overtired.

We don't have a big sandy beach on the island, because most of the land at the water's edge is very rocky and covered with trees, pine and otherwise (Maine *is* the Pine Tree State). But there's a small sandy beach where you can lie comfortably and watch the surf roll in—and swim if you're feeling either very very hot or very brave. The water temperature never gets all that warm.

We were enjoying having the time to ourselves to snuggle against each other. Everything was finally okay again, and it felt so perfect to be close to Ben like that. Nobody cuddled better than Ben. We fit together perfectly. He was gently moving strands of my hair off my face, and kissing me as he did that. I didn't know what I wanted more: to fall asleep with him holding me or to run off this beach and go somewhere more private together, like to a small cove, the way we did last summer when we ended up taking off our clothes and—

And then I stopped myself from thinking about it. Because that hadn't been Ben. That wasn't something Ben would do. It was too risky, too dangerous—what if somebody saw us? He'd never go for that idea.

That had been Evan.

A second later a shadow fell over us as someone stopped beside our towel.

Don't be Evan, I thought. *Please don't be Evan going for a jog and stopping by to say hello.* It would be just like him to do that, now that he knew I had a boyfriend, and now that I was lying here next to Ben—thinking about Evan. He'd be able to tell I was daydreaming about him; he'd see it in my eyes somehow. He was devious and horrible like that.

"You guys mind if I join you?"

I squinted up into the sun and saw Haley standing over us. "Hey!"

She lifted the beach towel that she'd been carrying on her shoulders and shook it out. "Is it okay?"

"No, we want you to go sit over there," Ben said, sitting up and resting on his elbows. He gestured to John and Molly Hyland, who were sitting underneath an umbrella where they'd both been reading and not speaking to each other since we got there. "With the Hylands."

"Shut up." Haley pretended to kick sand into his face. "How long have you guys been here?" She peeled off her T-shirt and shorts, revealing an orange floral bikini.

"Not long. Hey, is that suit new?" I asked. "It's nice."

"Looking good, lass," Ben teased her in a bad Scottish accent, for some reason.

"Again. Shut up." Haley grinned at Ben as she lay down on her towel beside me.

"Man, what a nice afternoon." Ben turned onto his side, looking at both of us.

"I feel like this is the part of summer we kept talking about all winter, when we were freezing our butts off on the ferry every morning," Haley said. "This was what kept us going."

"That and the thermos of hot chocolate my mom kept packing for me every day." Ben shook his head, embarrassed.

"Hey. At least she finally let you stop carrying that Superman lunchbox," Haley said.

Ben laughed and collapsed on his towel. "Oh, man. What'll she pack when I go to college?"

Neither of us said anything for a minute. Thinking about the three of us splitting up to go to different schools was a little daunting. We'd gotten so inseparable senior year. The three of us had even gone to the prom together.

"Maybe it's not too late to change our minds and transfer. What do you guys say? We'll do one of those Internet schools so we can all stay on the island." Haley rolled her T-shirt into a ball to use as a pillow.

Ben reached for my hand and squeezed it tightly. "Maybe we should. That way things could stay like this."

I turned toward him and smiled, but as fond as I was of the island—and there's no place on Earth I like more—I was looking forward to the changes ahead. If only that being away made me realize that I wanted to come back here to live, and to be with Ben. But I didn't want to just stop looking at other options yet.

I knew they probably didn't, either—it was just this building fear we all had of leaving, of possibly being so homesick for this place that we wouldn't be able to stand it.

I was working on a new collage on Monday when I heard a loud laugh coming from the front porch.

A very familiar laugh.

And then I heard Blair's voice saying, "I'll be right back."

I got up and peered out the window, but I knew I couldn't really see the porch, since it was below my window. That *laugh*, though. Had he come over to see me?

I heard Blair come upstairs and I opened my door, expecting Blair to be about to knock. But she wasn't. Instead, her bedroom door was just closing.

I went downstairs anyway. He had to be here to see me. Right?

The screen door closed behind me, and Evan asked, "So, you ready?"

"Ready for what?" I asked.

Evan looked up from the magazine he'd been reading. He had a baseball cap on and was wearing a pair of old, beat-up running sneakers without socks, khaki shorts, and an old Bobb's T-shirt that had a hole by the neck.

"Oh, sorry. I thought you were going to be Blair," he said.

"No. Not quite." I smiled. "A little shorter, a little less . . . blond."

We both looked at each other and did these awkward sort of nods. As in, Ahem, isn't *this* uncomfortable? At least I was uncomfortable.

Evan leaned back in his chair and stretched his arms over his head. He didn't seem uneasy at all. In fact, he almost looked like he was happy to be here.

"So this is the bachelorette house," he said. "Funny, it looks the same as it did when your parents were here."

"Yes, but have you been *inside*?" I asked. "We've painted the entire place pink." Or at least late-afternoon lupine.

"I've been inside," Evan said.

Before I could respond or even process that, Blair flounced through the door. "Ready!" she proclaimed. She was wearing a white polo shirt, blue shorts, and what looked like a brand-new pair of tennis sneakers. "Hey, Colleen. When did you get home?" she asked.

"I was . . . home," I said slowly.

How she could come out of that messy, dirty room where the floor was covered with clothes and old coffee mugs sitting on the dresser and look so neat and put together was beyond me. Of course, looking like Blair was beyond me, period.

And then they announced they were off to play tennis. Tennis, of all things. I hadn't noticed the racket propped against Evan's chair, probably because I was trying very hard not to look at him.

"You don't play tennis," I said to Evan.

"Sure I do," he replied with a laugh. "I've been playing since I was a kid."

"You have? But you never—"

"The thing is, *you* don't play tennis, Coll. That's the part you forgot."

I could have picked up his racket and overhead-smashed him, right then and there. Did he have to be so smug? When he was here picking up another girl—my housemate, no less? Did he have no respect for me?

"She does play a mean game of cribbage, though," Evan told Blair as she pulled her hair back into a ponytail and secured it with an elastic.

"Cribbage?" Blair scoffed.

"You know, fifteen-two, fifteen-four," Evan said, standing up.

"No. The only fifteens I know about are in tennis," she said.

"Then I'll teach you how to play cribbage. Come on, let's go. See you, Colleen."

"Yeah. Bye," I said. Good riddance. Have fun. Don't trip over the net. No, do.

And then they took off, just like that. Oh, wasn't that nice; he was going to teach her to play cribbage. He only knew how to play because of me, because I taught him!

Now he was the expert?

I hated him. I loathed him.

And Blair was definitely not one of my favorite people right now, either. She knew I'd gone out with Evan, so why did she have to flaunt the fact that they were hanging out by bringing him here?

Of course, I didn't have any dibs on Evan. I knew that. It was still really incredibly awkward, though.

It's not about Evan, I told myself. *It's about me and Ben. Just forget Evan.*

Still, I felt that I needed to blow off some steam, and also, Ben would be getting out of work soon.

I ran upstairs and cleared up my worktable. I put all my art materials away, closing the tubes and jars.

Then I got my bike out of the garage and started riding down toward the Landing.

On the way, I went past Betty McGonagle's house. Mr. McGonagle had died about five years ago, leaving Betty on her own. The house was at the top of a little bluff, and it had a gorgeous view of the water and the smaller islands in the distance. Betty was standing on her deck in front of an easel. Why did she even need to look at the ocean when she painted? I wondered. Didn't she have it memorized by now?

Blue here, white here, green here. This one would be called *Early Morning Sea Foam*, would be 5"x7", and would sell for $45. No, wait— $39.99.

Stop being such a snob, I told myself just as Betty looked up and noticed me approaching.

"Hello, Colleen!" she called to me. "How's

172

your summer going?" Betty was in her mid-seventies. She tended to wear big denim shirts that invariably had paint drops on them, and she wore a scarf over her short, completely white hair. When she worked, anyway—I hardly ever saw her when she *wasn't* working, except maybe at public suppers and the post office occasionally.

"Great!" I called back.

"Any new pieces to show?" she asked. "Anything I can see?"

"Not yet—maybe soon!" I yelled. Then I coasted down the hill, feeling terrible. *She* was supportive and nice and interested in my artwork; I was mean, judgmental, and cruel about hers. She was a real artist who'd actually made good money selling her paintings; I displayed my stuff at an elementary school—and only because both my parents *worked* there. I was really awful.

On my way to the Landing I had to ride past the tennis courts. I had to. Really. And . . . ick.

Blair was standing at the net, practicing her volleys. Evan was hitting shots to her, and Blair laughed as she smashed a tennis ball that hit Evan's leg and nearly knocked him down.

I rang the little bell on my bike's handlebars in approval. "Go, Blair!" I yelled. Keep that up, would you? She waved at me and smiled. Evan didn't look nearly as happy to see me. I was tempted to hang out for a while, because I had a feeling Evan was going to get beaten, slightly badly. That would be fun to watch.

But the ferry was coming in soon, and I wanted to be there to see Ben when it did. So I continued on my way, regretfully.

When I reached the Landing, the ferry had already docked. I saw Ben walking off, talking to the tall redheaded girl again.

Why did he have to get his stupid sea legs, so he could flirt with that girl every day? What was her deal, anyway? She didn't even have a frizzone. It was ninety-five percent humidity, and she showed no signs of it. Come to think of it, she'd *never* had a frizzone.

Which could only mean one thing: She was wearing a wig. Extensions—that had to be it. I had to cling to *something*.

"Who is that girl?" I asked Ben after I gave him a kiss hello.

"That's Holly," Ben said.

"And, uh, why does she seem to be on the ferry every afternoon?" I asked, trying to sound casual.

"Because she works on the mainland. She's doing an internship in a law office there, from eight to two every day."

"Hm. Really," I mused.

"Yes, really." Ben laughed as he put his arm around my shoulder. "Why is that so fascinating?"

"It's just . . . why did we never see her before?" I asked.

"She's older than us. She's in college, home for the summer. You know."

Yes, I did know. All about this painful pang of jealousy I was having, anyway.

First Evan with Blair, and now Ben and this . . . Holly. I was having a very jealous day. I didn't like feeling that way, especially on my day off, when I should be enjoying all things and not stressing about anything. It seemed shallow, and petty, of me.

But maybe that was how I was.

Chapter 14

Saturday night, Sam and I were walking home, both completely tired out. Blair wasn't with us because Erica had worked for her. Blair had said she had an urgent personal matter to attend to. That had us all curious, but we hadn't asked for details.

"This isn't how Saturday nights are supposed to be," Sam said. "We're supposed to be at the movies, or the mall, or out to dinner, or—"

"Asleep," I interrupted. "That sounds good, too, doesn't it?"

I heard a loud bass beat as we got closer to our house—the kind you usually hear coming from someone's car stereo.

"Where's that coming from?" Sam asked.

"Probably the Browns'. But they usually invite us to all their parties. Oh, well, maybe because Mom and Dad are away." Our neighbors were famous for their summer bashes.

"Coll? I don't think that's the Browns'," Sam

said as we passed by their front hedge and the music got even louder.

"What do you mean? That's *our* house?"

"I think so. Yup."

I cringed as we turned into the driveway and I saw a sign hanging from our birch tree: PARTY HERE.

"Okay, so this is an urgent personal matter? She wanted to throw a party without telling us about it?" I complained.

"It's very personal, all right," Sam said.

Dance music was blaring from the living room stereo, and someone had put a speaker in the window that pointed directly at the driveway. There were about two dozen people on the front porch—I recognized about half of them, but the other half? I'd never seen them before. Wasn't there a rule about "small gatherings only" and "not annoying the neighbors"?

In the kitchen, I waved to a few people I knew, then I peeked around the living room, looking for a sign of Blair—or Haley. Did Haley know about this, too?

The downstairs bathroom's bathtub was filled with ice and cans of soda—and beer, and some other bottled drinks.

Wasn't Rule 1 "No drugs or alcohol allowed"? How hard was that to understand?

Was it possible to break all of the house rules in one night?

I ran into Blair as I closed the bathroom door behind me. "What are you—I—we—we can't have a party like—" I was so angry that I couldn't complete my sentences.

"Hey, how's it going?" she replied with a smile. "I kind of invited some people over. What's the big deal?"

"I—we—can't do this."

"Colleen, relax. We *are* doing this." Blair grinned. "Isn't it great? Can you believe how many people showed?"

"No. *You're* doing this," I said.

"I did it for all of us. It's a surprise party! Come on, aren't you surprised?"

I stepped back as a couple of guys I'd never seen before pushed past us to get to the bathtub cooler. "Very," I said. "Why didn't you just tell me you wanted to have a party? Blair, my parents don't want anything like this happening here. They wrote it down for us, so we wouldn't forget."

"Come on. It's just one party. It's a couple of

hours of your life. Did you know today is the summer solstice? The longest day of the year. I celebrate it every year with a big party."

"Well, I don't. Why didn't you tell me you wanted to do this?"

"It was a spur-of-the-moment-type deal."

I frowned. If she planned it to celebrate the summer solstice, then how could it be spontaneous? Did she just find out that today was the summer solstice? I thought it was on the calendar. "You shouldn't have done it," I said.

"Look, do you *really* want me to ask everyone to leave? Or do you want to just try and have a good time, like everyone else is?" she asked.

I didn't like the way Blair had done this at all. But she was right—I had two choices: (1) Tell everyone to get out, and (a) be hated by a crowd and (b) be considered extremely uncool, or (2) get myself some potato chips and a Coke and just try to have fun while it lasted.

So. In other words, there really wasn't much of a choice at all.

"Okay. But could we turn down the music a little?" I asked.

"No problem!" she said breezily.

I grabbed a soda for myself and went outside to sit on the porch with Sam. That's when I saw Evan walking up to the house with his cousin Jake.

Oh, great. Of course. Of course Evan would be here.

Just as I was saying hello to him and Jake, Ben cruised up on his mountain bike. "Apparently we're having a party," I told him when he walked over to the porch steps where Sam and I were perched.

"I know—Blair called to invite me. But that was *after* I heard about it from Eddie down at the hardware store," Ben said.

"Eddie? She invited *Eddie*?"

"I guess she walked in and invited every-one." Ben laughed.

"Oh, my God. This is a nightmare," Sam said. "Well, except for the fact I like parties. And there are some cute guys here. But I mean, come on— we just got off work and we can't even shower and change for a party at our very own house." She smiled. "*Your* very own house, actually."

"Same difference," I told her.

"What's he doing here?" Ben gestured toward Evan, standing at the other end of the porch and talking with Blair.

"I don't know. She invited everyone, you said. They know each other from work," I said.

"Right." Ben shook his head. "You know, if your parents could see this place right now . . . They didn't even let you have a big graduation party."

"Tell me about it," I said. "I'm just hoping things wrap up before any real damage gets done. Do you think that's possible?"

"If you start kicking people out at midnight," Ben said. "Good luck with that." He patted my back and went into the house to talk to some friends.

Haley drove her family's rattling old pickup truck into the crowded driveway, saw there were no spots available, and went out to the road to park.

When she slammed the door and walked back to the house, she just stared at me and Sam with wide eyes. "What the . . . ?"

"Blair," Sam and I said in unison.

At about midnight, I went upstairs to get a couple of sweaters for me, Haley, and Sam. The night was getting chilly. The party had thinned out, but there were still about thirty people milling around, dancing, talking, singing, laughing.

When I got to the top of the stairs, I nearly bumped right into Evan. I hadn't even realized he was still around; I thought he and Jake had left.

"What are you doing up here?" I asked.

"Well, I was playing a chasing game with Starsky, and he ran up here, so I followed him. And then I had to visit Hutch, so . . ." Evan leaned against the closet door and gave me a small smile.

He hadn't been in the house—with me— since last year. And he was leaning against the closet. That walk-in closet.

"Actually, I wanted to see what you've been working on. Some pretty good stuff. Really good, actually."

One thing I always loved about Evan was that he was interested in my collage work. He didn't have to know there were a few I'd made about him. First, the romantic one. Then, the one with angry black brushstrokes all over the top of it. Those were, thankfully, safely stashed in a box in the closet—the Evan/last summer box. To be opened in the event of nuclear war only.

"I probably shouldn't have gone into your room without asking," he said as I just stood there, momentarily speechless as I thought about that box and whether it was hidden well enough under a pile of winter hats, scarves, and mittens.

"No, you probably shouldn't have," I finally said.

"Too late," Evan said. "What are you doing up here?"

"I live here?" I said. Then I laughed. "Actually, I came up to get some sweaters."

"You and your sweaters." Evan stepped aside so that I could open up the closet door.

"Actually, I think, ah, sweatshirts," I said, going into Haley's room and then Sam's to grab the sweatshirts they'd said they had hanging on the backs of their doors. Then I pulled my Bates sweatshirt off my bed, where I'd thrown it that morning.

When I came back out, I glanced awkwardly at Evan, who was now standing at the top of the stairs, apparently waiting for me. I didn't want to be alone with him, not like this. "We should get back," I said, starting down the stairs.

"Right behind you," Evan said.

When we walked into the kitchen, Haley was turning around from the sink, holding a bowl of freshly washed green grapes. She looked over my shoulder at Evan, then glared at me. "What are you doing?" she whispered after he went into the living room. "Why were you upstairs with him?"

"I wasn't . . . *with* him," I said. "We both ended up there at the same time."

"Whatever. Here, these are for Ben. Take them." She shoved the glass bowl at me.

I handed her the sweatshirt. "You're welcome," I said, annoyed by her tone. As if I were sneaking off with Evan while Ben was there. As if I'd *do* something like that. She was really selling me short if she thought that about me.

I went outside and handed Sam her sweatshirt, then held the bowl out to Ben. "Grape?"

"Look! Grapes!" Blair cried, stumbling over with a couple of slightly drunk friends of hers.

"It's going to be a long night," Ben murmured to me. "Or . . . morning."

I leaned against him and put my arm around his waist. "Please don't leave," I said.

"I can stay until one, but that's it," he said. "My parents are waiting up for me, you know."

"Maybe we should go to *your* house, then." I smiled up at him.

"Helloooooo! Colleen? Colleen!"

I blinked my eyes a few times and peered at the alarm clock beside my bed. Ten twenty A.M. Who was that yelling my name?

"Colleen! You up there?" my Uncle Frank's voice echoed over the stairwell.

"Oh no. Oh no." I remembered falling asleep with Ben sitting on my bed, stroking my hair. *Please let him be gone*, please, I thought. Ben and I had never had a sleepover, and I really didn't want today to be the first time he ended up in my bed in the morning.

I opened my eyes and slowly turned over and saw that he was gone. "Phew," I said out loud. I quickly threw on some shorts and a fresh T-shirt and called out the bedroom door, "Be right down!" I brushed my hair, slipped on some flip-flops, and hurried downstairs.

"Hey, you guys—what a surprise!" I said with a big smile. Which was the understatement of the year. I cringed at the pile of dishes in the sink and the trash can overflowing with plastic cups.

"We brought you some breakfast." Aunt Sue

185

held up a straw basket filled with blueberry muffins. "Hot, too! Well, they were."

"Thanks so much—those look awesome," I said. "So, what brings you by?"

"Good morning!" Haley said as she walked into the kitchen, looking as sleepy as I felt. I couldn't believe we'd all slept so late—then again, we'd been up pretty late.

"Hello, Haley," Uncle Frank said.

No sooner had he said hello than there were thundering footsteps coming down the stairs. A guy I vaguely remembered seeing at the party bolted past us with an awkward wave and ran outside.

Aunt Sue couldn't have looked more shocked than I felt. Was that guy coming out of Haley's room? The house rule was: no sleep-overs. Haley's rule had always been: no dumb, one-night things with guys. What was going on?

"Who was that?" Aunt Sue asked.

Uncle Frank was already out on the porch, watching whoever it was sprint down the road. If my uncle chased someone away from the house, I would feel very, very embarrassed. For both of them. And anyone who happened to see them.

"Oh, that was . . ." I hesitated. Who *was* that?

"That was Chuck," Haley quickly said.

Aunt Sue looked suspiciously at her. "Chuck who, Haley?"

I was wondering the same thing myself.

"Chuck, ah . . . Chuck Jacobs," Haley stammered.

I just stared at Haley. Had she really been with this Chuck Jacobs guy? And who was he?

"And what was he doing here at ten thirty in the morning, upstairs?" Aunt Sue asked.

"Well, uh, he came over to help clear the drains," Haley said. "In the upstairs bathroom. You know Blair, who lives here? She's got really long, thick hair, and it completely clogs the drains."

This was all starting to sound vaguely credible. I couldn't believe it.

Haley stretched her arms over her head. "So when I tried to take a shower this morning, everything was overflowing. I called Chuck."

"Well, why didn't you call us?" Aunt Sue complained. "We would have come right over. Frank is an excellent handyman," she said as my uncle walked back into the house, apparently having decided not to run down the mystery man.

Uncle Frank nodded proudly. "I like to think I have a knack."

"And where was this Chuck's van? And why wouldn't you just call your parents, instead?" My aunt can really grill a person when she wants to. I'd forgotten about that quality of hers.

"He's sort of a handyman type guy," Haley said with a shrug. "My family always calls him when there are plumbing emergencies."

"Chuck Jacobs, Chuck Jacobs," my uncle repeated, like a mantra. "Funny, I've never head that name. And we pretty much know everyone on the island."

"Not everyone," I said.

"Well, maybe not everyone, but . . . how did he get here? And where was his toolbox?"

"Oh, we've got all the tools he needed right here. We just weren't sure how to actually use them," I said, nervously looking around at the kitchen. The place was totally sloppy. The only good thing I could say was that there wasn't a bunch of beer bottles or cans lying around. Some people had been drinking last night, but I hadn't. I wasn't sure about Haley. I couldn't see her sleeping with someone, sober, just because she was so dead set against it.

Please don't let anyone else wake up and come downstairs, I thought. Especially not any boys. Or men. Or boy-men. Or book club targets.

"Well. The house is a mess, and a few things don't look quite right," Aunt Sue commented as she turned to my uncle. "Do they?"

He shook his head. "No. Your parents would be a little disappointed right now. No, check that. A *lot* disappointed."

"Aunt Sue, Uncle Frank? You just caught us on a bad day," I said. "This isn't what the place usually looks like, honestly. Sunday's our day off, so that's when we clean the house," I explained.

Aunt Sue gave the kitchen a look of disapproval. I glanced at the black cat clock on the wall. Its tail was switching back and forth, counting the seconds until she grabbed the phone and called my parents, dragging them out of a museum to let them know we were all living like heathens. "Girls, you'll have to do better," Aunt Sue said sternly.

I figured I had to do something to prove to them that we really were taking good care of the house. "Why don't you both come over for dinner tomorrow night?" I asked.

Aunt Sue and Uncle Frank agreed to the plan, and the second they walked out of the house, I jumped all over Haley.

"So who was that guy? That guy who almost got us in trouble by running out of your room and downstairs?"

"What? He wasn't with me!" Haley cried. "Are you serious?"

"Oh." Sam snapped her fingers. "Darn. I was hoping for some really good dirt on you."

"Forget it, I'm boring," Haley said with a sigh.

"So. The question remains. Who was that guy? And if he was running downstairs, why wasn't Blair? And what about the no sleepovers rule?" I groaned.

My parents would find out about this from my aunt and uncle. They'd be on the first plane out of Milan, or whatever the city du jour was. I'd have to check the itinerary on the fridge.

They'd no doubt hear about the party, too. The downside of living on an island is that everything gets back to everyone eventually. We're not very good at keeping secrets here.

Chapter 15

"What do you think I should get?" I asked Ben as we pulled into the Bobb's parking lot. I'd picked him up at his house five minutes before. Since he was coming over for dinner, it would be fun to hang out for a while together before Aunt Sue and Uncle Frank descended.

I'd tried to make something at home, but it hadn't exactly worked out. All those cooking lessons my mom had given me. She'd tried so hard. And I had no talent at all.

Erica was working all day to cover for Blair, who needed the day off so she could go to the mainland for something. (She'd never explained about the guy who slept over. She claimed to not even know who he was.) That left me holding the potholders.

It was one of those times when I really wished that I didn't live on an island. If I could just drive to some restaurant, or takeout deli, and get some pasta and salads. If there were a

McDonald's or Wendy's anywhere in sight. Yes, I could buy grinders at the general store, and cheeseburgers at the Landing. But that didn't exactly say "Meal home-cooked by Colleen with care."

Neither did takeout from Bobb's, but it was the only option left.

"You know, I can cook. I'm not bad, either," Ben said. "I make a mean mac and cheese. Or we could just throw some burgers and hot dogs on the grill."

"I know, but I feel like I need to do something a little more special for them," I said.

"But don't your aunt and uncle eat at Bobb's all the time?" Ben asked.

I shook my head. "Not really, no. They think it's overpriced. My uncle once went on a ten-minute tirade about how the side salad was too small to cost a dollar ninety-nine. Then he insisted Trudy take the dessert off the check because the ice cream melted a little before it got to the table."

Ben laughed. "Yeah, that sounds like him."

"So this will be kind of a treat for them. And I really appreciate that you're doing this with me." I reached over and squeezed Ben's knee as

I parked in front of the restaurant.

All of a sudden I remembered that Evan was working. Okay, so I'd known that, but I suddenly realized that I didn't really want Ben to come in with me and see Evan and wonder if that was why I'd come up with this plan to stop by Bobb's for food. Because it wasn't. Because I'm the world's worst cook, and if I didn't buy food here I'd be serving shredded wheat cereal to my aunt and uncle. That wouldn't get me back on their good side. I needed to be on their good side.

"I'll just run in and get a container of clam chowder and some other things," I said to Ben. "Okay?"

"You need help?"

"Nah. It'll only take me a sec." I grabbed my wallet from on top of the dashboard and leaned over to give Ben a quick kiss. "Thanks."

"Wait," Ben said as I closed the door. "Coll, hold up."

Please don't come with me, please don't say you want to come with me, I thought. I leaned back in through the window. "Yeah? Do you want me to get something for you, too?"

"No. I just want the keys," he said. "That way I can listen to the Sox game while I wait."

"Right. Sorry!" I tossed the keys to him and hurried down the sidewalk into the restaurant.

When I walked into Bobb's, I waved to Erica, then Trudy. Samantha was busy waiting on a table. In the kitchen, Evan was sitting on the freezer, eating a basket of fried clams.

"Hey. Did you start missing the place?" he asked.

"I need to buy some food for dinner," I said. "I'm having my aunt and uncle over." I cleared my throat. "I mean, ah, we are."

"We?" Evan repeated.

"Me and Ben," I mumbled.

"Is he a glutton for punishment or something?" Evan laughed. "Why don't you just bring them here for dinner? It'd be fun. I'll get your table, and I can make them laugh so that they cheer up and get off your back. Or if I don't make them laugh, then I'll give them something to complain about instead of the food prices."

"I know. How about they come here for dinner and I stay home?" I suggested.

"Come on, they're not so bad," Evan said. "I mean, besides being ridiculously judgmental, and the fact they wish you'd never gotten older than nine." He slid off the freezer and dropped the empty plastic basket into the dishwasher. "Why *are* you having them over for dinner?"

"Well, you know how we had that party on Saturday night," I said. *Because you were there and you kept talking with Ben, and then looking at me, and then putting your arm around Blair?*

"Yeah?" Evan asked.

"Well, they sort of heard about it. I guess the Browns called them when things got loud, and they called but I didn't hear the phone. Which is sort of bad, I guess. But they decided it was no big deal, that the Browns were just exaggerating, so they went to bed. So instead they showed up on Sunday morning, really early, to check on me," I said.

"You're kidding. How early?" Evan asked.

"Okay, not that early. Ten thirty. But that's early on a Sunday, when it's your day off." I felt my face turn red. "The place was trashed, and then some guy came running downstairs while they were *standing* there, so they're convinced we're like heathens. Haley tried to cover by saying he came over to fix the sink."

"Haley should never be the one to cover," Evan said. "She's a terrible liar."

"I know," I said.

"So. What guy?" Evan asked. "Wait a second. Not Ben, was it?"

There was this weird look we exchanged when he said that. Because if I said yes, Ben was the one who spent the night, it would somehow change things between us. I don't know what it was.

Finally I just smiled. "Don't you think my aunt and uncle know what Ben looks like? It'd be kind of hard to make up a story about that."

"Right." Evan nodded. "Of course."

"Anyway, I don't know who the guy was. Since Haley and Samantha insist he wasn't with them, and I know he wasn't with me, I have to assume he either passed out in the hallway or spent the night with Blair."

"Really." Evan nodded.

I watched his face for any sign of surprise or disappointment. He and Blair had been spending a lot of time together. Were they an item or weren't they? I really wanted to find out without asking.

"Yeah," I said. "We actually didn't hear one way or the other yet."

"Interesting. Was the guy anyone we know?"

I shook my head. "Not that *I* know, anyway.

Oh, well, if it's important we'll meet him, I guess. Anyway, I have to convince my aunt and uncle that I'm doing just fine on my own and that the house is doing just fine, too. I've been cleaning since dawn, I think."

"You? You hate cleaning."

"Not as much as I hate cooking," I complained.

"You are so domestic. It's frightening," Evan said.

"I know."

"So after you got busted . . . did your parents call to tell you they're canceling their French château tour and coming home tomorrow?"

"No." I laughed.

"So forget about it," Evan said with a wave of his hand. "It'll blow over. These things always do. Everyone panics, and then a week later no one even remembers."

What a refreshing attitude. Of course, Evan didn't care much what other people thought of him, and he wasn't the one who'd get a parental lecture. I'd never met his parents, in fact. I had no idea what they were like.

"All I think of when I remember your aunt is how she threw a fit last year when she caught us drinking," Evan said. "Remember?"

I laughed, "Oh, my god. She was ready to send us to jail and a rehab clinic just because we sneaked one glass of wine at that end-of-summer party. One glass! And we split it."

"And she ran and told your dad, and he was like, well, it's a holiday, and they're walking home, and it was only one glass, and they're leaving now," Evan said. "Your dad is so cool."

"Yeah. But of course, when we left . . ." That was the night of the lighthouse incident. Why did I have to bring that up?

"Well, yeah. But nobody knows about that. Right?"

"Right," I said quickly. I might have confided in a friend or two, but *he* didn't need to know about that. In fact, sometimes I wished that I couldn't remember that. It made me feel sort of stupid. That I'd misinterpreted the way we acted toward each other as something serious and lasting, instead of just a . . . what? A "fling"? But it wasn't.

"So," Evan said, glancing over my shoulder. "What are you picking up to eat?" he asked quietly.

I followed his gaze and saw Ben walking into

the kitchen. Oh, no. I'd been in here too long, and now I didn't even have what I'd come in for. "Food. Right!"

"Let me check if your order's ready," Evan said. "Hey, Ben. How's it going?"

"Hi," Ben replied, a little stiffly. "What's going on?"

"All the cooks decided to go on break at the same time. Should be just a second," I added.

I smiled at Ben, thinking this was terrible. Evan and I were lying to him over something as stupid as why it took me so long to pick up some takeout dishes. Why did we have to lie? But we'd already done it, instead of just saying that we'd gotten caught up in talking. That meant we felt like we had something to hide from him. But nothing was going on, so what were we hiding?

"I am so sorry. I am like the slowest shopper in the world." I grabbed Ben's hand and squeezed it tightly. "So what sounds good to you?"

Ben looked confused. "Didn't you already order?"

"Well, yeah—a few things. But if there's something special you want . . . ?"

"No, just you." While Evan went around

collecting various containers for us—I had no idea what he would pick out—Ben put his arms around my waist and nuzzled my neck. He was usually physically affectionate with me, but not *this* affectionate, not in public. It was almost as if he was looking for some kind of reassurance that he was the one now, and Evan wasn't. And I was supposed to prove it to him, right now, in front of both of them.

"You know what I was thinking? I was listening to the radio and I heard an ad for this inn up on Mount Desert. We should both ask for a couple of days off at the same time," Ben said. "So we can go away on a trip together. Before summer's over and we go off to college. You know?"

"That sounds nice," I said, still distracted by the thought of what had just happened. I felt like I'd gotten caught cheating on Ben. Just because I was having such a good time with Evan that I literally could not tear myself away. I was in Bobb's, on my day off, *lingering*. Usually I didn't come within a half-mile radius on my day off. Not that I hated the job—I didn't, at all. I just enjoyed my time away from it.

"We could go to Acadia, spend a couple of nights camping."

"Yeah, sure."

"You don't sound that excited about it. Is it because camping requires cooking?" Ben teased.

Normally I would have made several jokes about my cooking and envisioning the disaster that taking me camping could turn into. But I just didn't feel like even playing along. Going off with Ben, by ourselves, didn't sound that good to me. That was crazy. A couple of months ago I spent days begging my parents to let us do just that. I'd even managed to convince them to let us go to Portland for a couple of days; we stayed at Erica's house—in separate rooms, of course, and under the supervision of Erica's parents. Still, it had been a romantic type of getaway because we'd never done anything like that by ourselves before.

But now? I didn't want to leave the island. Not really. Not at all. And not with Ben.

I should have heard alarm bells ringing as loud as a foghorn. Or at least I should have done everything in reverse and started the day over. The last place I wanted to be was standing in the kitchen at Bobb's with both Evan and Ben.

"Let's go outside and wait," I said, backing out of Ben's embrace. "Come on."

"I'll find you, you know!" Evan called after us. "You can run, but you can't hide."

I turned around and gave him a quizzical look. So did Ben.

Evan held up a brown paper bag. "When your food's ready."

"Riiiiiight," I said. "When the food's ready."

Chapter 16

"Guess what? Trudy just called," Samantha said when I walked downstairs for breakfast. "We get a catering gig next week, and guess who it's for!"

I sleepily rubbed my eyes. "Orlando Bloom?"

"Close. Remember that guy we saw get off the ferry a couple of days ago—with the blond hair and the goatee and the white T-shirt and the khaki cargo shorts, and he asked us where he could rent a mountain bike?"

"Um . . . sort of," I said.

"You remember. We said he was the first actual book club sighting of the year," Sam said. "Actually, that was what I said."

"The party's at the Hamiltons' house, and I saw Mr. Hamilton coming to pick him up at the ferry," Haley said.

"You mean . . . *the* Hamiltons?" I asked. "The ones with the little cottage on the hill?"

Haley laughed. We both knew how really

wealthy people referred to their summer homes around here. "I have a cottage," they'd say, and that was our clue that it was at least a five-bedroom, six-bathroom house. "Exactly," she said.

"You really cleaned up the kitchen nicely last night," Sam commented as she put a filter into the coffeemaker.

"Yeah, well, it's easy when you don't actually cook anything. I mean, it's not too hard to rinse out plastic containers for recycling." I smiled, thinking of how much my aunt had teased me for picking up carryout food the night before. For some reason she thought it was the most amusing thing she'd ever heard of, and she couldn't wait to E-mail my parents and tell them how I'd had them over for takeout.

The whole time I was trying not to laugh because I kept thinking of how I had no more idea what we were going to eat than she did. I hadn't bothered to open up the containers before she and my uncle came over. I'd expected the clam chowder and lobster salad on a bed of lettuce. I hadn't expected the cold French fries—and so many of them—that Evan had picked out for us.

"So what was the verdict?" Haley asked.

"Did they decide we're not such horrible people after all?"

"Yeah. They inspected everything," I said. "Well, everything downstairs. I didn't let them see the upstairs. I didn't want them finding out about the new paint job in my parents' room."

"Good plan," Sam said as she took out three mugs from the cabinet.

"Yeah. Besides, I didn't exactly clean my room or scrub the upstairs bathroom, either." I smiled. "So what are you going to do with your day off?" I asked Haley, who was busy making herself a slice of toast.

"Absolutely nothing," she said. Then she laughed. "Yeah, right. I'll be at my mom and dad's, and they'll rope me into helping out, as usual."

"You should just get out of here and go to a movie or something," I said.

"Yeah, but it's no fun doing that by yourself." She wrinkled her nose. "You know?"

"You wouldn't be totally by yourself. At least not on the ferry," I said.

"True. Maybe I could convince Ben to—"

Samantha held up her hand for Haley to be silent. We all sat and listened to a car pulling up in the driveway. "What's that sound?" Sam asked.

I got up and looked out the screen door. A car was very definitely pulling up in the driveway. And it was the old Volvo—*my* old Volvo. Which meant that I was definitely not the one driving it, because I was standing in the kitchen. And it couldn't really drive itself, which meant . . .

I watched as Blair climbed out of the driver's seat and slammed the door shut. *Easy!* I wanted to say. If you close the door too hard, rusted pieces of the car fall off!

As I stepped back and watched her walk from the car to the steps, I wondered: Didn't I leave the keys on top of my dresser last night, where I always left them? So had she really come into my bedroom and taken them off the dresser? And now what? Did I have to hide the keys somewhere whenever I wasn't going to be around or awake? Should I sleep with them tied around my ankle?

I mean, who sneaks into someone's room when they're asleep and takes something?

"Hi, guys," Blair said as she strolled into the kitchen carrying a small plastic bag.

"Where were you?" Haley asked.

"I had some errands to run," Blair said.

Blair picked up a mug from the ones we'd gotten out for ourselves and poured herself some coffee.

"Funny, I was just about to have some," Sam muttered under her breath.

"Errands? Really important errands, I hope. Extremely urgent errands," Haley said. "Like, someone on the other side of the island needed CPR."

"I was out of conditioner." Blair held up the ends of her hair. "It's hard to figure out what kind to use out here because it's so humid. You know?"

Haley cleared her throat. "So I'm wondering, Blair. Did you not *read* the list?"

"What list?" Blair asked.

"The rules. The ones posted right there." I pointed to the poster board on the wall. "The ones I gave you to look over the day you came to visit the house for the first time, and you said okay to, that you said were like something your parents would make you do."

Samantha removed the pushpin and pulled the list off the wall. "Here. Read and review." She put it on the kitchen table, next to Blair's freshly poured mug of coffee. "It says that only

Colleen drives her car. It also says no big parties."

"God, you guys are so uptight sometimes," Blair said as she shook her head. "I mean, really. What's the big deal? It's not like anyone can check on us."

Except my ever-present relatives, I thought. Not that Blair would know about them, because she hadn't been around that Sunday morning, even though her overnight guest still had been.

"Yeah, maybe not, but it's still cheating," Sam said. "It still means breaking the rules."

"Anyway, it's not just about the list. It's about respecting the basic principles of the house and being a good housemate," Haley said. "You left like four wet towels on the bathroom floor yesterday. You left your laundry in the washer for three days straight."

"So?" Blair asked. "Just put it in the dryer."

"And fold it when it's dry? Like the last three times I did laundry?" Haley scoffed. "No thanks. When I want to do my laundry—okay, maybe *need* is a better word than *want*—I don't want to do yours, too."

"I'm sorry," Blair said. "I've been really busy."

"And we're not?" I asked.

There was a very awkward silence for a minute or so. Then Samantha picked up the jar on the counter that we used to collect and store "house money." It was empty. We each contributed twenty-five dollars every two weeks. Now it was time for everyone to refill the jar. Haley passed it around the table, and everyone contributed—except when the jar was passed to Blair.

"I don't have it, but I'll get it to you later today," she said.

"Didn't you make some tips last night?"

"Yeah, but I had to pay back Evan," Blair said.

"You too?" I blurted. "For what? I mean, um, did you ruin something of his?" Why was I asking? Maybe I didn't want to know the answer.

"No. He loaned me money when we took the ferry the day before. We went into town and had lunch and bought some stuff, and I didn't have enough cash on me."

I nearly choked on my coffee. Since when was Evan so flush—or generous? And why hadn't Ben told me he saw them together on the ferry?

Then again, it probably wasn't important to Ben. Probably he'd been glad to see the two of them hanging out together, because it might mean that Evan was attached to someone else now. Or had he been too busy flirting with Boat-and-Tote-Bag Girl to notice Blair and Evan?

This was turning into a semi–soap opera—without the international intrigue, romantic sex, and extreme close-ups.

"So, is that okay?" Blair asked.

The fact you're broke? Or the fact you're totally going after the guy I used to be in love with? No—and . . . no.

"Sure," I said, forcing a polite smile. "That's fine."

"You know what? I'll put money into the jar—I'm always over here." Erica handed me two twenty-dollar bills. "Here, Colleen."

"You don't have to," I said.

"I know, but I want to," Erica said.

I handed her back one of the twenties. "This will be great," I said as I stuffed the other twenty into the jar. "Thanks."

"You know what took me so long?" Blair said. "Some old lady fell and broke her arm and wrist or something. Everyone was talking about it at the store. She had to go in to the hospital last night on someone's boat and get it set. There was this really long line because everyone was talking about it."

"Yeah, you can't even sneeze around here without people talking about it," Samantha said.

Which was sometimes a very annoying thing, but it meant that if Blair ever took the car again without asking, at least I'd find out about it.

"Who was it? Did you get a name?" Haley asked.

"No. Well, Betty something."

"You're kidding. Betty McGonagle?" I asked. "Was that it?"

"Yeah, that sounds right." Blair refilled her coffee mug, draining the last drops left in the pot.

Poor Betty, I thought. But maybe it wasn't her painting hand. Then again, maybe it was.

"Hello, Mrs. McGonagle?" I knocked again and called into the house. "Can I come in?"

"Only if you call me Betty!" an irritated voice called back.

"Okay. Betty." I smiled and opened the screen door. "How are you?" I asked as I walked into her living room. She was sitting on the sofa with her right arm propped up on the side of it. She set down the book she had been reading when I walked in, and looked up at me. She was thin, with short, bright white hair that almost looked dyed that color, as if it were one shade short of platinum.

"Well, I've got a claw now," she said, holding up her right arm, which was wrapped and bandaged and partially in a cast. "Other than that, perfectly fine, same as always."

"Sorry to hear about your accident," I said. I hadn't been to her house since the last time I trick-or-treated, which must have been five years ago. I didn't remember all the abstract paintings on the walls. "Did you do those?" I asked.

"Most of them. Now, what can I get you? How about a cup of tea?" Betty said, starting to get to her feet.

"But I'm here to help you—to see what *you* need," I said.

"Nonsense. Don't need a thing," she said. "Now, what have you been up to this summer?"

"Well, you know. My parents are in Europe. I'm working at Bobb's."

"Well, I know all *that*, I'm not living in a

cave," Betty said. "Honestly, Colleen. I'm old, not dead," she snapped.

"Sorry," I said.

"Oh, it's not you. It's my idiot son. Wants me to leave the island, move in with him, in Bangor. Told him I'm not leaving this place. Just because I hurt myself, he thinks I'm helpless."

"You're not," I said. "Obviously."

"It's not as if I can't get help when I need it. Which I don't," she insisted. "Except last night when I had to call Cap and get him to take me in to the hospital in his boat. But that worked. That worked just fine."

One thing I really like about our island is that everyone takes care of one another. They might grumble about it, but they'll do it. And we might talk about each other too much, but at least we keep up with each other's lives.

"So how did you hurt your arm?" I asked as I followed Betty into the kitchen. "How long will it take to heal?"

"Six weeks or so." She groaned as she filled the tea kettle with water from the tap. "An eternity, in other words."

"Well, you'll tell me. If there's anything I can do to help, I mean," I said.

"You could come by now and then," she said. "Bring me some of your work. If I can't paint, then I can live vicariously through you. Right?" She smiled as she took mugs from the cabinet above the counter.

I wonder if Evan's working tonight. I stirred my spaghetti around my plate, and stared off into space, picturing Evan working with Blair, wondering whether there was anything going on between them, or if it already had. I should never have asked Blair to live with us. Not just because of the Evan thing, although that was awkward, too.

Suddenly I remembered a big fight Evan and I had had last summer, when I thought we were going out exclusively, and he had spent an entire day sailing with this girl named . . . Kelley.

Wait a second. No wonder she'd left Bobb's for the summer to work at the Spindrift B&B. Somehow, she'd gotten the heads-up that he was coming back for the summer. It wasn't about wanting to make muffins or beds. No, she was the *smart* one on the island.

I am a horrible, terrible person, I thought. I was sitting with Ben's family, having dinner, and I was thinking about Evan.

I was pathetic. It seemed as if I couldn't stop having these thoughts. What was wrong with me? Had I repressed all these things for months, and now they were taking their revenge? But did it have to happen mid-spaghetti? One strand went down the wrong way, and Ben nearly had to give me the Heimlich maneuver to save me from choking.

"Are you all right?" Ben asked.

"S-sure," I said. "Sorry. Don't know what I was doing. I just spaced out there for a second."

"You're tired, that's all," Ben's mother said. "In fact, you two are both working too hard this summer. I don't see how you've had time to just have fun together."

"It's been hard," I agreed. Not to mention complicated.

"How *is* your job going?" Ben's father asked.

"Good." I nodded.

"Busy?"

"Very. Well, not every night," I said. "But most of them."

"So you're making some good money?" he asked.

"Definitely." Unless you counted the

expensive-Birkenstock-sandals deduction. Or maybe it was more of a Colleen-impulsive-act-of-stupidity deduction. If he'd gotten mad or upset, the ninety dollars would be well worth it. But no, he'd enjoyed being tossed into the drink.

I looked up from my salad bowl and smiled at Ben's mother, who was watching me for some reason. Could *she* tell, somehow?

Meanwhile, Ben reached over under the table and put his hand on my leg. I was so surprised that I nearly kicked their dog, who was lying at my feet. Ben hardly ever did anything like that—not in front of (or under the table of) his parents and family.

I glanced at him and gave him a small, questioning smile.

After dinner, we had planned on watching a movie together, but I just wasn't in the mood. I felt too restless to sit still—like I needed to be out on a walk or something.

Hanging out with Ben like this, sitting around and listening to music . . . it was all fun and good and wonderful, when Evan wasn't here. But he *was* here now. And I was sitting on the sofa with Ben, wondering what Evan was doing that night. Not the *whole* time, but wasn't even part of the time bad enough?

Suddenly I couldn't take it anymore. I just needed some time to think, some time to breathe.

"You know what? I know we planned on watching a movie and everything, but I think I need go check on Betty and see how she's doing," I said, standing up.

"What?" Ben asked. "Check on Betty? McGonagle?"

"Yeah. I was over there yesterday, and she just . . . she needs some help," I said. "I promised I'd stop by, so I'd better do that before it gets too late."

"But . . . you always made fun of her," Ben said, getting up to follow me outside.

"I know. And that was really horrible of me. She's actually very nice," I said. "And she showed me a lot of her other paintings yesterday. I mean, she paints so much more than just . . . oceans. The stuff she sells at the gift shop, you know, that's just to support herself. She does abstract stuff; some of it's really incredible." I'd spent more than an hour at her house, looking at her work. I'd had no idea she was more than just . . . rolling surf.

"Yeah." Ben had never really been that

interested in art—mine or anyone else's. "So . . .
wait. Are you serious? You're going over there
right now?"

"Just to check on her on my way home," I
said. "Why? Is that okay?"

"It just seems strange, that's all." Ben stood
in the open doorway. "Are you sure that's where
you're going?"

What was he trying to say? Oh, no. He
thought I was leaving because I was going to see
Evan. I could see why he'd think that, but it
wasn't true. I might be confused at times, but I
wasn't a liar.

"Yes, I'm sure," I said, trying to keep things
simple. I didn't really want to go into it right
now. "Do you want to come with me?"

He shook his head. "No. Not really."

"Okay, well, I'll see you tomorrow?" I
walked back and gave him a quick kiss on the
lips.

"You want a ride?" Ben offered as I started
down the driveway.

"No, it's okay—I want to walk," I said.

After a quick visit to Betty, who looked at me like
I was crazy for coming by twice in one day, and

assured me she was still fine, I went home, walking the long way. I just felt like I couldn't be home tonight, I couldn't be with Ben. I dropped by to say hello to Haley's parents when I went past their place. I stopped in to say hello to my aunt and uncle. I even had a semi-okay thirty-second visit with the grumpy John and Molly Hyland, who were out for their evening stroll.

I'd never done so much socializing in my life, but mostly it was because I wanted to keep moving and I didn't want to stop. I didn't know why I had so much energy or what, exactly, I was looking for.

When I finally gave up and went home, Hutch was lying on the end of my bed, curled up on my red sweatshirt. I changed into my pajamas and lay down beside him. I scratched him behind the ears, and he turned over and stretched out on his back. Then I rubbed his belly. It was a good five minutes of cat therapy before Hutch turned and looked right at me. He stood up and rubbed his face against mine.

"I know, Hutch," I said softly. "I don't know what I'm doing, either."

Chapter 17

Saturday morning, when I went downstairs to make myself breakfast, I saw a body stretched out on the sofa. I almost didn't want to look—did we need any more unidentified overnight guests in this house? But then I quickly realized that it was my big brother lying there, curled up under a blanket.

"Richard! When did you get here?" I squealed. I ran over to give him a big hug. I hadn't seen him in a few months, and hadn't even realized how much I missed him until, suddenly, there he was.

"I caught the last ferry last night. I thought for sure I'd wake you guys up when I came in, but—well, I guess I perfected the art of sneaking into this house late at night a long time ago." He sat up and rubbed his head. "Though I did hit my head coming in the window." His short, wavy blond hair was a floppy, curly mess, as if it had absorbed half of the ocean on the way over on the ferry, as if he'd been at sea for weeks. If my hair became a frizzone, Richard's turned into a curlizone. He nearly had *ringlets*. Which could have been embarrassing if he didn't have such good cheekbones.

"Why didn't you call or E-mail before you came?" I asked. "I would have come to pick you up, if I knew when to."

"I wasn't sure I was going to make it. Then a guy I work with rented a car, and I drove up with him. He's in Machias now. Anyway, don't worry about it." He stretched his arms over his head and yawned. He was wearing a white T-shirt and shorts. "I met this girl on the ferry last night—"

"Oh, no," I groaned. "Here we go again."

He grinned. "She gave me a ride. She's staying at the Ludlows' this weekend. Do we know the Ludlows?"

"Richard." I picked up a pillow and bashed him on the head with it.

"'Cause we should, I think," he said, laughing. "That name sounds familiar. Where's the phone book?"

"You are horrible. You're so horrible," I told him. "Don't you have like a serious girlfriend in New York?"

"Correction. Had," Richard said.

I rolled my eyes. That was Richard for you. Every girl was perfect, every girl was the one he'd been waiting for, the one he wanted to marry. And then . . . he'd be on the ferry and there'd be someone cute and his old relationship would be history.

At least he was nice to them while he dated them. The problem was that they weren't prepared for how short an attention span Richard had for relationships. It was like everyone came with an expiration date. "I don't know where he gets it from," Mom would say, "but it's not from me."

And then Dad would get sort of red and flustered and mumble something about "skipping a generation," but I'd always start wondering what exactly happened when they met in college. Dad was so mild-mannered and sweet and . . . well, goofy . . . that I couldn't picture this cloud of women around him, fighting over him. No, not in a million years.

Richard, on the other hand? That I could see. I *had* seen it. He'd dated so many girls on the island that he'd run *out* of them. And he didn't even have a bad reputation. If a girl ever did what he did? Well, never mind. He was here now, and I was very excited to see him. "This is going to be so cool. I'm working tonight, so you should come in and eat for free. Bring . . . whoever. Then we can all go to the fireworks together. You, me, Evan—I mean, Ben—"

"Whoa. What's up with that?" Richard sat up a little on the sofa. "Now we're getting to the good stuff."

"There's no . . . stuff," I said. I was about to tell Richard the situation when Blair came downstairs.

"Hello. Who are you?" she asked Richard. The thing that killed me about Blair—okay, one of the things—was that she could look good no matter what time of day it was. Sure, she spent tons of time in front of the mirror to do it, but the thing was that it paid off. Me? The more time I spent, the worse I looked, it seemed. I'd make too many second guesses about my makeup and end up ruining my face, or hair. Or both.

"This is Richard. You know, the guy in all the pictures?" I pointed to the living room wall, where the photos of Colleen and Richard Through the Ages—from the cute to the embarrassing to the okay to the good—were displayed.

"Oh, my god. Of course you are. And Colleen said you might be coming for the weekend.

That's great!" She walked over and held out her hand. "Hi, I'm Blair."

"Nice to meet you, Blair," Richard said as he slowly shook her hand.

"Hey, would you like some coffee?" Blair offered.

"Sure. Sounds great." Richard smiled at her. "Thanks." Then he turned to me. "It's really strange being in our house and being waited on by someone I don't know. Not to mention sleeping on the sofa."

I didn't mention that it was also really strange, because Blair never made coffee. Or did anything around the house, actually. Except occasionally borrow the car without asking and use up groceries she didn't pay for.

"Did you see Haley?" I asked. "She would have had to be at work already."

"Horrible Haley? No, I didn't," Richard said.

"She's staying in your room this summer," I said.

"Yeah, you told me that. Your E-mails have kind of dropped off lately, though. Anything I need to know about?"

"Ah . . . Betty McGonagle broke her arm?" I said.

Richard sighed and snuggled back under the blanket. "Slow news day on the island, as usual."

"No, but I feel really bad for her," I said. "I've been visiting her."

"Huh?"

"Come on, get up—let's have breakfast. Then maybe you can get to work. We've been saving up some stuff around the house for you to do. The hinge on the screen door is busted, for one."

"Oh, great. That's what I want to do on my long weekend," Richard complained. "It better be *good* coffee."

"Don't count on it," I told him.

"How about a Bobb's bib?"

Richard looked up at me with his eyebrow raised. He was having lunch at Bobb's with a couple of his old high school friends. "How about no?" he said.

"Come on, you have to wear a bib," I said. "If you order the lobster, you get a bib. Free of charge. No, really."

Carl leaned over to Richard. "I know I asked you this before, but is that gorgeous girl your sister?"

I'd had such a crush on Carl when I was ten

and he was eighteen. He always teased me like that, whenever I saw him. Now he was already starting to lose his hair at twenty-five. It made me feel old.

"No, that's not my sister, that's an annoying waitress," Richard said. "Colleen, when is the last time you saw me wear a bib? Never."

I shook the plastic bib in front of him, the way you'd shake a towel that had sand on it. "Come on. For me?"

"No. I think I can eat a lobster without ruining my shirt."

"And I had my camera ready and everything," I complained. "I was going to take a picture of you in the bib and E-mail it to Mom and Dad."

"Well, forget it. So that's your boyfriend, right?" Richard pointed at Evan with a lobster leg. "I remember him from last summer."

"No, it's not," I said. "I'm with Ben. You know Ben—you met him at Christmas."

"Oh, right. Ben." He stared at me and gestured for me to come closer. He lowered his voice and said, "Coll, reality check time. That guy is either your boyfriend or he's going to be—"

"No!" I interrupted. "He's my *ex*-boyfriend. Evan. Remember how upset I was last fall? How

226

I was crying and miserable?"

"No." Richard shook his head. "Sorry, but I don't."

"Oh. Well, that was all *his* fault." I glared at Evan, who was cheerfully greeting a large table of twelve guests.

"Uh-huh. Well, I don't know what happened back then, but he seems to kind of like you now. I saw the way you guys made sure you got in each other's way? Just to get through the door?"

"We did not," I said, remembering how I'd had to squeeze past Evan. Wait! *Was* one of us going out through the in door? On purpose? And was that one of us . . . me?

"It's not like that," I said, but I was wondering. Was it like that? Evan had never given me a reason to think he wasn't still maybe interested in me. We were just not seeing each other now.

"Well, why don't you bring me another lobster?" Richard said as he cracked a claw.

"Are you serious?" I asked. "Two lobsters?"

"Yeah. Completely serious. And when you get it for me, try not to touch that guy," Richard whispered. "I want to see if you can pull it off."

"Richard!" I whispered, slapping his shoulder. "Quiet."

"Don't hit me," Richard said.

"Yeah, hit me instead," Carl said. "And you can bring me another lobster while you're in there, okay, Colleen?"

Luke was busy chewing, but he held up his hand and signaled for another for himself, too. Richard and his friends always ate *so much*, I thought as I walked into the kitchen. They hadn't changed at all since last summer, or the summer before that, or . . .

"Did you see him?" Samantha asked when I nearly crashed into her. She was standing right by the door, peeking through the window in it. "Did you see how cute he is?"

"Who?" I asked.

"That blond guy at table seventeen. I'm waiting on him," she said. "Remember, the guy Mr. Hamilton picked up from the ferry?"

"Oh, yeah. Now I remember," I said as I checked him out.

"His name's Troy Hamilton." Samantha nodded. "And guess what? They're here to evaluate the catering menu because they hired Bobb's for his cousin's engagement luncheon next week. And I was right—we're totally invited. As caterers, that is."

"Sounds fun," I said.

"Well, sort of. Does walking around offering trays of mini crab cakes count?" she joked.

When I got back to Richard's table with the tray of three lobsters, Richard was on the other side of the restaurant, talking to someone at another table. I glanced over just as a woman's arm shot out and she doused him with a glass of water, right in the face.

Richard stepped back, looked shocked, and then came walking back over to his table. The front of his faded navy polo shirt was drenched.

"You should have gone with the bib," I teased as he sank into his chair.

Carl and Luke were laughing at him. "What happened?" Carl asked.

"I was trying to talk to that girl from the ferry last night. The one staying with the Ludlows?" Richard dabbed his face with a napkin. "Ludlow, Ludlow . . . what Ludlow do I know who would want to throw water at me?"

Carl snapped his fingers. "Emily Ludlow, you idiot. You went out junior year."

"Right! Right. But that was like ten years ago." He rubbed his neck. "Why is she still holding that against me?"

"You stood her up for the prom," Luke said. "Does that ring a bell?"

"Oh, crap. This place *is* small," Richard complained.

"You know what?" I said, thinking of my own predicament, being stuck on an island with my current and my ex. "We should live in Montana or California. Even Rhode Island would be bigger."

"Why do you think I moved to Manhattan?" Richard replied, casting a nervous glance over his shoulder at Emily Ludlow's table.

"Wait a second, wait a second. I know all about Richard, but why do *you* say that?" Carl asked me.

"Oh. Uh, looks like another table needs me." I escaped before they could ask any more questions. I could just see those guys having a field day with my situation. Before they left Bobb's, they'd probably harass Evan to no end. I didn't want them doing that.

That was *my* job.

Richard was catching a ride back to the city on Monday morning with Luke, who was driving down to Portland, where Richard could get the train.

I hadn't seen him too much the night before, when everyone on the island had gone to watch the fireworks. Ben and I hung out together, while Richard ran around with his friends. They'd stayed out until at least two in the morning. I wasn't surprised that Richard was looking a little the worse for wear as he got out of the car and we walked slowly toward the ferry. We both waved at Luke, who was already on the boat, waiting for him.

"I know I should be a better big brother. I don't really set a good example." Richard took a sip from the can of ginger ale he'd grabbed on the way out the door, and made a face. "But I do have to give you some advice."

"Don't drink heavily the night before you have to get on a ferry and then be in a car and then on a train?" I said.

"Ha ha, very funny. I'm *fine*." He scratched the blond stubble on his cheek. "It's just—look, Colleen. About you and that guy at the restaurant."

"There is no 'about' us," I said.

"Just think about what you really want. Because if you don't *know* what you want, you're just screwing around with other people's feelings."

This would have to be ironic, coming from him.

"No offense, Richard. But I just don't know how much you know about real relationships."

"Ooh. Ouch." Richard pretended to dab his face, as if I'd punched it and given him a bloody nose.

I laughed. "Well, sorry, but it's true."

"It might be true, but I do know no one likes being lied to. I mean, once it's over . . ." He shrugged. "It's over."

"Yes, but it's not over until it's over," I said.

"That makes no sense." Richard leaned over to give me a hug. "But whatever works for you, Coll. I'm off to make my fortune."

"That's what you said last time. Send me some *checks* already."

"I'll come visit you at Bates in the fall!" Richard called as the ferry started to pull away. "Make some cute friends, okay?"

"You're horrible!" I yelled.

That was all I needed, Richard, Mr. Short Relationship Attention Span, hitting on my college roommates and breaking their hearts. And being way, way too old for them—only he wouldn't think so.

But as I watched him go, I had to wonder: Did Evan and I really act that obviously toward each other that even my brother had to comment on it? Was I still as attracted to him as I used to be? And if I was . . . then what was I doing with Ben?

Chapter 18

"Rich much?" Blair asked as we climbed out of the Bobb's catering van. I stood next to her and looked up at the "cottage" in front of us. It was a large, white house overlooking the ocean, with green shutters, a wide porch that wrapped around the entire house, a gorgeous rose garden, a shuffleboard court, and a three-car garage and a little carriage house. The Hamiltons probably put more money into mowing their lawn than my parents put into our entire house.

"So this is how the other half lives," Evan said, getting out of the backseat of the van.

Samantha walked around from the driver's seat. "Wow. The Hamiltons do all right, don't they? I'm so jealous, I almost hate them."

"As long as they keep inviting cute grand-nephews here, who cares?" I whispered to Sam.

"No doubt. So I've been thinking about what this year's excursion should be," she said as we started to unload the van, carrying trays of food into the house. "You know, last year we did the sailboat cruising thing. What should we do this year?"

"I haven't really thought about it," I said. The memory of Ben asking me to go to Acadia with him flitted through my brain. That was a summer getaway excursion plan, and for some reason it didn't make me want to . . . excurse. It made me want to *excuse* myself.

"I have two ideas," Sam said. "One, we take a road trip somewhere we've never been before. It could be Maine, it could be Canada—Nova Scotia, maybe. Or two, *we* have a party catered by Bobb's. And Trudy has to wait on *us*."

"That sounds good," Evan said. "Am I invited?" He pulled open the back door we'd been instructed to use, and held the door open with his foot for the rest of us.

"No," Sam said bluntly.

"Come on. I got to go last year," Evan complained as I walked past him.

"That was then—" I began.

"This is now," Evan said. "Why was *then* so much better than now?"

Don't, I thought. *Don't do that*. He was really turning it up a notch with the flirting lately. As I bumped into him in the kitchen, struggling to set down the tray I was carrying, I thought about what Richard had said, how we couldn't get through a shift at Bobb's without touching each other. Was that true?

I tried to keep my distance while we got ready for and then worked the party, which was held on a large deck overlooking the ocean. Everyone was very nice to us, except for one grumpy older man who kept insisting the shrimp were no good, that he expected *prawns*, not "itty bitty shrimp."

"But jumbo shrimp is an oxymoron," Evan said. "Sir."

He grunted at both of us and then turned away to get another glass of champagne, or whatever he was drinking. They'd hired a bartender from somewhere else, since (a) all of us were underage, and (b) Trudy's selection of liquor was limited to Geary's Ale and a few domestic beers.

I saw Blair laughing with Troy Hamilton, and Sam gently interrupting to tell her to go to the kitchen for the cheese puffs. Then Sam and Troy leaned against the deck railing for a couple of minutes, talking. *Good for her*, I thought. *Go, Sam, go.*

                    *   *   *

"Hey, Sam? Could you drop me off here?" I asked as we drove past the Landing on our way back to Bobb's. I was thinking that I could see Ben when he finished work, and in the meantime I could visit with Haley.

"Sure thing," Sam said, pulling over and stopping. "Tell Haley I said hi!"

"Yeah, for me, too," Blair added.

I climbed out of the van and was about to close the sliding door behind me when Evan stopped me. He hopped out of the van. "I could really go for an ice cream. All that small talk and politeness gave me a sore throat," he said, as if that explained why he was following me.

"Yeah. Sure," I said as Sam drove off in the van with Blair. I felt kind of bad that they'd have to unload everything without us now. But most of it was empty trays and dirty silverware.

"Sure what?" Evan laughed as he fell into step beside me. "You sound like you don't believe me."

"Should I?" I asked.

"I have no idea what you're talking about."

"Never mind," I said. "It just seems like a coincidence, that's all. I get out of the van, so you do?"

"Okay, so. In your . . . fantasy world . . . a person wants a little mocha chip and suddenly it's a plot?"

I started laughing, despite myself. Okay, so maybe my ego was getting a little out of control. Evan was allowed to crave mocha chip. It didn't have anything to do with me. Although . . . if he really wanted the ice cream, why hadn't he jumped out of the van first?

We walked over to the Landing's takeout window. Haley was leaning on the wooden shelf with her elbows and staring out at the water.

"Pretty boring between ferries, huh?" I asked.

"Hey, Coll!" she said, her face lighting up when she saw me. Then her expression changed a bit. "Oh. Hi, Evan," she said coldly.

"Haley. What's up?" Evan asked.

"Not much." She sighed. "Pretty slow. How was the catering thing?" she asked me.

"Fabulous," I said.

"Yeah, fabulous for them, because all the chicks were lusting after this guy at the party," Evan said.

"No, we all weren't," I said. "Sam likes him, and he likes her—"

"Same old, same old," Evan said.

"Yeah. It is getting old," Haley said. She stared at Evan. "Really old."

She was acting very standoffish toward him. I realized she probably hadn't seen him much at all this summer. She was no doubt still angry with him for making me cry last fall. She can hold a grudge longer than you'd think it's humanly possible.

"Anyway, aren't you guys supposed to be at work?" she asked.

"We get a break before dinner," I said. "So I thought I'd come see you."

"I think I'd go home and chill by myself for a while," Haley said with a pointed look at me. "If it were me."

"Uh, maybe you're right," I said as I heard the ferry horn. "Maybe we should get back to work."

Evan shrugged. "Okay, but I want the mocha chip first."

"Cone or dish?" Haley asked. She quickly got Evan a double cone, and me a single dish of praline pecan. I wanted to get out of there before Ben showed up. I felt this nervous energy, like I was doing something wrong.

Relax, Colleen. It's only ice cream. And you're not even sharing a spoon.

"We'd better get going," I said, heading for the road.

"Yeah, we'd better," Evan said. "It's a bit of a walk from here. Want to call a cab? Or, wait. Even better—let's hitch."

"I don't hitch rides," I said.

"Don't worry. You'll be safe with me," Evan said.

Somehow I doubted that, as he hailed an old station wagon that was driving past. It felt like we were running away together—except for the fact that we were carrying ice cream and wearing black-and-white catering uniforms. Which kind of took some of the thrill of adventure out of it.

We got into the backseat of the station wagon against my better judgment. Two guys I'd never seen before, a skinny one with long straggly hair and a large-ish one with a crew cut, both (sadly) bare-chested, turned around and nodded at us. "Right on," they said in unison.

"Where are you headed?" the straggly-haired guy asked.

"Bobb's restaurant," Evan said.

"Right on." The crew cut guy nodded in approval.

Evan and I glanced at each other. "Is there any other answer?" I whispered.

"Right on," he replied, and we both grinned.

We were halfway through the dinner shift at Bobb's when Trudy said she wanted to talk to me in the kitchen. I had no idea what it was about. I'd brought out the wrong salad dressing a couple of times that night, but it wasn't like her to get on my case about small mistakes.

"The Hamiltons just called," she said. "Olivia Hamilton, to be exact."

"And?" I asked. I was expecting praise, expecting her to have said she wanted to hire us for another event. "The party went really smoothly—did she say that?"

Trudy wiped down one of the prep tables while she spoke. "Not exactly. She has a problem." ·

"Problem? What kind?" I asked.

"Some of her jewelry's missing. An entire box, I guess."

I put my hand to my throat. "You're kidding!"

"I wish that I were." Trudy frowned at me. "This is very serious."

"Okay. So who do they think is responsible?"

"Well, that's just it, Colleen. And believe me, I hate to say this. But I've talked to everyone else already—Sam, Blair, Evan. And you were the last one in the house, and—"

"What? But I didn't—I wouldn't—"

"I didn't think you did, either. But there are witnesses."

"Witnesses?" Why was this turning into an episode of *Law & Order*? I was being accused of a crime. What next—I was supposed to hire a lawyer, wasn't I? *Were* there any lawyers on the island? "Trudy, the only reason I was the last person in the house is that I was the last person in the van, because Blair forgot a tray on the deck and I ran back in to get it."

"Well. The fact remains that you were in the house after everyone else—"

"But the entire family was still in the house!" I protested. "So how would I even know where to look or what to steal? I don't think like that. I've never stolen anything."

"I promise I'll check into this. I'm not letting you go right away," Trudy said. "No one's going to press any charges until there's some more facts. But this is the story right now, so far. We'll see what develops in the next few days."

"Trudy! How can you even *think* I'd do something like that? You've known me for *four* years. Have I ever—"

"I'm sorry, Colleen. But—"

"You know what? Never mind. I can't believe this. I didn't take *anything*, and I can't believe I even have to tell you that!" I stormed out through the back doors and ran to the end of the dock. I was so upset that I started crying.

I heard footsteps clomping down the dock toward me. I turned around and there was Evan, reaching out for me, putting his arms around me, holding me close. I didn't bother to resist. I didn't have the strength to—besides, I needed him.

"She thinks . . . she thinks . . ." I sputtered.

"Don't worry." Evan stroked my hair. "I know you didn't do anything. Trudy will find that out."

"But why would she . . . ?"

"She had some woman call up and yell at her," Evan said. "Ten to one, Mrs. Hamilton finds her jewelry tonight."

I kept sniffling, and he kept running his hand over my head, and then he kissed my cheek.

"And you know what? The stuff she was wearing today was so gaudy that I'm surprised it could even *go* missing. I mean, it could light up an entire town."

I smiled. "True." I brushed his T-shirt sleeve against my face to dab away the tears, and it was so soft, and smelled just like I remembered him.

Suddenly, out of the corner of my eye, I saw someone else on the docks.

My eyes widened in horror. That figure in the dark was *Ben*.

And as soon as I recognized him, he turned and ran.

Chapter 19

"Ben! Ben, wait!" I called.

Evan was still holding my arms, not letting me go right away. I twisted my way out of his grasp just as I heard a car peeling out of the parking lot. I teetered on the dock, nearly tipping over. Evan caught my arm to keep me from falling into the water, but I shook him off. "Let me go!" I said.

I ran inside and found Trudy as quickly as I could. She was at the host stand with Erica, inserting the sheet with tomorrow's lunch specials printed on it into the menu.

"Trudy, I—I have to go," I said. "I can't work the rest of my shift."

"Colleen? You can't just leave," she said.

"I have to!" I said.

"Colleen. We still have to talk about this missing jewelry issue. And you've got a shift to finish. I really don't think this is the time for you to be taking off—"

"But I have to. Trudy, you know me, you know I'd never do anything like steal—anything to break the law—come on!" I insisted. "And this is a really important personal issue and I have to deal with it now. You always say that we can have time off for personal days. Well, I need some personal hours—now."

"Colleen! It's too short notice. What are we going to do if you just take up and leave because you feel like it?" Trudy said.

"Trudy, I'll work for her," Erica said.

"But you're hosting," Trudy argued.

"That doesn't take all of my time—anyway, the evening's winding down, and we're only seating tables for another hour. I can handle it," Erica said.

I loved her for sticking up for me.

"We'll split her tables," Samantha said, walking up. "Go, Colleen. Do what you have to do."

"You guys are the best."

"Colleen? Consider yourself suspended," Trudy said. "I don't want to see you here tomorrow. Is that understood?"

"Yes, ma'am," I grumbled. I could care less about my job right then, and besides, I was still mad at Trudy for not trusting me. I wished she'd suspended me about two hours ago.

I pulled off my apron and handed it to Erica, then I quickly went over with her and Sam which tables I had and what they still needed. Then I was on my way. I had to catch Ben before any more time went by. He was thinking terrible, horrible things, and they weren't true.

"Hey, Coll! Where are you going?" Evan called as I hurried past him, out the door.

"Where do you think?" I said, still moving, going down the dock beside the building. I didn't want to talk to him right now. Maybe he hadn't meant to, but he'd ruined things for me—again. Just like he was always ruining things for me.

"Look, maybe you shouldn't go over there right now."

"I have to," I said.

"I know you *want* to, and you think you have to," Evan said. "But give the guy a second to deal with it. If it were me, I'd be really angry—"

"But it wouldn't be you, would it?" I said. "You don't understand. You don't know what it's like—Ben's a nice person, too nice to do stuff like what we just did to him."

"I didn't mean anything by it. I was only trying to make you feel better—"

"I know. I *know*. But look—not right now." I started jogging toward Ben's house, which was about a mile and a half from Bobb's. Good thing I always wore running sneakers to work.

"Colleen?" Ben's mother stared at my outfit, at the flush in my cheeks. She stepped aside to let me walk past her into the house. "Have you been exercising?"

"I—I was in a hurry," I said. I didn't want to get into the details with her.

"Did you get out of work early?" She smiled at me. So, she didn't hate me yet. That must mean Ben hadn't told her anything. Of course, why would he? It wasn't the sort of thing you went around bragging about. *I saw my girlfriend with another guy.*

"Um, yes," I said. Not in the way she thought, but the fact was I *had* gotten out early. "It was sort of a slow night." Except when it came to me messing up—in that respect, it was a very busy night.

"Well, I'll run upstairs and tell Ben you're here. He just got home," she said.

While she was gone, I paced around the living room. Through the doorway to the den, I could see Ben's father sitting in front of the TV, watching a Red Sox game. I waved to him, and he smiled and waved back. It was about nine o'clock, and Ben's younger brothers, Colin and Philip, were no doubt already asleep, or at least in bed.

I was checking out the crystal figurines in their hutch display when I heard footsteps coming down the stairs. My hand shook and I nearly knocked over a crystal swan. That was all I needed—to break the collectibles on top of everything else.

I took a deep breath and turned around.

"I'm sorry, Colleen. He's already gone to bed," Ben's mother said.

I bit my lip, trying to decide what to do next. Maybe Ben was just angry, and he needed some time to recover—the way he had when I'd first told him about Evan that day on the ferry. (Which felt like months ago, instead of weeks.) It had taken him two days to talk to me about it. Maybe I should let the whole thing blow over this time, too.

Then again, if I just left, I'd have no chance of explaining what had happened. Ben would assume the worst. Like he already apparently had.

"I hate to ask you to do this. But do you think you could wake him up?" I asked. "It's really, really important."

"Is it an emergency? Is everything okay?"

"Well, no. It's not. I have to talk to him," I said. "Tonight."

I guess she could see how desperate I was, because she nodded and said, "All right. I'll try again."

Try again. That meant he wasn't sleeping, that she'd asked if he could come down and see me, and he'd said to *tell* me that he was asleep. Wow. He'd never done that to me—never lied. At least, not that I knew of.

When he finally came downstairs, I could tell he hadn't been sleeping at all.

"Hey," I said.

He ran his hands through his hair and just looked at me.

"Can we . . . can we go for a walk or something?" I asked, thinking about his father in the den, and his mother somewhere else nearby—and she knew something was up.

"Sure."

We went down to this really big rock beside the road, where we often sat and talked. I was walking slightly behind Ben, and as I looked at his back, I felt like I was about to start crying.

I remembered one of the first nights we went out on a date, to the winter dance, how Ben had been sitting on this rock, waiting for me when I pulled up in the car, and how he was carrying flowers in the dead of winter, how he had mittens on with his dark suit, and how I was wearing my mother's thick wool coat over my dress and attempting to drive—and walk—on the ice in heels, and how Ben had picked me up and carried me into the school.

Ben leaned against the rock, and I tried to stand next to him.

"I saw you run off tonight," I said. "I know you saw me and Evan and you thought we were . . . I don't know what you thought, actually, which is why I came over to explain. It was just a quick hug. Really."

Ben didn't say anything for a minute. I bit my lip, wanting him to understand, wishing tonight had never happened. "It lasted five minutes," he finally said, his tone cold.

"What? No, that's impossible." I shook my head. "Look, what happened was—"

"I don't care what happened or whatever

spin you're going to put on what happened," Ben said. "I know what I saw, and it wasn't some ten-second hug. Five minutes, Coll."

"But . . . it's important," I said. "Please, listen. See, we had this catering job—you remember, at the Hamilton house? And they reported some jewelry missing, and someone actually said *I* was responsible. Me."

Ben crossed his arms in front of him. "Well. Were you?"

"Ben! Come on. I'd never steal," I said. "Do you really think so poorly of me?"

"I shouldn't have said that. I'm sorry," Ben said.

"No, *I'm* sorry. I was just—I was upset when the whole thing came up and Trudy accused me—and I—I went outside. Evan followed me and I just—I turned to him because I was so upset. I mean, Trudy . . . of all people. You know?"

"You could have turned to Samantha. Or Erica," Ben said. "Couldn't you?"

"Well, yeah, of course, but they weren't right there—"

"Or you could have just called me. That's sort of what I'd expect you to do," Ben said. "If you were upset. I wouldn't expect you to be all over your ex-boyfriend, in front of me, in front of everyone eating at Bobb's—"

"I didn't know you were there," I said.

That sounded terrible, as if I were going around hugging Evan whenever I knew Ben wouldn't be there. "I mean, I wasn't thinking! It wasn't a *plan*. It was a gut reaction. I would have hugged Cap, or John Hyland, or Eddie from the hardware store . . . if he'd been out there. I would have hugged a seagull, if it was possible."

"You're not being honest. I know what I saw, and I know it didn't mean . . . I know it meant *something*," Ben stammered. "And in a way, it wasn't even surprising. I mean, it was so . . . obvious what was going on. What's been going on all summer."

"Nothing!" I said. "Nothing's going on now, nothing's *been* going on—"

"Yeah. It is," Ben said.

"But . . . no. It isn't," I insisted. "And Evan— and I—we're not. That's the only time we ever hugged—there's nothing between us."

"There's something," Ben said slowly. "Which really sucks. Because this was supposed to be such a great summer for us. You know?

Yeah. Turned out really great."

"Hasn't it?" I asked.

"No. You've changed, Colleen."

"What? I haven't *changed*," I said.

"Yeah, you have. You used to be so . . . reliable. Stable. Now you're all over the place. You can't even commit to going on a trip together because you can't make up your mind what—I'm sorry, who—you want from one day to the next."

"That's not true," I said. Reliable and stable? As if I were a car or something. That sounded boring. Maybe that was how I acted, or how he perceived me, but that didn't sound like the way I *felt*.

"Look, we're not going to be together next year anyway," Ben went on, as if he'd made up his mind. "Let's stop kidding ourselves—this isn't going to work out then. It's not working out now. Let's just forget about it. Stop seeing each other."

"No. No!" I said. "Don't say that." I reached for his arms and tried to pull him toward me, but he wouldn't budge.

He just glared at me. "You can't hold on to me while you decide which of us you like more.

I don't want to be the backup boyfriend. You know, for whenever this year's summer fling—which was exactly the same as last year's fling—is over," he said bitterly.

"It's not like that!" I said, starting to cry.

"No. Actually, it's worse than that. Because the fact that you guys are still spending time together after the way things ended between you means you still have feelings for him, even though he treated you like—like an afterthought for months. So you want someone like Evan, who's here today, gone tomorrow. Okay. Whatever. I'm not that person."

I was sobbing while he said this. "No, that's *not* what I want. It's . . ." What was it? Did I need to prove to myself that I *could* get Evan back? That he had tried to reject me, but it wouldn't work because I was too irresistible? What was my problem?

But if I couldn't, right then and there, say that I didn't want Evan, and that I wanted Ben . . .

I couldn't do it.

Ben was the completely good and logical choice for so many reasons.

Evan was not.

And I was giving up on Ben when I didn't

even have anything with Evan.

"Bye," Ben said as he started walking up his driveway.

I couldn't say anything. I wanted to ramble on, explain myself ten times over, tell Ben how much I loved him—because, despite everything, I did love him. But maybe I wasn't *in* love with him. Maybe he knew more about how I felt than I did.

When I got home, Haley was sitting on the porch. I was so glad to see her, because I wanted to tell her what happened, but I didn't know if I could. I'd spent the entire walk home crying. It was embarrassing, really.

"What are you doing up so late?" I asked.

"Just thinking about things." Her legs were propped on the porch railing, and she was holding a glass of lemonade. "Where have you been? Wait—why aren't you at work?"

I started crying all over again. I sat down in a chair next to hers and buried my face in my hands.

"Colleen! What is it?" She shook the arm of my chair. "Come on, tell me—what happened?"

I took a tissue out of my pocket and dabbed the tears from my cheeks. Then I told her about how I was a suspect now, and how Ben had seen me hug Evan, and how Ben and I had broken up. When I finished the story—the short version—I looked over at her. I couldn't wait to hear what she had to say. She was always so supportive of me, especially when I messed up.

She shook her head as if she couldn't believe what she'd heard.

"I know, I know," I said. "Isn't it awful?"

"Yeah." She nodded. "God, Colleen. You really have been acting like a royal jerk."

"What?"

"You deserve to feel this bad." She tossed my crumpled tissue onto the porch. "You deserve everything that's happened tonight. If I were Ben, I'd hate you, too."

"What?" How could she talk to me like that? I knew she could be mean, and stubborn, with other people, but she'd never been this way to me. Never.

"As soon as Evan got here, you acted like Ben was just . . . runner-up. You know that?" she asked. "As if you had a contest: Who can date the great and wonderful Colleen—"

"There was no contest," I said, her words stinging me. "That's a terrible thing to say to me."

"Well, you treated Ben terribly. You completely dropped him. Like, summer boyfriend, winter boyfriend. Like you can just shut off feelings, like—like—like it's as easy as closing all the outdoor taps over the winter. Ben really, really cared about you—"

"And I cared about him!" I cried. "I *still* care."

"Obviously *not*," she said. "You know what? You're just like Richard."

"What? I am not."

"No, you are. I didn't see it before, but now I do."

Haley stood up and walked into the house, the screen door slamming loudly behind her. I'd forgotten to make Richard help me repair that loose hinge.

Me—just like Richard? Since when? And where did Haley get off, telling me I was holding a contest and that I didn't care about Ben? I wasn't, and I did.

I sat on the porch for a while, thinking about everything that had happened that night, listening to the crickets, watching moths fly around the porch light. I was glad nobody else would be home for a while. I needed time to recover.

Chapter 20

The next morning I was in my room, lazing about in bed, enjoying my dictated day off. I had no reason to get up early because I had the whole day ahead of me. And I hadn't slept well the night before, so if I dozed back to sleep, who cared?

"Suspended." Who gets suspended from a waitress job? I'd made it through high school with no suspensions, but apparently I couldn't make it through the summer without one.

As if my life weren't bad enough right now, with Ben hating me, Haley disapproving of me, and Evan . . . hugging me. Okay, so that last one wasn't bad. In fact, it had felt pretty good at the time.

But it was horrible that it came about because Trudy suspected me of stealing. As if I would. I'd worked for her for four years now, and suddenly I couldn't be trusted? What kind of sense did that make?

If Trudy wanted to think I was a thief, after everything I'd done for her, after the countless Bobb's bibs I'd fastened, the silverware I'd bundled, the onions I'd chopped until tears streamed down my face—to say nothing of the way I pushed the cups of chowder (not that I needed to, really) to customers and the fried seafood Fisherman's Platter—well, I wasn't so sure I wanted to go back to work tomorrow, even if she said it was okay. Maybe I'd just take the rest of the summer off.

And do what, exactly? I thought as I stared at my drafting table and work area. I'd go crazy after a couple of days without working.

Okay, *more* crazy.

There was a knock at the door, and I sat up on the bed, not wanting to be seen looking as hopeless as I felt. "Yeah?"

Samantha strode into the room and put her hands on her hips. "Are you *ever* going to get up?"

"Eventually," I said with a yawn as Erica walked in behind her. "Why?"

"We have great news!" Erica said.

"What?"

"Blair's gone!" Erica cried.

It was funny to hear someone as nice as Erica say something that catty. "What do you mean, she's gone?" I asked. "I can't believe it. She *left*?"

"Her room's cleared out," Erica said. "In fact, I think I could even move in right now."

"Would you please?" Sam asked her. "Because one lying, cheating, deadbeat house-mate is enough for one summer."

I raised my eyebrows. "What?"

"You won't believe this," Erica said, sitting in my desk chair.

Sam grabbed a pillow off my bed and sat on it on the floor. "Yeah, she will," she predicted.

"You know that whole thing yesterday . . . about the catering? And the missing jewelry?" Erica asked.

I nodded. "How could I not know? I took it, remember?" I rolled my eyes. "Trudy. How could she—"

"Blair was the so-called witness," Erica said.

"No. You're kidding," I said.

Erica shook her head. "Not only that, she's the one who stole the stuff. And Sam's the one who busted her."

"How?" I asked. "Come on, I haven't seen you guys in like twelve hours. And all this happened?"

261

"I just had a feeling about her, you know?" Sam said. "A very, very *bad* feeling. I mean, first I considered the whole theft story could be made up, or a setup or something. You never know when someone's going to have a grudge against someone on this island."

I thought about Mrs. Boudreau's feud with Trudy. There were numerous long-standing disagreements like that around here.

"Then I thought about the group of us who went on the job. You, me, Evan, Blair. Who else would be a witness?" Sam asked. "That cranky old guy who insisted on *prawns*? And it just didn't make sense to me. And remember how we didn't see Blair for like ten minutes at one point, and when we did, she said she had to use the bathroom and she went on and on about the house and how rich they were? So I had Erica distract her with some bogus credit card mistake, and I snooped in her backpack at work. I know I shouldn't have, that it was *completely* wrong. That stuff never holds up in court or whatever. But I just couldn't stand her anymore. I couldn't stand that she was accusing *you*, of all people."

"So you found the missing things?" I asked.

Samantha nodded. "Oh, yeah. Plus three

CDs of mine and a shirt I think is yours."

"So . . . what happened?" This was sounding too good to be true. I still couldn't believe it, though. I had invited her into my house, and she'd framed me?

"I confronted her with it as soon as the restaurant closed. She had to confess. She apologized to Trudy for everything, and then Trudy fired her," Erica said. "We all just stood there, totally speechless for a second. Then after she walked out everyone was all buzzing about how you should never have been suspended and I don't know what happened, but I think Trudy gave Blair a serious earful."

"Why didn't you guys wake me up last night to tell me all this?" I cried.

Erica and Samantha looked at each other. "I didn't think you were home, actually," Sam said. "I thought you were with Ben."

I shook my head. "Nope."

"And I don't know where Blair went last night—I never heard her come home—but she's gone now."

"Do you think she left the island?" I asked.

"It would have been too late last night to get a boat out. But we can easily find out if she left this morning. We'll just go ask Ben."

"Um . . ." I murmured. "Maybe not."

"Uh-oh." Sam shifted on the pillow and leaned back against the bookcase. "This doesn't sound good. Tell us what happened."

I gave them a brief description of our talk, skipping over the really painful parts. Which made it extremely brief, actually. I explained what Ben had seen, and what he had said. They knew part of the story already, because of last night.

"You really broke up with Ben?" Erica asked. "You're kidding."

"No. Actually, he really broke up with *me*," I said. "And now Haley's mad at me because she thinks I was mean to Ben. She's like . . . furious, in fact. She was sort of mean about it."

"Well, she and Ben are really good friends, too," Erica said. "I mean, you guys did everything together. Right?"

"Yeah." I nodded.

"She's sort of stuck in the middle," Sam said.

I sighed, thinking about how much damage Blair had done with her stupid, unfounded allegation. "I can't believe Blair got me in trouble, which is why I was hugging Evan, which is why

Ben broke up with me, which is why Haley hates me. That all happened for nothing—for no reason!" I said.

Erica and Samantha glanced at each other.

"What?" I said.

"Maybe she did cause things to speed up," Sam said tentatively. "But it did happen for a reason. I mean, that's what prompted you and Evan to hug . . . but maybe that was going to happen anyway."

"What are you saying? That I *wanted* to hug Evan?"

"Well . . . yeah," Erica said. "It seems like you did."

If even Erica, the nicest person in the world, thought that about me, then it must be close to true.

"Didn't you?" she asked when I didn't respond.

"I don't know. In some ways, yes." I thought about how attracted I felt to Evan, how I'd been sort of fighting that feeling ever since he came back. But then I thought about how I didn't approve of the way he treated me, and how he was about as reliable as his friend's car that had broken down on the highway. When Ben said he'd be somewhere, he was there—early. When Evan said that, I knew I couldn't believe him. He might be there, and he might not. And he wouldn't pick a time.

So the question was, how important was that to me?

"And in some ways, no?" Erica pressed, sounding a little hopeful that I wasn't being completely sucked into the Evan phenomenon again.

The telephone rang just then, and I reached over to grab it. "Templeton residence," I said.

"Templeton? As in Colleen Templeton?"

"Mom!" I felt a huge smile spread across my face. I'd E-mailed her last night, just before I went to bed, that I hoped she could call me today.

"Everything all right?"

"Sure, everything's fine." I waved at Erica and Sam, who were leaving my bedroom so that Mom and I could talk in private. I wanted to celebrate being unsuspended with them as soon as I got off the phone. Of course, that meant I'd be going in to work, and I'd kind of been excited by the prospect of spending the day by myself, gluing, pasting, maybe visiting Betty again.

"Are you sure?" Mom asked. "Because you don't sound fine, and neither did your E-mail."

"I'm all right," I assured her. "It's just . . . certain things aren't going all that well, actually, Mom." I didn't want her to worry, and I didn't want to ruin any fun they were having. I didn't want them to come home, either. I could handle this, but I just needed to talk to her. I definitely wasn't going into the whole evil housemate/Colleen's-nearly-getting-fired-and-jailed story. She didn't need to know that until she got home. And maybe not even then.

"Oh, no. Why not?" She sounded immediately concerned.

"Ben and I . . . well, we broke up," I said. "Last night."

"What?" Mom sounded completely shocked, as if all the breath had gone out of her. "You and Ben? Are you joking? I'm sorry—I take that back. Of course you wouldn't joke about something like that. Oh, honey. I'm sorry. What happened?"

How could I possibly explain long-distance? And did I even want to? "It's a long story," I said. That sounded ridiculously vague, though, so I went on. "But remember Evan? Of course you remember him. Well, he's around again this summer."

"Evan." I could hear the disapproval in her

voice, coming all the way from overseas. Across an ocean, after a year, Evan was still doubted. "That Evan?"

"Yeah. That Evan," I said.

"Ah. That must be awkward."

She's always had a great gift for understatement.

"Actually, in retrospect? The awkward part was the easy part," I said. "Once we got past that was when things got complicated and weird."

My mother cleared her throat. "So . . . I almost hate to ask. But are you and Evan . . . ?"

"No, we're not—not at all. But maybe . . . we could be . . . I don't know. I don't even know what I want." I sighed. "That's okay, right?"

"Of course that's okay," she said. "You know, Colleen, they both care about you. They're both probably confused, that's all—just like you are. Love is confusing."

"I'll say," I muttered.

"You know what, honey? Just relax. Let things take their course," Mom said. "You're moving in a month, and you might as well *not* be serious with anyone right now."

That was so logical. It sounded right, easy, fair. But it didn't sound fun. Did it?

*   *   *

"Hey, Coll. Look what a nice afternoon it is!" Sam said cheerfully, walking into the kitchen.

"How was work?" I asked. Trudy had given me the day off, with pay, after all. She'd actually come by to apologize in person and bring me my favorite, the fried fish sandwich, and an entire strawberry-rhubarb pie. Which I wasn't sharing, at least not yet.

I'd spent the day lounging, painting, collaging, and visiting Betty, while keeping a very low profile around the island. Extremely low. I was glad I didn't have to go to work, because I didn't want to see Evan yet. And I wasn't going near the post office, the general store, or anywhere anyone else might be.

"Nothing too exciting," Sam said. "Come on, Erica's waiting outside for us. We've got to hurry to make the three o'clock."

"The three o'clock?" I repeated.

"Hello, it's Friday. There's someplace we need to be," Sam said.

I shook my head. "No thanks. I don't want to see Ben."

"So you won't," she said. "We can be busy talking when he gets off the boat. Heck, we can

269

even be gone by then. We just have to stick around long enough to see if Orlando Bloom's on the boat."

"He's not coming!" I laughed. "Doesn't he live in New Zealand or something?"

"Hey. We *saw* him last year," she insisted.

"Sam, I'm sorry. I just—I don't care who gets off the ferry today. I'm not looking for anyone else to date."

"Who cares about you? You've *had* your share. This is about us—me and Erica," Sam declared.

"But you found your dream date," I said. "Troy."

"Yes, but—come on, it's a tradition. Book club. Your contributions are vital to the discussion." She grabbed my arm and started pulling me toward the door. "Come on."

"So, let's talk about the worst thing a guy ever did to each of us," Sam declared when we sat down on our designated book club bench. They should add a plaque to it, after we leave, if any of us ever became famous or known for anything. COLLEEN TEMPLETON SAT HERE. REPEAT-EDLY.

"That'll make you feel better," Sam said. "Trust me."

"They didn't do anything," I mumbled. "It was me."

"So you're indecisive. So what?" Sam said. "That isn't a crime. Unless you're sitting at one of my tables and you can't choose from the menu and you take like twenty minutes to order." She laughed.

Erica went over to see if Haley could come join us, but she said no. That didn't surprise me. If she had been mad at me last night, she was still going to be angry today. In fact, it might take her a week or more to forgive me. The whole thought of that was just depressing.

"Does she know about Blair yet?" I asked Erica as she sat down beside me.

"Yeah, we told her," Erica said.

I thought about what Betty said when I told her about the situation. "She's lucky she left. I'd have taken her out myself with this claw." Betty had waved her broken wrist in the air like a weapon. "What an ungrateful wretch."

"What am I doing here?" I asked now. "Haley doesn't want to see me, and I don't want to see

Ben when his shift ends."

"You're here because if he does want to see you, well, you're making it easy for him," Sam declared.

"Okay, but doesn't it make me look sort of pathetic? Like I'm hoping he'll talk to me?"

"Well, aren't you? Pathetic or not?" Sam asked.

I wasn't sure. I knew that a lot of the things that Ben had said to me last night were true. That my heart really wasn't in it anymore. That I was stringing Ben along while I sort of waited to see whether Evan and I got back together again.

Which made me a real cretin.

I didn't necessarily know what a cretin was, but it sounded despicable, and I felt that I deserved that sort of insult right about now.

I stirred my chocolate shake halfheartedly as I heard the ferry's warning horn. It was approaching the landing. Then it was turning and backing up to the ramp. I knew the routine by heart, which was good, because I didn't want to watch. I was *afraid* to look over there. What sort of look would Ben give me if our eyes met? Or would he just stay on the ferry when he saw me, and wait for me to get the message and get lost?

Or would he walk past holding up a life preserver in front of his face so I wouldn't see him?

"Hey, who's that with Ben?" Erica asked.

I rolled my eyes as I saw the red-haired college student with the white-and-blue boat-and-tote bag striding off the boat beside Ben. They were talking and laughing like they did every other day.

"Oh, God," I groaned. "It's that beautiful girl on the boat with him every single day. Great, now she can move in, if she hasn't already."

"Colleen. She's holding hands with the guy next to her," Samantha said.

"She and Ben are holding hands?" I blurted.

"*No*. She's holding hands with the guy on her left. The guy in the business suit?" Sam said. "I don't think you need to worry about her and Ben."

"Oh." What a relief. On the other hand, it would have been nice to have something to be angry about. I'd feel less guilty if I knew that Ben had already moved on to someone else.

I watched Ben and Haley say hi to each other, and I felt this huge pang of regret. Why did I have to go and ruin everything?

It was killing me. What was really sad was

that I was hiding behind my sunglasses. Yes, the same ones that I got cat food on. They didn't smell like cat food anymore, because I'd run them through the dishwasher to get rid of the smell. Unfortunately, they'd melted into a strange, wavy shape, but I didn't have new ones yet, so I was wearing them anyway.

They were the official bad-luck sunglasses of the summer.

Of course, there are those who believe in making your own luck. And if you're running around in stinky, melted sunglasses, you're not exactly a recipe for success.

But at least they still sort of hid the tears welling in my eyes.

"Well, *she's* definitely thrilled to be here," Sam commented as a woman with short black hair spotted someone on the dock and started jumping up and down, waving wildly.

There could not have been a bigger contrast between the way *she* felt and the way *I* felt. "Ever seen her before?" I asked Erica.

Erica shook her head. "No." She glanced around, looking slightly uncomfortable. "So, you guys want to get going?"

Samantha coughed. "Maybe we should go

see Haley. I could use a cup of ice water."

They both sort of tried to herd me from the bench where we were sitting.

"Hold on, hold on," I said as I spotted a pair of familiar-looking legs on the dock. They weren't Ben's. "Is that Evan over there?"

He was wearing a baseball cap and a T-shirt that was too big for him. It was like he was intentionally trying not to be seen.

I watched as the excited woman with short black hair dropped her red duffel bag and shrieked and sprinted into his waiting arms.

Chapter 21

"So, I hear we've got an AWOL co-worker." Evan arranged some butter pats into a small white bowl, then put the bowl onto his tray next to a plastic lobster trap full of dinner rolls. "What made her do it, anyway?"

I just kept putting salads into bowls. I couldn't talk to him and pretend everything was the same. I couldn't do the flirting thing or the weird looks. I wasn't going to act like a freak anymore.

"Is anything missing from your house?" Evan asked. "You know . . . have you checked for Starsky and Hutch? Or wait. They were probably on the case. Right? They busted her."

"Ha ha, very funny. She owes me money and a repainted bedroom," I said.

"So. There's an extra bedroom. Is that what you're saying? 'Cause Jake's place *is* getting a little cramped." He left his tray on the counter and walked over to me.

Don't get any closer to me, I thought. *Any closer*

276

and these salad tongs go right in your . . . face. "Yeah, I can see why it would feel cramped," I said.

"Why's that?" Evan asked.

"With an extra person," I said.

"Meaning . . . me."

"And," I muttered. *Her*, I thought.

He just stared at me for a second as if he were trying to figure out what I was talking about. "Hey, do you think you could make up a side salad for me? I've got to make a couple of cappuccinos. Who wants cappuccino with fried clams? That's disgusting, but okay."

"No, actually, I can't." I put the tongs back into the large bowl of premixed salad.

"You can't?" Evan turned around from the espresso machine. "Or you won't?"

"That's not my table," I said. I knew I was being juvenile, but I just couldn't help it. I was sick of the whole game. Him taking stuff to my tables, me making salads for him—it was so fake. Especially when you considered how he'd spent his weekend.

"I'm totally swamped, Coll. Could you just give me a break?" Evan asked.

"Why should I?" I replied.

"You know, a lobster has big claws, but that

doesn't mean it actually has to *use* them constantly," Evan said. He stared at me, waiting for some sort of reaction, or explanation, for why I was acting so difficult.

"I can't believe you," I suddenly blurted. "Why didn't you just tell me she was coming?"

"Tell you who was coming?" Evan looked sort of confused, but I knew it was an act. He might only come here in the summer, but he had to know that we lived for gossiping about who gets on and off the ferry—with whom. Did he really think he could just hide her, that he could bring someone to the island without *someone* finding out? And we'd been there and seen it happen. And I'd seen how he was trying not to be recognized, because he *knew* it would get back to me, but he wanted me to think he wasn't seeing anyone. Why?

"You know. That woman with the short black hair carrying a red duffel who practically tackled you on the dock?" I said. "Does that ring a bell? The reason you took the entire weekend off, so you could be with her?"

Evan took a step back. "God. Why are you so angry?"

"Because you're such a liar!" I said. "Why

couldn't you just tell me about her? Why didn't you just say, Hey, I have a friend coming for the weekend. A *girl*friend."

"I didn't lie about it," Evan said.

"No, you just chose not to tell me," I replied. "Just like you chose not to tell me why you suddenly dropped off the face of the Earth and stopped E-mailing. I mean, I'm sure some other girl was involved then, too, but you didn't tell me about it, either."

"We were living in separate states, Coll. Did it matter? Did you really want to know?" Evan asked.

"I wanted to know *some*thing. Some reason for why you vanished."

"Hey, I didn't vanish. You did!" Evan said.

I'd heard of revisionist history, but this was ridiculous. "I vanished? Since when?"

"You said you were coming to visit, but you didn't," Evan said.

"Are you serious? I never visited because you never told me when, or how. You quit E-mailing. Obviously because you had a girlfriend."

There was a long pause. Evan focused on finishing making the cappuccino, and I was about to go back over to pick up my tray—I'd been in here way too long already—when Evan put his hand on my arm. "Look, Colleen. I only started seeing her—Dahlia—in May."

Dahlia? What kind of name was Dahlia? I thought. (Okay, so it's a very nice name actually, I was just feeling a little jealous at the time, especially since she was as pretty as her name.) "And then you left town in June, to come here? Hm. Sounds familiar."

"Colleen, come on. We went out a few weeks—she wanted to see the island," Evan said. "It's not *serious*. It's not like you—"

"No, of course not," I said. "Nothing's ever serious with you."

"What did you expect? Did you think I was going to move to the island so we could be together?"

"No. Of course not. I know. I know you had to go home. But . . . look, never mind." It was already the end of July. We'd all be leaving in a month, or less than that. "It's just—" Part of me wished we could go outside and keep talking until we got this straightened out for good. And part of me wished we could go outside so that I could push him into the harbor again. I looked down at his stupid new pair of Birks. When had he gotten them? I couldn't risk his losing those sandals again. It wasn't about the money, although I definitely didn't want to shell out any more where Evan was concerned. But I couldn't take the risk of being in contact with Evan like that again.

"I don't really get where you're coming from. We're not together," Evan said. "Do you want to be? Because you've been dating someone else all summer—hey, all year, even—"

"Yeah, well. Ben and I aren't together anymore. Thanks to you," I said.

"Oh, no. No way." Evan shook his head. "I'm not taking the blame. Coll, I'm not responsible for that."

"Yeah, you are. Because you came back here," I said.

"Well, I didn't come back here for you," Evan said.

Ugh. Did he have to be so brutal? I was going to say "brutally honest," but I wasn't sure he *was* being honest. If he didn't come back here for me, then why was he here?

I was starting to wonder why *I* was here, as I picked up the tray of salads and went out into the dining room, plastering a phony smile on my face. Maybe I could meet my parents in Italy. Why not?

Because you invited your friends to live with you, and you can't just bail on them, even though one of them isn't talking to you right now. And you can't just bail on Trudy, the way Blair did, because you're not like her. And you can't just bail on Betty, because she needs you.

Why was my life being dictated by older women with old-fashioned-sounding names?

In the morning I got up early and rode my bike to the Landing. Haley hadn't been staying at the house since last week, since our fight. Having both her and Blair leave at the same time had been strange. I didn't like the fact that it had been nearly a week and we still weren't talking. I was determined to make things up to her. Whatever she needed me to say, I'd say it, but I wasn't ending the summer like this.

As soon as I got to the Landing, though, I felt almost panicky. Why was I even down here? Ben hated me. Haley wasn't talking to me. I couldn't have felt *less* welcome.

There was Haley's old green pickup truck. I rode over to it and leaned my bike against the truck before I walked up to the window.

"Haley. Where've you been?" I asked.

She was in the middle of making a pot of coffee, and she didn't answer me right away. "I've been here," she said when she finally turned around. "Why—were you here earlier?"

"No. I mean . . . I haven't seen you around the house for a few days," I said. *Obviously.*

"Yeah. Well." She just kept going about her business while I stood there, stupidly, stubbornly, waiting for her to talk to me. If she could be stubborn, so could I. She should know that by now. She wasn't going to get off the hook by just making herself busy behind the counter. I'd stand here and repeatedly order stuff if I had to.

Which I would probably have to, because I could see people heading off the ferry toward the window for their morning cup of coffee. Come to think of it, I was feeling pretty hungry after my bike ride. Maybe I'd pick up some breakfast pastries for me and Sam, drop off a couple of muffins with Betty.

"So, is there anything I can do to fix things?" I asked. "I mean, you have to tell me what I did wrong. Because I can't apologize if I don't know. Is it the Ben thing, still? Because I apologize if I acted badly. But you said a lot of other things that night, too."

"It's not that," she said.

"Then what?" I asked. "You can't be mad at me for the Blair thing."

"It's nothing," she said.

"Really," I said.

"I just wanted to spend some time with my mother the past few days. She hasn't been feeling well, so . . ."

"Really. I'm sorry to hear that. I hope she feels better soon." Now I knew she was lying. I mean, you might think that was cold of me, that I should have asked how her mother was feeling—and it wasn't that I didn't care. But I could tell she was making the whole thing up, because I'd seen her mother at the store yesterday when I went by with Erica to rent a video. And she was completely fine. She didn't even complain about a sniffle or a headache.

Haley was the one who hadn't been feeling well. About me, her former best friend. Man, could she hold a grudge. So I'd made a mistake. How long was she going to hold it against me?

I wanted to tell her that the house wasn't the same without her, that she should come home and celebrate the fact that Blair was gone, that it was just me, her, and Sam. But she'd been gone as long as Blair had. The house felt empty with just me and Sam rattling around inside.

For the benefit of sleepy customers, I stepped aside and waited a few minutes, alternately watching Haley pour coffee for them, and staring out at the ocean.

"So. Will you be at the house later?" I asked once she got through the line.

Haley shrugged. "I don't know."

"Don't you need some clothes or something? You practically moved all your stuff in there," I said.

"Yeah, well, maybe I'll see you later, maybe I won't," she said. "Next!" she called over my shoulder to another customer.

So much for conversation. I walked over to the dock and stared out at the ferry, rocking gently on the waves. Moby looked sort of sad today. Or maybe it was me.

I loved the sound of the ropes and bells clinking and knocking against the boat as it floated, nestled against the dock. I wondered if Ben was working this morning. I took a few steps closer to the ferry, then stopped. What would I say to him if I saw him? Hello? How are you? That would sound stupid. But I did want to know how he was doing. I missed him. We'd spent all our time together for the past eight months or so. Now there was this hole. Ben wasn't there to ask me how I felt, or to tell me I looked great, or to listen to me complain or worry about Haley and how she was acting. I needed Ben to confide in, but I was completely on my own in this. It had been a while since I was on my own, I realized. And I didn't mind *being* alone . . . but I didn't like *feeling* alone. Especially now that Haley wasn't speaking to me, too.

When I heard a male voice saying "Hi" behind me, I nearly jumped. I turned around and saw Troy Hamilton standing there.

"Oh, hey," I said.

"Hi. Again." He smiled sort of cutely.

"How are you?" I asked. (See, I knew it would sound stupid—whether I said it to Ben or to someone else.) If there were a way I could have instantly summoned Samantha down to the Landing, I would have.

"Good." He nodded. "You're Colleen, right?"

I nodded.

"So, sorry about that crazy stuff with my grandmother. The theft thing. That was a huge mistake," he said.

"Yeah, it was. But it's okay now," I assured him. "Don't worry about it."

"Okay, but I'm sorry. So, I heard you live here year-round?"

I nodded. "Yeah."

"What about your friend—you know, not the rude one. The, um . . . ?"

"Beautiful one?" I suggested.

His ears turned slightly red. "Was her name Samantha?"

I nodded.

"Does she live here year-round, too?" Troy asked.

"No, she only comes for the summers. She lives in Richmond the rest of the year."

"Richmond, Maine?"

"Is there one?" I laughed. "I have no idea. But she lives in Virginia. She's going to college at UVA."

"Oh, yeah? Cool. I'm going to UNC. I guess it's not all that close, but it's in the same time zone anyway."

This definitely sounded promising. He was

interested in Sam, even if he was trying to be casual about it. There had to be some way I could get them together again without suggesting his family host another catered event or telling him to come into Bobb's. That would be tacky, and besides, he wouldn't really get to spend any time with her.

I knew what I'd do—I'd have the party this time. Not a loud beer bash, like last time. A dinner party—something simple we could do, like a barbecue. And I'd invite him, on Sam's behalf. Only . . . who else could I invite, so he wouldn't be the only guy there?

Not Evan.

Not Ben.

Definitely not Uncle Frank.

Maybe we ought to make it a huge, raging party, so that it wouldn't seem like such a formal setup. I could invite everyone from Bobb's, plus other island friends. A Sunday barbecue. I'd made a killing at work that week and could afford to be generous—we were hitting peak tourist weeks. And I'd make it such a big deal that Haley would have to be there, too. She wouldn't be able to say no or not show up. I'd have Sam invite her and stress that it was a group event. I'd be killing—or uniting—several birds with one stone. (Not that I'd decided on barbecued chicken yet.)

"So, you're here for a while yet?" I asked Troy.

"One more week," he said.

"Cool. Well, how'd you like to come to a party?"

I chose the date off the top of my head—that Sunday night. I wrote down the house address and handed it to him. "Six o'clock. Be there, okay?"

When I walked back over past Haley's take-out window to get my bike, Haley called out, "Two guys weren't enough for one summer?"

"What?" I couldn't believe her. "No. He's not— Look, I'm trying to fix up . . . Oh, never mind." I didn't want to bother saying it. What was the use explaining when she was so mad, so ready to see the worst in me?

Chapter 22

"So, how many people are coming?" Sam asked as she set out a column of plastic cups next to a stack of paper plates. We'd learned from our first party—well, Blair's first party—not to use the good stuff. One, it created a lot of dishes for us to wash; and two, we'd lost a glass or two that night—cheap ones, fortunately, that we had several others of. I didn't think my parents would miss a couple. At least, I hoped not.

"Well, besides the guest of honor—" I began.

"Troy, you mean?" Sam interrupted.

"Yes," I said, smiling at her. "Besides him, probably about ten or fifteen people, some from work and some Haley and I know from school. You're not mad, are you? That I sort of set this up?"

"As long as there are a few more people than Troy here, it's not a setup, or at least it won't look like one," Erica said.

"Uh-huh. I hope not," Sam said.

"Look, we already know you guys like each other," I said. "Everyone knows that, including you and him. So just relax."

"Right. No problem." Sam gave a nervous smile, then went into the house.

Meanwhile, I went over to the black kettle barbecue to check on the coals. They were almost ready, so I went inside to get a plate of burgers and a package of hot dogs. People started wandering up as I was cooking, and Erica helped everyone to lemonade and iced tea and soda. After a while, Haley showed up. It was good to see her, even though she was still angry with me.

"This is going to be a lot nicer—and quieter—than the last party here," I predicted as she and Erica came to check on the food and see if I needed help.

"I wonder where she is now," Haley said. That was typical, that she'd talk to me when someone else was around.

"Blair?" Erica said.

Haley nodded. "Yeah."

"Probably moved into someone else's beach house, working at some other summer place," I said.

"She *was* good to work with," Erica said.

"Yeah, it was her best quality. Too bad we met her there, so we didn't realize she wasn't like that at home." I laughed.

"I'm sorry. It's my fault," Erica said.

"Shut up, it's not your fault," Haley said.

Erica nodded as she set her cup of lemonade on the porch railing. "Yes, it is! You said we didn't know her at all, that we shouldn't have asked her—remember, the first time she came over?"

"Yeah. But she seemed all right," Haley said. "Except when we realized she wouldn't do a thing around the house but use things up and not pay us back. She's just lucky she didn't steal anything from us. I mean, I would have tracked her down, you know?" Haley's face suddenly lit up, and she smiled.

I looked over my shoulder and saw Ben walking up. Haley went over to say hello to him, and the two of them headed into the house together.

"What's he doing here? Who invited him?" I asked.

"I did," Erica said. "I thought maybe you guys wanted to make up."

"No, we don't," I snapped. When I saw the hurt look on Erica's face as she turned to leave, I reached out and grabbed her arm with my hand, which was covered with a potholder. "I'm sorry," I said. "I shouldn't have said that."

She shrugged. "It's okay."

"No, it's not. I'm sorry," I said. "I just—I got really stressed when I saw him. But I appreciate what you were trying to do."

I looked up at the porch as Ben walked back outside by himself. He headed to the table and started helping himself to some chips and dip. He looked really cute in his black T-shirt, long khaki shorts, and unlaced tennis sneakers. *Go talk to him*, I told myself. But I couldn't.

"Coll? I think something's burning." Erica waved her hand in front of my face and pointed down.

I looked down at the grill, where a hot dog had just fallen victim to a raging inferno of hamburger drippings. "Why am I doing this? I'm horrible at this!" I said as Erica and I laughed at the charred food.

"We've got salad," she said, taking the tongs and potholder from me. "Don't worry."

A couple of hours later everyone had eaten, and they were either sitting on the porch and talking, roasting marshmallows for S'mores over the dying glowing coals, or playing croquet in the backyard. Troy and Samantha seemed to be getting along great. They'd been together ever since he arrived.

And me? I was sitting next to Ben, chatting about things. Nothing serious, mind you. I'd mingled with everyone else and it was just time for me to talk to him. We discussed this and that—what his little brothers were up to, what country my parents were in, and, you know, the weather. When all else fails, you can talk about the water temperature and the tide.

We weren't about to have a reunion or anything, but it was nice to just be civil, even if it felt awkward. But then, just before dark, Evan showed up.

Ben's eyes narrowed as he watched Evan stop and talk to some friends from Bobb's at the grill. "What's *he* doing here?" he asked. He sounded exactly like I had when Evan had shown up at Bobb's that first day.

"I didn't invite him," I said to Ben. "Honest."

"That's what you said at your last party," Ben complained.

"I didn't invite him then, either! Blair did," I

reminded him. "And come to think of it, I didn't even invite you to that party—it was Blair who invited the entire town."

"Yeah, but that was different. This is private," Ben said.

I could tell it was hurting him, seeing Evan here. But I had nothing to do with it, not really.

"So. He's just the type of guy to crash parties?" Ben asked. From the tone in his voice, I could tell that he hated Evan. And I could understand why. But it made me not like Ben, because he wasn't giving Evan a chance.

"Yes. That's the kind of person he is," I said.

"And Haley said he made you hitch a ride back to Bobb's the other day. Is that true?"

"He didn't *make* me," I said. "It was his idea. Spontaneous, you know." Actually, Ben wouldn't know.

"Colleen, he could have put you in a dangerous situation," Ben said.

"Maybe," I said.

"And you went out with him for *how* long?"

I stared at Ben. I didn't like the way he was acting. I knew he had every right to be that way, but it still made me mad because (a) he didn't know Evan, and (b) he wasn't like Evan.

That was what had drawn me to Ben in the first place—the fact that he was the opposite of Evan. Now, I didn't find that quality all that attractive.

"I'll see you later," I said as I got up. I knew that I'd hurt him and maybe he felt the need to hurt me back. But I didn't have to sit there and take it any longer than I already had. I glanced around the yard, where Erica was laughing with some other friends of ours from Bobb's, then I went out back to say hi to Samantha and Troy. Samantha had just knocked her croquet ball through a hoop and Troy was congratulating her with a high-five. After they slapped hands, they held on for a while, looking at each other. Well, I definitely wasn't needed back there, I thought with a smile as I headed in the back door.

Evan was standing in the kitchen, helping himself to a cup of water. "Hey, Coll."

"Oh. Hey," I said.

"Nice party," he said.

I walked over to the trash can and dropped my empty plastic cup into it. "Yeah. It is, isn't it? I should probably clean up or something."

"Yeah, but people are still hanging out," Evan said.

I leaned back against the counter and sighed.

"Hey, you want a S'more?" Evan offered. "I'll make one for you."

I shook my head. "Nah. But thanks. I already had two."

Evan smiled, walking over to me. "I think you have a little marshmallow. Right there." He reached out his finger and dabbed at my upper lip.

I grabbed his hand. "Don't do that."

"Why not?" he asked.

"Because," I said. A little lame, considering I could give him a thousand reasons why not. Because the last time we really talked, we were fighting. Because you just had a girl visiting last weekend. Because of Dahlia. Because you said you didn't come back here this summer for me.

And because Ben was still out on the porch and I wouldn't throw this in his face.

"You—you know what?" I stammered, getting completely flustered by how close Evan was standing to me, how he nearly had me pressed up against the counter, how he'd just touched my mouth.

"No. What?" Evan asked.

"I think I'm going to go upstairs and get a sweater. Sam's cold," I said. "I told her I'd get her something warm to wear."

"Is that your second job this summer?" Evan joked as I edged away from him. "Getting sweaters and sweatshirts for other people?"

"What?" I turned around at the bottom of the stairs.

"Well, it's just that's what you were doing the last time I was over here for a party," Evan said.

"So I'm predictable!" I called over my shoulder as I started walking up the stairs. I opened the walk-in closet door in the upstairs hallway.

"What are you really doing up here?" Evan asked as he came up the stairs behind me.

"Sweaters. I'm getting sweaters." I reached out and petted Hutch, who was lying on top of my favorite black V-neck. He'd left a layer of golden-tan fur that was about a quarter of an inch thick.

I heard the closet door close behind me. And then Evan was behind me, his arms around my waist, kissing the back of my neck. "So, which sweaters are you going to get?" he whispered.

For a second, I panicked. I didn't know what I should do, whether to run out the door or turn around and start kissing him back.

"No, actually, I'm . . . hiding up here," I said as a shiver of pleasure went down my back. "I just . . . I kind of couldn't take it down there."

"Why not?" Evan asked.

"Because I just—I don't know," I said. "I don't know what to do anymore."

"I do," Evan said, gently turning me to face him. "Look, about what I said the other day. When I said I didn't come back to the island because of you. I mean, not *just* because of you. But when I thought about you and us? It did make me want to come back. It was the reason I changed my plans."

"So, why . . . why couldn't you just say that when you got here?" I asked.

"Are you joking? You hated me. You loathed the sight of me," Evan said. "And I couldn't even blame you. But then you were with Ben, and . . ."

"I guess it was kind of complicated," I said.

Evan traced the edge of my face. "You're even more beautiful than you were last summer. You know that, don't you? That you've been torturing me?"

I laughed. "I have? I don't think I've ever tortured anybody before. Is it a good thing? Am I good at it? Just like that, right off the bat?"

"You could practice some. Like, if you tell me you want me to leave right now, and you insist

299

on it. That would be perfect torture." He leaned down and kissed my neck, first on one side, and then the other, and then my shoulders.

"Yeah. I agree," I said softly, enjoying every second that his lips were on my skin. "For both of us."

Evan looked into my eyes. "Is this okay?"

"Very okay," I whispered, and our lips met in a passionate kiss, our bodies were pressed together, and we were moving backward, toward the shelving where Hutch lay innocently sleeping.

"Hutch," I murmured between kisses. "Hutch needs his privacy. We don't want to wake up Hutch."

Evan took his hands off my hips and reached for my hand. "How about we go to your room this time?"

I nodded, unable to speak, not wanting to discuss anything anymore, just wanting to stay in the moment. As we walked into my bedroom I felt excited and scared, as if I were taking a risk I wasn't sure that I wanted to take.

And then Evan was closing the door and kissing me, and I knew that yes, I was completely sure I wanted to.

Chapter 23

When I got up the next morning, I sneaked out of the house.

Afterward, after . . . Evan . . . I hadn't gone back downstairs. I wondered if everyone knew. I wondered if anyone had seen Evan leave, and if they had, what time it was. I wasn't sure when he'd gone. I'd woken up in the middle of the night, around three A.M., and I was alone. I hadn't been able to get back to sleep. I was happy, I was worried, I was excited, I was a thousand different things.

One thing I didn't feel was guilty about what I'd done. But I didn't necessarily want to talk about it, or analyze what had happened or why. Not even with Sam, and especially not with Haley.

So at dawn I tiptoed out of the house. I took my bike instead of the car. It was a misty, cloudy, humid morning, and I could feel my clothes becoming damp as I rode.

I wanted to bring Betty something to eat—I'd promised I'd drop by with something for breakfast. But I couldn't cook, I hadn't baked, and I couldn't go to the Landing and see Haley—I was too embarrassed. Also, I didn't want to be yelled at by her for being with Evan.

I dropped by the general store and browsed through the rack of Drake's baked products. Hm. Would Betty like Devil Dogs or Ring Dings for breakfast?

"Colleen!" Aunt Sue's voice rang out behind me. "What are you doing up and about so early?"

"I'm going to visit Betty," I said.

"Well, isn't that sweet of you. I'd heard you two had become buddies," she said.

I couldn't quite picture Betty ever referring to herself as anyone's "buddy." She was a bit too curmudgeonly for that.

"I actually was hoping to pick up something to eat. She always makes tea for me, so—"

"Why don't you take her a couple of muffins? No, wait. I'm out of muffins." Aunt Sue tapped her chin as she thought. "How about a lemon-blueberry pound cake?"

"Yum. That sounds great. But did you have

plans for it?" I asked.

"No, don't be silly. Now come on." She paid for her half gallon of milk and we walked down the road to her house, which was only a quarter mile away or so. I walked my bike beside her.

"So, anything new?" she asked.

"Not really." I shrugged.

"Have you been riding a lot this morning?"

"No, why?"

"Your cheeks are awfully pink," she commented.

"Oh. Well, I think I got a little too much sun yesterday," I said as we approached her house.

"Really? What were you doing yesterday?" she asked.

Again, I could feel myself blushing, so I glanced at my watch and said, "You know, I really should get going. Betty's expecting me, so . . ." That wasn't the truth, but I didn't see how that little white lie could hurt anyone.

"Well, just wait a second and I'll get you that cake!"

Aunt Sue hurried inside her house and came out carrying a loaf shape wrapped in aluminum foil. I put it into the wicker basket on the bike's handlebars. Maybe that was why my grandmother had put this basket on her bike—to carry Aunt Sue's pound cakes home. It fit perfectly in the basket.

"Thanks—see you later!" I called as I rode away.

I'd escaped two things: (1) Telling my aunt about sleeping with Evan, not that I would ever do that, unless someone was sticking pins into my skin, and (2) Telling my uncle I was going to see Betty, and hearing "You should paint, Colleen, why don't you paint!" for the thousandth time.

"How many blueberry recipes does your aunt know, do you think?" Betty asked as I unwrapped the aluminum foil and started to cut us some slices of pound cake.

"Twenty? Fifty? A hundred?" I guessed.

"Oh, no. Got to be at least a thousand," she said. "She should open a bakery instead of handing it out for free all over the island. How does she even find enough berries?"

"I think she has Cap buy flats of them for her at the farmer's market near the wharf. I'm not totally sure, though."

"Hm. Well, at least she's good at it. Everyone

should be good at something. And baking is an art, just like cooking's an art. You've got to be creative."

"Yeah, I guess you're right. I never looked at it that way," I said.

"What, did you think you were the only one who inherited some of your grandmother's talent?" Betty asked.

I hated to admit it, but I guessed I did.

She took another bite of pound cake. "Do you know that you're sort of glowing? You look so happy today. What's new? And don't tell me it's this pound cake."

How did these women know that I'd had sex? Was it the way my skin looked? The way my hair looked? This was not sex, this was humidity, people. A frizzone. I pulled my hair back into a ponytail. "Nothing's new," I said.

"Has something old changed, then?"

"Uh. Um." I didn't know what to say, or whether to say anything. I didn't confide in Betty about my love life, or at least I hadn't yet. I didn't necessarily want to start. I liked that we talked about a couple of subjects—like art, and independence, and her annoying son. Couldn't we just keep it at that? Then again, I enjoyed her take on things. Maybe it would be worth asking what she thought.

"Colleen." She refilled my mug of tea. "I don't subscribe to a satellite dish or to the island grapevine. You know that. You could tell me you were madly in love with Pastor Cuddy and I wouldn't tell a soul."

I burst out laughing. "It's not Pastor Cuddy!"

"Then who?"

Was it Evan? Was I in love with him? Or was it just that I'd done something I'd really wanted to do? "I don't know. Does it have to be someone? Can't it just be me?"

Betty nodded. "Sure it can."

But I still couldn't get Evan out of my head. On my way home, I stopped by his cousin's to see if he was around.

"Hey, Colleen, nice party last night," Jake said when he opened the door.

"Um, thanks," I said, suddenly feeling ridiculous. Evan had come to the party with Jake. He definitely hadn't left with him. If anyone knew what went on between us, it was Jake.

"Looking for Evan? He actually went to town today," Jake said.

"Oh. Really?" What was he doing there? Why hadn't he mentioned it to me earlier?

"Yeah. Should I tell him you were here?"

"No, that's okay." I thought it over for a second. Didn't I want him to know I was looking for him, that I expected him to be around? "Well, yeah. Tell him I came by."

Samantha, Erica, and I spent the afternoon at the beach. It was one of the few times we'd all been able to do that on our own. I kind of liked not spending all of my day off with Ben. I had a lot more options.

I was still feeling a little guilty, though, about the way I'd acted, about how I'd slowly but steadily pushed Ben away. On our way home, when we had to drive past his house, I mentioned it to Erica and Sam.

"Coll, look. You know as well as I know that there's no point staying with someone just because he's *nice*," Samantha said. "Nice only gets you so far."

"Same with charm," I commented.

"Yeah, okay. But you and Evan had this . . . I don't know. Fire. Passion."

"Which also only goes so far," I mused.

"Unless you're not careful," Sam added. "If you know what I mean."

We all started laughing, and I glanced at Erica and Sam as I turned into our driveway. Did they know about me and Evan and last night? If they did, they were acting as if they didn't. I hadn't told them yet. It felt like something so private, and so strange, that I had to hold on to it myself for a while yet.

And then, as we got out of the car, we all saw it. This giant bouquet of red roses sitting in a glass vase on the porch. There must have been at least two dozen—maybe three.

That's why he went to the mainland, I thought. To get flowers. I ran over to the bouquet and plucked out the little white card.

"Are they from Ben?" Erica asked excitedly as I read the card. "Are they from Evan?"

I felt my heart sink and shook my head. "No. They're for you." I smiled and held the vase out to Sam.

"*Me?* No way!" She read the card out loud. "'Dear Samantha, thanks for a great vacation. I'll be thinking of you, Troy.'"

I was so happy for Sam and so overemotional myself that I felt tears filling my eyes.

Why was I hoping for something from Evan that I knew he absolutely refused to deliver? Not just flowers. A whole, intact relationship. Evan wasn't about romance, though, not in the sweet, present-giving, thoughtful way.

I went upstairs to my room and stared at the bed. Hutch was curled up at the end of the bed, on top of the blanket. I sat down next to him and petted his fur. Maybe I felt confused, I thought with a smile, but what about Hutch? How much had he seen in his lifetime, how many things had he witnessed that he didn't want to see? No wonder he'd stopped sleeping in the closet.

Maybe I should *start* sleeping in there.

I pictured Evan's body, his shoulders, his chest, the little hollow were his shoulders met his chest. . . .

I was hopeless.

I couldn't fall asleep that night. I was too revved up. The air outside was thick with humidity, the kind of humidity where towels don't dry and everything is just heavy with dew. The sheets were sticking to me. I'd turned off the light at eleven, and it was midnight now.

I hadn't heard from Evan all day, and it was

killing me. I couldn't stop thinking about him and about last night. How was he feeling about it? Had he taken off for Philadelphia on the first ferry? Or was he lying in bed at his house, feeling like this?

I wanted him to be here. And wanting that as much as I did terrified me. I didn't want to feel like this, as if my life were on hold until I saw him again. I'd thought I was past this, somehow. And yet it was more physical than emotional. I didn't need him, I realized, as much as I just wanted him.

But it was still frightening to want someone so badly. Especially Evan. Especially after last year.

I turned on my light and read for a while to make myself sleepy, to stop myself from thinking about my life. It worked. I switched off the light and was about to drift off when I heard a creaking sound. Like a hinge that wasn't quite working right. The screen porch door, I realized, sitting up in bed. We never locked our doors on the island.

I heard a cat meow outside in the hallway. And then my bedroom door opened.

In the dark, Evan made his way toward the

bed. "Hey." He sat on the edge and leaned down to kiss me. He ran his fingers down the side of my cheek.

"Hey," I said.

"Did I wake you up?" he asked.

I shook my head. "I couldn't sleep."

"Yeah. Me either. You know what? I really can't stay away from you," he said.

I smiled, glad that he felt the same way I did. "Where were you?"

"Running," he said. "I've actually been trying to stay away from you all day."

"So, you succeeded," I said as I pointed to the alarm clock beside my bed. It was 1:15 A.M. "It's tomorrow now."

"*Finally.*" Evan kicked off his sandals and climbed into bed beside me.

Chapter 24

It seemed like I had been asleep for only a few minutes when I woke up again, but I guess it had been a little longer.

The weather had changed. Now the wind was blowing fiercely, and a branch kept scraping against the window. The leaves of the trees around the house were rustling in the wind, and when I glanced out the window I saw a flash of lightning in the distance. There was a low rumble of thunder.

Somehow Evan could sleep through this. Neither he nor Hutch had moved yet. Hutch was curled up at the foot of the bed—lying right on Evan's ankles, if I wasn't mistaken. So. Even Hutch was drawn to those ankles.

I gently pulled off the top sheet and quietly walked to the door. I closed it behind me and went downstairs.

Starsky hated thunderstorms. He was sitting

on the kitchen counter, where he knew he wasn't supposed to be, his pupils completely black and dilated as I switched on the overhead light. "It's okay," I whispered, rubbing his head.

I poured myself a glass of milk and stirred in a spoonful of chocolate syrup. When I sat down, I found that I was face-to-face with the infamous poster board of house rules.

I felt this nervous gnawing in my stomach that the milk wouldn't help. I was *really* breaking the rules here. My parents trusted me *so much*. They'd felt okay leaving me here for ten weeks because they did trust me, because I was almost always responsible. And now, what? My boyfriend, or whatever Evan was to me, was asleep upstairs.

All I could say in my defense? Sticking to the rules wasn't nearly as easy as it looked. I went down the list.

1. No drugs or alcohol allowed.

Well, okay, I'd had a beer or two, but nothing that harmful. And it had only been because Blair had brought it into the house.

313

2. No sleepovers. Especially of the
   boyfriend variety.

Ahem.

3. The house will be kept clean. To
   that end, the house will be cleaned
   once weekly.

Also ahem, but we were doing a lot better since
Blair moved out.

4. No loud parties. Small gatherings
   are fine, but do not annoy the
   neighbors.

We'd broken this one once.

5. Each girl will be responsible for her
   own long-distance phone calls made
   on the house phone, as well as for
   excessive Internet connection
   charges.

No problem.

6. Any damage done to the house—not
   that there will be any—will be
   repaired by the time we get home.

Which meant I needed to get started really soon.

Maybe my parents thought that writing things down would make me stick to them. They were expecting a lot. And how could I let them down this way? I didn't think any of the rules were as important, to them, as number 2. As far as they knew, when they left, Ben and I were dating. Maybe they trusted me so much because they knew Ben and I weren't going to have "sleepovers." Ben and I cuddled, we snuggled—but we never got carried away by our feelings, we never fought, we never had to make up, we never felt like doing anything outrageous.

It was all really sweet and romantic with Ben, but it was also really safe.

That's who my parents thought they were leaving me with. Not Evan. Would they have gone away if they'd known we'd be together again? Because I'd told my mom, anyway, that I'd had sex with Evan, so I'm sure she told my dad. We'd talked about it and I'd told her that I'd learned I wasn't ready for that, that I'd gotten too close to Evan too fast. So I'd held off with Ben. I'd waited.

And now?

I unclipped their printed itinerary from the fridge. They were in London for a week now. That was five hours ahead, timewise, and it was three-thirty here, which meant they should be eating breakfast there, or in their hotel room getting dressed.

I took a deep breath and dialed. "Mom?" I said when she answered the phone.

"Colleen?" Her voice sounded bright and cheerful. "Hi!"

"Hey, how's it going?" Now that I had her on the phone, I didn't know what exactly I planned to say.

There was a bright flash of lightning—and a second later a loud crack of thunder. A branch fell somewhere close by, and suddenly the overhead light went out. The fridge switched off, the microwave clock went dark. Starsky let out a long, plaintive yowl.

"Mom? We're having a huge storm here," I said into the telephone as I went to pick up

Starsky, but I couldn't find him in the dark. "Mom? Hello?"

The line was dead. She was gone.

We'd lost both our power and our phone line. I stood at the window looking out at the rain that was building in intensity, hammering against the house.

I saw a flicker of light reflected in the window and turned around. It was Haley, carrying a candle. I was so glad to see her, so glad to know she'd come back to stay. Sam was right behind her. "I'm freaking out!" Sam said.

"Don't worry," I said. "We're going to be fine."

I watched as Hutch strolled sleepily into the kitchen and went right up to Starsky, who was huddled against a cabinet, trying to get inside to hide. They touched noses, then Hutch gave Starsky a lick on the head.

Hold on. If Hutch was downstairs, that meant . . .

Evan walked into the kitchen wearing a T-shirt and shorts, his hair sticking up on the back of his head. "What's going on?" he asked.

Haley and Samantha both turned to me. Even in the semi-darkness, I could see their shocked expressions. "Yes. What is going on?" Sam asked, raising an eyebrow.

"The storm—it knocked out the phone lines and electricity. I'm glad you knew where a candle was," I told Haley.

"I didn't think I'd ever say this, but I'm really glad you're here," Haley told Evan.

The four of us all gathered by the living room window, watching lightning flash across the sky.

"I wonder how high the water's going to get," Haley said. "I hope my parents are ready."

When the heavy rain paused for a few minutes, Evan stepped out onto the porch. "Come on!" he called back to us. "It's wild!"

We watched as he grabbed one of the heavy Adirondack chairs to get his balance. The wind had nearly knocked him down. The little white folding table had already blown off the porch and was lying on its side on the driveway. Plastic cups we'd left outside were flying around like kites. The trees were bowing and swaying in the wind. The barbecue kettle was rolling around and spinning on the ground like a top.

"I'm staying inside," Sam said. "Funny, I didn't hear anything about a hurricane coming."

"This isn't one," Haley said.

"You're kidding."

"No. This is just a storm. A severe one, but no hurricane."

I stood and watched Evan step out from under the porch into the falling rain. He turned around and waved at us, laughing and making a motion as if he were about to dive into the water on the lawn.

"Coll?" Sam said.

"Yeah?"

"You have weird taste," she said.

"Agreed," Haley said as we watched Evan skip through a puddle.

I couldn't believe they weren't going to give me more of a hard time about Evan's being here than that. But they didn't.

"Agreed," I said.

I woke up on the living room couch, alone, to sun streaming through the window. Sam was crouched beside me, holding a mug of coffee under my nose. "Come on, sleepyhead."

I rubbed my eyes and struggled to sit up. "How long have you been up?" I asked.

"Since last night. Maybe you can sleep through a tornado, but down in Richmond we don't have those kinds of storms."

"Is the electricity back on?" I asked, taking the coffee from her.

"Nope. But since your stove runs on propane, I heated the water and made you a modified French press coffee."

I took a sip. "Does French press mean bitterly strong?"

"Hey, as long as it gets you up, what are you complaining about?"

I took another sip and rubbed my eyes. I must have slept about two hours total. "You know what? I don't think we're even going to have to work today. It's like a snow day."

"How come?" Samantha asked.

"No electricity? No Bobb's," I declared. "So, ah, where's everyone else? Still asleep?"

"Heck no. Evan went home after you fell asleep. Haley went to check on her parents and the pier and stuff. I think we should go find her, see if we can help. I already did some cleaning up around the yard, but I'm sure there's more we can do."

"Okay—I want to check in on Betty, too, make sure she's okay."

"Sounds good," Sam said. "And on the way?

Maybe you can tell me when you started sleeping with Evan."

We both started laughing. "Yeah, okay," I said. "I'll tell you all about it."

"Then let's get going," Sam said. "I'm dying for a good story."

The road was littered with branches that we cleared as we walked. It seemed as if every resident was outside, clearing their property, repairing docks, collecting debris, and talking about the storm—where they'd been and what they'd seen.

The sun was out, and there was a stark blue sky. There was almost no wind, which was very strange. It felt eerie, almost, looking around at all the damage on such a gorgeous sunny morning.

Only the ocean still looked angry and violent. All of the storm remained in the water, which was riled up—the waves were high, and water pounded against the dock pilings and splashed onto the rocky coast. I remembered something my grandfather used to say: "The sea has a longer memory than an elephant."

Down at the Landing, Haley wasn't behind the window, working. There was a sign on the window that said CLOSED FOR REPAIRS.

Over at the commercial dock, the ferry was still tied up, rocking in the rough waves. "Hasn't made its first trip of the day yet. Too rough," someone commented behind us.

I pictured Ben trying to work with such massive waves and getting seasick. And then I saw them. They were tying up beside the dock, in an old aluminum boat that belonged to Haley's family. Ben had his arms on Haley's waist. He was helping her out of the boat, and when he helped her up to the dock, they held on to each other a second too long for friends.

Ben and Haley. Haley and Ben. It sounded right. I didn't think they'd been having an affair or anything, I knew neither one of them would ever do that. It just seemed like there was more to them than friendship. And that was a good thing.

That night, Evan and I were sitting on the porch, playing cribbage by the light of a lantern. It reminded me of when I was little, and I would come here to visit and my grandfather taught me by candlelight one night when a storm knocked out the power.

At the table beside us, Sam and Erica were playing backgammon. After each game, we'd switch and play a different game and/or opponent.

I nearly jumped when the telephone rang inside the house. "Well, sounds like the phone's back," I said as I reluctantly got up from the table.

Evan gave my arm a squeeze as I went past. "Whoever it is, get rid of them," he said.

I picked up the phone. "Hello?"

"Colleen! Oh, thank goodness. I'm so glad to hear your voice. Is everything okay? I was so worried when the phone went dead," Mom said. "We've been trying to call all day!"

"Everything's fine—just a storm." I glanced over at Evan. *And a few other stormy things*. "We didn't have phone service until just now. We still don't have electricity, so we're all sitting outside, playing games by lantern."

"But everything's okay?" she asked.

"Sure. Everything's great." Through the screen door, I could hear Evan giving Sam a hard time about the way she was playing. "How's London?" I asked.

"Well, it's lovely, but we've made a decision. We had to tell you right away."

"A decision?" I asked.

"Yes. We miss you too much, so we're

cutting our trip short. We'll be home the day after tomorrow."

"You'll be home the—the day after tomorrow?" I repeated loudly, through the screen door. "Really?"

Evan, Sam, and Erica all stared at me, then looked at each other with widened eyes.

The day after tomorrow?

Chapter 25

"Don't worry, we'll get it all done."

That was the first thing Erica said the next morning. It was good to have such a positive person around; otherwise, I'd probably give up and throw in the towel. Especially the dirty ones.

The four of us were sitting at the kitchen table drinking coffee at six A.M. (Fortunately, the electric power was back, and the coffee was a lot better.) I didn't get up at six A.M., unless school was involved. But this was almost more important than school.

Haley had to be at work at seven; the rest of us had to be at work from eleven to two. Then we'd have two free hours to get the house completely ready before the dinner shift.

How could we possibly get it all done?

Erica had called her grandparents last night and they'd come over with supplies so we could prepare my parents' bedroom for painting. We'd stayed up late taping around the windows and the doors—I noticed Blair hadn't done such a neat job—and putting down the drop cloths. I would paint; Erica would clean and scrub other parts of the house; Sam would do laundry and help me paint.

As soon as the hardware store opened, I drove down to pick up a couple of gallons of paint. I still couldn't remember the right color, but it turned out that Eddie had found a record of it in his customer file. "You have a file on us?" I'd asked. I didn't want to think of the implications of that, but it was a lifesaver right now.

"Here it is," Eddie said, showing me a chip. "So Blue Over You."

"Seriously? My mother picked out a color called So Blue Over You?" It sounded like a country-western song, not a color for my happy-go-lucky parents.

"That exact color isn't available anymore," Eddie said. My heart started to sink, but then he smiled and said, "They just changed the name to Bluebird On My Shoulder. I'll mix some up right away."

When I walked in the front door, excited to share the good paint news with Sam and Erica, I saw my aunt and uncle working in the kitchen.

"What are you doing here?"

"Just baking a few things to welcome them home," Aunt Sue said. "The blueberry loaf will be out in a jif, and I'm working on a cobbler or two. And I think I'll make some muffins for everyone who's working so hard."

"I'm on cleanup duty." Uncle Frank held up a spray bottle and a sponge. "You really haven't wiped down the cabinets in a while, have you?"

"Um . . ."

The telephone rang, so I set down the paint on the kitchen table and picked it up. It felt like everything was happening all at once.

"Colleen. I heard your parents are coming home tomorrow." It was Betty McGonagle.

"Ah yes, the good old island grapevine," I said, laughing.

"Yes. It's still got a few grapes on it. But next time you create gossip, make it a little more exciting, would you? My TV went out in the storm and I'm bored to tears over here," Betty said.

"I'll try," I said. I could tell her about yesterday and Evan, but I probably wouldn't. Especially not with my aunt and uncle in the same room.

"Now, what can I do to help?" Betty asked.

"Oh, nothing, Betty. Really."

"Colleen. You are a wonderful person and a fine artist, but you're the worst caretaker I've ever seen." Betty cleared her throat. "Why don't I come over and fix up the garden for you?"

"You don't have to do that," I said.

"Yes, I think I do. I was going by yesterday and I saw weeds that are taller than I am. I'll be there in an hour," Betty said.

"Okay. See you soon." I hung up the phone and smiled.

"Who was that?" my aunt asked. "Ben?"

"Ah . . . no," I said. "That was Betty. She's coming over to help with the garden."

"Betty McGonagle? You know, she really cleans up at that gift shop. Boy, does she make a good living. You ought to think about doing some paintings," my uncle said as he spritzed the window over the sink. "Colleen, have you thought about painting some nice seascapes?"

But I was already on my way up the stairs. I'd be painting, all right.

"So I finally figured out what our excursion should be this year," Sam said. We were halfway through applying our first coat of paint. Because the lupine color was darker, we'd have to put two coats over it—one now, and one in the afternoon.

"What?" I asked, putting the roller into the pan to pick up some more paint.

"Tell me if we can pull this off," Samantha said. "We go to Portland to the museums, and then we take the train to Boston and go to the Museum of Fine Art. We'd have to stay over, probably—either we get a hotel in Boston or we rack our brains and think of someone we know there."

"Are you serious? I'd love to do that," I said. "But do we have time?"

"You would have to be practical." Samantha stopped to dab the brush into the gallon she was working from. "Okay. I know. How about if we just have a showing of your work here? The Colleen Templeton Gallery. No—we'll sell your stuff at Bobb's! Trudy would definitely have an art show for you."

"That's not much of an excursion. I mean, it doesn't sound like fun for anyone else," I commented.

"What are you talking about? We organize it, we have an opening—make it a major end-of-summer island event," Samantha declared. "We circulate with crab cakes. You just stand there, mingle, and make *money*. People would buy your stuff for souvenirs of the island. You know, quaint native art."

"You know what?" I smiled. "That's brilliant. But do I have enough pieces to show?"

"You have a closet full," Sam said.

"Yes, but is any of it *quaint*?" As I turned around to dip the paint roller again, I saw Starsky on top of their dresser, walking back and forth. He was swishing his tail against the wall. "Starsky—no!" I cried.

But it was too late. His gray-black tail was now streaked with blue paint, and the wall had a swirled, marbled effect—with cat fur mixed in.

"Starsky's helping. That's cute." Sam laughed.

Starsky knocked a pen off the dresser, then jumped down to play with it, waving his light-blue tail behind him. I grabbed a wet rag and tried to clean his tail, but he thought it was a game and kept running under the bed.

"We could sell Starsky at the art show. He's quaint *and* native," Sam suggested.

"No, let's sell cat paintings," I said. "Tourists would be all over that. Maine coon cat paintings!

He's not a coon, but you know, it sounds good."

"Anyway, it's not going to be a meet-and-greet-the-artist type event," Sam said. "They won't know. We'll take a picture of him and then we can alter it to make him look bigger and furrier."

I pictured Starsky presiding over a show of his art, wandering around and playing with women's (and maybe men's) earrings and jewelry. Lapping a glass of milk and signing autographs with his paw.

Sam and I both started giggling so hard that we ended up lying down on the plastic drop cloths, laughing until we started to cry. Maybe it was the stress of trying to get the house ready, I don't know. But every time I thought about Starsky, the painting Maine coon cat, with a little black beret on his head, doing a meet-the-artist event, I started laughing all over again.

"Don't do that to me."

I was slicing pieces of a banana cream pie at lunchtime when Evan came up behind me and started kissing the back of my neck. "Please don't do that to me," I said as I tried to correct the jagged cut I'd just made.

"Don't?" Evan asked.

"No, do. Just . . . not right now." I served a new, more cleanly cut slice of pie onto a plate, and put the pie back into the refrigerated case. "Not today." I turned around to face him.

"You know, we won't have a chance to see each other that much when your parents get home," Evan said. "How about we go swimming between shifts today?"

"Swimming?" I asked. "But I'd have to go get my suit."

"No, you wouldn't," Evan said. "I was running last week and I went down this abandoned trail—I found a new cove. Total privacy."

That sounded tempting. And freezing. And impossible, in broad daylight. And not likely, given the work I had left to do at the house. "No, I can't," I said as I hurried over to the coffee machine to fill a carafe.

"Why not?" Evan followed me.

"Because I have to paint some more," I said, placing a small white bowl of creamers and sugar on my tray.

"But . . . can't you do that tonight?" Evan asked.

"No, not really. I'm working, and then—"

Erica was in the kitchen to fill some glasses

with water, and she came up beside me. "It's okay—Sam and I will finish the painting. If you guys want to go do something this afternoon, we'll do the second coat."

"No, I can do it," I said. "I'll just have to go really fast."

"Which will ruin everything!" Erica said, laughing. "Come on, Coll, it's the least we can do. You invited us to stay in your house for the entire summer."

"But you didn't live there," I pointed out.

Erica waved my comment away. "Technicalities. Go do whatever, and we'll see you back here at five. Oh, and did you hear? Sam talked to Trudy about selling your art. She's totally psyched to do it."

"Really?" I asked as I hurried past both her and Evan with the pie and coffee.

Erica nodded.

"You're the best!" I told her.

"Thank you!" Evan replied. "I know!"

Evan and I spent so much time hanging out at the private beach together that we barely had time to stop by his cousin's to pick up some fresh clothes before work. I'd used my T-shirt to dry myself off after swimming, and it was soaked.

I pulled on the T-shirt Evan tossed to me, and we nearly sprinted side by side to Bobb's so we wouldn't be late. My hair was still slightly wet when we walked into the kitchen.

"You're so lucky you got here in time!" Sam greeted me when I walked into the kitchen. "It's not Orlando Bloom, but it's close."

"Who is it?" I asked, wrapping an apron around my waist and checking over the specials for the night.

"Graeme Helman," she said. "The guy from the movie with—"

"The really incredible body?" I interrupted.

"Hey," Evan said. "Keep it down over there."

"He's in *your* section, too," Sam said. "You can thank Erica later. Plus, my section was full, or I would have killed her." She shoved an order pad into my hand. "Now, go. He's got water already and I'm sure he's ready to order."

"Thanks!" I said, laughing as I headed for the swinging doors to the dining room.

"But—wait—Colleen—" Sam said. "Hold on. You can't go in there like that!"

I turned around, shaking my head. "No way, I'm not giving you his table. He's in *my* section, and I'll wait on him."

"Should we tell her?" Evan asked.

"Tell her what?" I said. I peered through the little peephole window. "He's alone? Oh, wow. Here's my chance."

I walked out into the restaurant and went straight to Graeme's table. (I was already calling him "Graeme," as if we were close.) He looked even better in person than he did in the movies and on TV. He had wide shoulders, a face with perfect-looking-enough-to-be-sculpted features, and dark brown eyes. Why on earth was he dining *alone*? Why on earth was he at our little island?

"Welcome to Bobb's," I said. "Have you heard about our specials?"

"Yes, thanks," he replied in a deep voice. "But I think I'll go with my standard. The Fisherman's Platter."

"Your . . . standard?" I asked. "You've been here before?"

"Sure. Not for a few years, though." He grinned. "You probably weren't here then. Hey, nice T-shirt."

"Oh, uh, thanks," I said, glancing down at the shirt. Something about it looked weird, but I couldn't place it. "Anything to drink?"

"Iced tea," he said. "Extra lemon. Oh, and extra tartar sauce and extra lemon slices for the platter, too."

"No problem! Be right back with your iced tea," I promised.

When I turned around and headed for the kitchen, I saw Erica and Samantha huddled by the host stand. Sam was laughing so hard that she couldn't stand up; she put her hand on the wooden counter to balance herself.

Erica's face was bright pink as I walked over to them, and she was trying not to smile.

"What's so funny?" I asked. "Does my hair look that bad? Oh, no, it's a frizzone day, isn't it? I shouldn't have gone swimming."

Erica burst out laughing. "Colleen, you might, ah, you might . . ." She reached into the glass counter next to the host stand. She rifled through a stack of Bobb's T-shirts and pulled one out. "Go to the bathroom and put this on."

"Why? Did I spill?" I asked, peering at my T-shirt. This time I actually looked at it long enough to read the upside-down script: "Dip Into Something More Comfortable," it said, with a butter dish.

Oh no, don't tell me. Then I twisted the shirt around so that I could read the back. There it was, in large blue letters: "Boob's." Not Bobb's.

Evan had given me one of his mock "funny" T-shirts to wear to work. No wonder Graeme had said "Nice T-shirt." No wonder everyone was laughing at me.

I hated him. With every fiber of my being.

And then some.

I tried to say good-night to Evan outside the restaurant, but it took us so long that Erica and Sam went home without me. "Evan, I just can't break the rule about no sleepovers tonight, not when I'm going to see my parents tomorrow," I said as we walked down the road toward my house.

"Do you really think they'd care?" he asked.

"Um, *yeah*?" I said.

Evan laughed. "Yeah, probably they would. Sorry. I just . . . I can't stand that they're gonna be here, and we have two weeks left, and I . . ." He leaned closer to me and whispered in my ear, "I want to spend every night with you."

I didn't say anything. I wanted that, too, but I knew it was impossible.

"So let's go somewhere tonight," Evan said. "If we spend the night together somewhere else, that isn't technically breaking the rule, you know."

"But I can't!" I laughed. "And anyway, the house is mostly fixed up and neat and perfect, but I have to make sure it stays perfect because I have to go pick them up tomorrow morning . . ."

Evan put his arm around my shoulders as we walked. Then he started gently pushing me in the direction of the path to the beach. "The house is in great shape. It's never been in better shape. Don't worry."

"Yeah. But I have to worry," I said as we stepped off the road onto the path. It was like trying to resist the tide, or the undertow maybe. An impossible thing to do, but I felt like I should at least try to resist, as if giving in right away was not really playing the game. "Plus I'm still mad at you for giving me that stupid shirt and letting me wear it in public for ten minutes, so I could embarrass myself."

"You're *mad* at me? Come on. I think it made Graeme *like* you," Evan said.

I wrinkled my nose. "I actually don't think he noticed."

"Oh, he noticed." Evan nodded. "He noticed, all right."

"I hate you," I said.

"I know. You really hate me. You can't *stand* me." Evan slipped off his sandals and ran straight toward the ocean.

"Pretty much!" I called as I sprinted to catch up with him and push him into the water.

Chapter 26

"So. This is what it's like down here at seven in the morning," I said. "I kind of forgot." The days of catching the ferry to school at seven seemed like a long time ago. In fact, had that even been me?

"It's usually a lot colder and foggier," Haley said.

"Uh-huh," I said.

"No, really!" Haley insisted.

"Yeah, I'm sure it's really awful." I grinned at her.

"What are you doing here?" Haley asked. "Oh, right. How could I forget? You're picking up the kids in Portland."

"Yup." I stretched my arms over my head, then reached down to touch my toes. "Is Ben working today?" I asked when I straightened up.

"Um . . . I don't know," she said.

I just stood there and waited for a second for her to answer me.

"Okay, I think I do know. He has today off," she said. "But why did you want to know?" She sounded suspicious.

"Oh, I just wondered if he'd be on the ferry," I said. "That's all."

"Right. Of course." She seemed a little relieved, as if she'd been afraid I was down here to find Ben and try to win him back or something. That was the last thing on my mind. Maybe it was a little bizarre to think about the two of them as a couple, but I'd get past that. I was already halfway past it.

"You know, Haley? It's okay if you and Ben . . . you know," I said.

"What?" Haley asked, a little flustered.

"I saw you guys the other day. I noticed the way you just sort of *fit*." I'd thought that before of me and Ben, but it wasn't true. He and Haley fit. I loved him, but it was as a friend. And I loved him for being with Haley, because I knew what a great person she was and that deep down they made a better match, they were more alike. It had so often been the three of us. And maybe it still could be, sometimes, but things were rearranged now.

"I could never do that to you," Haley said.

"Ever. I'd never—"

"No, it's okay."

"But . . . come on, Coll. He doesn't even like me that way—"

"Sure he does. Just ask him." I couldn't believe I was saying that. I felt like I was standing on this tiny island of my own, only it was about as sturdy as a lily pad or a piece of paper. I was giving up the sure thing, or what used to be the sure thing, anyway. Everyone had always assumed Ben and I should and would get married someday, after we finished college. And I had no guarantee of anything permanent, or safe, with Evan.

In fact, it was almost guaranteed we *wouldn't* stay together. Evan wasn't in it for the long haul—not now, anyway, and maybe not ever. He was sort of like my brother, in fact.

And maybe I was more like them than I wanted to believe.

But I had to be okay with that. And surprisingly—to myself, more than anyone else—I was.

My life wouldn't be as predictable in the future as it had been in the past. None of our lives would be. It was scary, terrifying, and exciting. Like being with Evan.

"Well, I'm not like rushing into anything," Haley said. "I mean . . . wouldn't it be really awkward if me and Ben were . . . you know, together?"

"Yeah, kind of," I said. "But we'd get over it. If things got weird, I could always give him a hard time about almost puking on us a year ago."

"I can't believe that was a year ago," Haley said. She took a sip of coffee. "And now this summer's almost over. It went so fast. I mean, here you are, going to get your parents, and it seems like they only left last week—"

"Of course, they did decide to come home two weeks early," I said.

"Yeah, that does make the summer seem a little shorter," she said, laughing. "Especially since I had to move back in with my mother yesterday."

"Sorry," I said.

"No, I was just kidding. It'll be good for me to be at home for a week or two before college. It'll make me appreciate college even more, right?" she asked. "With my luck, I'll get a roommate who's just like my mother. She'll probably tell me to clean all the time."

"Can you believe there's only a few weeks before we leave?" I said. As the day I was required to be at Bates got closer and closer, I seemed to be having a harder and harder time fathoming it.

"I can't believe it. I don't want to, I don't think, in a way. But I'm excited about getting to Dartmouth. I can't wait, actually. I'm just doing a good impression of someone waiting patiently."

"It's going to be hard. Saying good-bye to . . . everyone. You know?" I felt my eyes fill with tears. I was feeling really emotional about leaving the island. About leaving our life here behind—if not for good, at least for a while. Nothing would be the same in a few weeks. And Haley had always been there for me, from that very first day of school, when I felt scared and alone, in third grade.

She'd been there that day on the ferry when we both met Ben. She was the one who'd pulled out the Tums after the cinnamon-raisin bagel didn't really help. How could I forget? Now we'd be nowhere near each other, and neither would she and Ben. I wondered how much things would change and how we'd all deal with that, whether this time next year we'd all be here again—or somewhere else completely.

Me? For now, I was planning on being back here. Maybe someday working at Bobb's Lobster would get old, and I'd be even more aggravated by having to deliver dinner rolls in quaint trap-shaped baskets and serve "chowdah" and tie Bobb's plastic bibs onto complete strangers. But until then, I'd be happy to live on the island whenever I could.

I sort of felt like today was dress rehearsal, as if I were getting a chance to practice leaving home. I glanced at my watch. It was ten minutes before the ferry would leave.

Last night Evan had said he'd meet me down here, to see me off—he'd promised, in fact, to buy me a cup of coffee and a couple of dough-nuts and sit and hang out with me, but at the time, I hadn't really believed him, even as he said it and even as I said, "That would be so nice." Evan had a habit of vanishing just when things mattered to me.

But at five minutes to seven, I saw him jogging down the hill toward me. I smiled, even though I couldn't help feeling a little disappointed that he was so late.

"You missed the coffee," I said as he stopped in front of me. "And the doughnuts."

"Yeah, well. I'm trying to cut back on dough-nuts." He patted his extremely lean stomach.

"Yeah, you need to do that." I reached out to pat his stomach, too.

He grabbed my hand and pulled me toward him. "What time do you think you'll be back?"

"I don't know—late afternoon, I guess?" I snuggled against his chest. "But you know my parents—we'll probably hang out by ourselves tonight, just the three of us. I know you want to see them, but it'll have to wait a couple of days."

Evan stepped back. "Don't tell me. Slide show. World War I battle sites. Castles. Cathedrals."

I laughed. My parents had bored Evan a few times last summer with slide shows, one set from a visit to the Museum of Fine Art in Boston, and one from their colonial inns tour. How they could be so fun sometimes, and so dull at others, never ceased to amaze me. I hoped I wasn't anything like that, that it wasn't written into our genetic code like the lack of good timing.

Speaking of which, the ferry was leaving in a couple of minutes, and I really needed to get on board.

"But I really do want to see your parents. Tell them that, okay?" Evan said.

"I know, I know. And you will, just not tonight."

"Okay." Evan leaned forward and whispered in my ear, "But I might sneak over later."

"You wouldn't," I said.

"Coll."

"Okay, you would, but don't. Not tonight, anyway. We'll see about later."

"All right." He sighed loudly. "Now, if you're on your way to pick them up and that old car of yours breaks down—"

"What," I interrupted. "You'll come get us?"

"No. But I know a couple of nuns in New Hampshire."

"Yeah. I bet you do." I shook my head, laughing at him.

He put his hands on my waist and pulled me toward him. He ran his fingers down the side of my cheek, and we kissed just as the ferry horn blew three times, warning me there was a minute left before she sailed. I'd already driven the car onto it, so I didn't have to worry about that. I had a space and my ticket, and all I had to do was jump on.

But I didn't want to stop kissing him. This wasn't our big, sad good-bye scene—that was coming in a few weeks. But somehow I knew I would be ready for it this time. This wasn't

Casablanca, and we weren't Humphrey Bogart and Ingrid Bergman.

And I wouldn't fall apart this time.

"You'd better go," Evan said now.

"I know," I said. "I really should."

There was one more—the final—blast of the ferry horn, and I wriggled out of Evan's arms. I sprinted toward the boat, losing a sandal on the way. I turned around, ran back to slip the sandal back on, and saw Evan grinning at me. Then I took off my sandals and dashed barefoot toward the boat. I dodged a couple of kittens roaming around the docks, nearly falling facefirst onto the gangplank as a big calico cat got in my way. I waved at the guy collecting tickets that morning as I hopped on board. Half a minute later, we were untied from the mooring and starting to pull away from the dock.

I climbed up the stairs to the upper deck, which wasn't that crowded—it was a Tuesday morning, post-early-rush.

"Colleen! You almost didn't make it," Cap Green said, leaning out from the cabin.

"Yeah. I know!" I sat down in the back and gazed out at the water, and at the island disappearing behind us. The way the sun was shining on the ocean reminded me of something. Maybe one of Betty's paintings.

All of a sudden I thought I heard a baby crying. That was weird, because I hadn't seen anyone with a baby. I listened again for the crying.

It wasn't crying, I realized as I turned around and saw a cat crouched under one of the bench seats across from me. It was *mewing*.

I crept over to look more closely. It was the calico cat I'd almost fallen onto a minute ago, right near the gangplank. It had sneaked onto the ferry. But that didn't make sense. What did a cat want on the mainland?

The cat came out and rubbed against my legs. It had black-colored fur around its eye that almost looked like a pirate eye patch.

How did the cats get to the island? One took the ferry; one came from a pirate ship.

I smiled. I couldn't wait to see Dad and Mom.

From *Spanish Holiday* by Kate Cann

Oh, God, he's pawing at her face again. Oh, God, stop him. If he does that thing he does—where he paddles his fingers down her face and grabs hold of her cheeks and squidges her mouth up . . . I'm going to kill him. I'm going to have to.

I watch helplessly as Tom squeezes in Ruth's face and makes her mouth look like a duck's bill. I stare as he kisses her, saying, *Ooo-ooh, Roofy-Roofy*. And I don't make a move to even slap him, let alone kill him.

I'm demoralized, that's what I am. Passive, helpless, and demoralized. I've been on this Spanish trip one week three days, and that's approximately one week one day too long.

Tom, Ruth, Yaz, and I are sitting in a fake touristy taverna at a table for four, drinking ready-made sangria and waiting for our sham paella to arrive. Yaz and I are silent, and the canned flamenco music is happily too loud for us to hear what Tom and Ruth are whispering about. Although I can guess. They're kind of gurgling and gnawing at each other across the red-checked tablecloth, and then Tom comes up for

No, it wasn't, but I was anxious to see it, to get settled in. Still, I did slow down as we walked along a wide corridor, which closely resembled a boulevard. Stores and restaurants lined both sides. Plants, statuettes, artwork, festive lights, and a domed ceiling created an openness that I hadn't expected within a ship. It was like touring a gigantic mall—one of my favorite places to hang out. With so many people mingling around, it was like a bustling city floating on the ocean. I was a little overwhelmed by the crowds and the vastness of the ship.

"It's just not fair that I have to work and can't go on this cruise with you," Julie lamented.

Those words had become Julie's mantra ever since I'd told her that I was going on my trip.

"I'd give anything if you could come," I said. We'd shared everything since kindergarten. I couldn't imagine not sharing this, too.

"I know. You have to send me a postcard from every port," she commanded.

"I will. I promise."

"And since you are so into making lists, I expect a report listing all the yummy details about every guy you meet."

I laughed. I *was* a little obsessed with lists. I

From CARIBBEAN CRUISING
by Rachel Hawthorne

The Enchantment   Night One

"I can't believe it! Everything is totally amazing!"

I couldn't believe it either as Julie Barnes and I gazed around one of the atriums of *The Enchantment*. The name suited this ship. I was definitely enchanted. It was huge and luxurious. I figured it would take all ten nights of the cruise simply to walk from one end of the ship to the other.

"Come on," I said, nudging Julie's arm. "Let's check out my cabin."

Julie was my best friend. Like me, she had blond hair. But her eyes were blue, while mine were green. And she was a little shorter than me, which meant she had a difficult time keeping pace when I was in a hurry like I was in now. I just wanted to see everything as quickly as possible. There was so much to take in. My time here would be short, and I didn't want to waste a single minute.

"Slow down, Lindsay," Julie ordered. "Your cabin's not going anywhere."

air and asks, "Well, I said I'd get us here, didn't I girls, eh?" and Ruth says, "I know, I know, you're *brilliant*, baby."

I try to make sickened eye contact with Yaz but she's staring straight ahead.

"Senor—senoritas—dinner is served!" Two waiters swoop four microwaved plates down in front of us—*crash-crash, crash-crash*. I look at the vicious yellow of the rice, the scattering of what might be seafood, and feel ill.

"Looks good!" announces Tom, as he forks a great slimy mound of it into his face.

"Yeah," agrees Ruth, lovingly. "This place is lovely."

"Although I wouldn't mind a steak, tomorrow. Or a burger or something. I'm getting a bit sick of all this Spanish crap, to be honest."

"This isn't Spanish crap," I snarl. "This is tourist crap. No Spaniard would be caught dead eating this."

"Oh, here we go again," sneers Tom. "Lors the expert on Spain."

"Don't call me *Lors*."

"Just 'cos you got your GCSE in Spanish, it doesn't make you an expert."

"I'm not saying I'm an expert. I'm just saying

we should eat somewhere *real* for once, and not go in the most *touristy* place in the town!"

"You need somewhere where they've got the prices up in *English*," says Tom slowly, leaning toward me as though explaining to a backward child. "So they can't rip you off."

"Actually," I snap, "that place we walked by that *I* wanted to go in—that was cheaper. I checked the menu."

"Yeah, yeah. Understood all of it, did you?"

"Most of it. Well—some of it."

"Octopus guts and pig's colon—know the Spanish for that do you? Yum."

Ruth starts giggling as though he's hilarious, and I shoot her a look that says *traitor* and hiss, "It looked good. There were Spanish people in there."

"What's good about that? They eat all kinds of rubbish. Anyway, you should've gone in on your own if you felt that strongly about it."

"Oh, come on, Tom," says Ruth. "We've only just got here. We agreed we'd stick together tonight."

Tom splats a kiss on the side of her head, and says, "Yeah, babes, you're right, we did agree. So shut up moaning, Laura. You were outvoted, okay?"

even though (as Tom gloatingly reminded us just about every single time he filled it up) petrol was cheaper here than at home. Or maybe I hated it because the car was the principal reason for us all being here together, and I'd started to *really* hate that.

God, what a mistake it was, agreeing to come.

I glare at Tom, out of words. He smirks, triumphant. Ruth looks pleadingly across the table at me and says, "Oh, come on, let's enjoy the meal, shall we?" And there's the briefest of pauses, then we all start forking up the day-glo paella and shoving it in our mouths.

It started as a joke, Tom getting the casting vote because he owns the car. It was funny about twice, then it got to be really grating. We'd pull up outside some gruesome place offering pizza at the top of the menu, and Tom would say, "Looks okay. Less than a fiver a head." And I (or sometimes Yaz) would say, "Why don't we go on a bit farther, see if there's somewhere more interesting?" And Tom would answer, "Okay—put it to the vote. I say eat here." And Ruth (of course) would echo, "Yes—here looks great." Yaz would usually back me up and want to go on, and Tom would say, "I'm the driver, I get the casting vote."

And he'd park the car.

I'd started to hate that bloody car.

Maybe I hated it because we were stuck in it so long each day, all through the loveliest, warmest part of the day, because Tom had this touring fixation. Maybe I hated it because it guzzled so much of my holiday money in petrol liked organization and had compiled several different lists as soon as I found out I was going on a cruise: everything I needed to buy before I came onboard, all the items I needed to pack, and everything I planned to do while I was on this cruise.

"Maybe I'll just send you a list of their names. I'm hoping there will be so many that I won't have room on the postcards to tell you about all of them."

"That's a definite possibility," she said. "Have you ever seen so many cuties in one place?"

"Nope." From the moment I'd checked in and we'd started our quick tour of the ship, I'd seen at least a dozen guys who I thought I'd like to get to know better. Each one was smiling, laughing, or talking with someone.

"I think it is so romantic that Walter is going to marry your mom on a cruise ship," Julie said.

"He's definitely gone all out."

Walter Hunt was quiet and reserved, but when he spoke, people listened and did as he asked. Mostly because his name appeared on a famous list of the top one hundred wealthiest people in the world.

Hence the cruise. A special honeymoon for

him and his new bride—who just happened to be my mom—and anyone else who wanted to tag along. Of which I was undeniably one.

They say that most people are introduced by a friend to the person they'll marry. That's how Mom met Walter. She was attending a friend's funeral. Her friend had worked for Walter's company, so Walter had gone to the funeral as well. He and Mom met, hit it off, and now my life was on the verge of changing forever in ways that I'd never really anticipated. And truthfully, it's something I was having a hard time comprehending. For as long as I could remember, it had always been just me and Mom. Now it would be me, Mom, and Walter.

Still, Walter was nice and I liked him. I thought he'd be good for my mom. I was heading off to the University of Texas in the fall, and I'd been a little worried about Mom dealing with the empty nest. So I was definitely in favor of her marrying Walter.

And I was going to be a bridesmaid for the first time in my life. I had no doubt that I was embarking on a summer of firsts. And I planned for most of them to take place on this cruise.

I wanted to go places I'd never gone. And I

didn't simply mean traveling to islands. I wanted to explore all the different facets of myself . . . and boys. I wanted to cut loose and do things that I'd never done.

The cruise seemed the perfect place to try new things, because even if I made a fool of myself, I'd never see any of these people again, so it didn't really matter if I made mistakes. I could be wild and crazy. And no one would know that wild and crazy wasn't the real Lindsay Darnell.